Dropped from Heaven

Copyright © 2007 by Sophie Judah

All rights reserved. Published in the United States by Schocken
Books, a division of Random House, Inc., New York, and in Canada
by Random House of Canada Limited, Toronto.

Schocken Books and colophon are registered trademarks of
Random House, Inc.

Library of Congress Cataloging-in-Publication Data

Judah, Sophie, [date]
Dropped from heaven / Sophie Judah.
      p.   cm.
ISBN-13: 978-0-8052-4248-5
1. Jews—India—Fiction.   2. Bene-Israel—Fiction.   3. India—
History—20th century—Fiction.   I. Title.
PR9510.9.J84D76 2007   823'.92—dc22   2006026003

www.schocken.com

Book design by M. Kristen Bearse

Printed in the United States of America
First Edition

2   4   6   8   9   7   5   3   1

Sophie Judah

Dropped from Heaven

SCHOCKEN BOOKS, NEW YORK

In memory of my two sons,
Ezekiel and Barak

CONTENTS

Dropped from Heaven is a collection of stories about the Bene Israel Jewish community of India. The origin of the community is shrouded in mystery. Some scholars claim that the Bene Israel belong to the tribe of Zebulun, who made their way to India after the conquest of the Kingdom of Israel by the Assyrians, who then sent the ten tribes that made up the kingdom into exile. The two tribes that made up the Kingdom of Judea survived for another two centuries, but after the destruction of the Second Temple by the Romans, they also were sent into exile.

There is no written history of the exile of the ten "lost" tribes, so the legends of the arrival of the Bene Israel in India cannot be proved. These Jews lived on the Konkan Coast, on the southwestern side of the Indian subcontinent, cut off from the rest of the Jewish world for centuries. But they observed Jewish laws such as *kashrut,* circumcision of baby boys on the eighth day, Shabbat, and not intermarrying with the Gentile community. Children of mixed marriages were never accepted by the community. This is why the community is small in comparison with other Jewish communities.

Jwalanagar is an imaginary town, and the River Murli does not exist. I placed the town in the Hindi-speaking area of central India for the simple reason that it is the language I am most comfortable with when I use the vernacular. The landscape of hills and caves is true to the geography of the central states. I have not described the caves in any detail, as then they could be confused with the Ajanta, Ellora, or Elephanta Caves and would give the town a definite location on the map, something I have tried to avoid doing in order to make the stories more "Indian" and less localized to one of the states.

This collection of stories is divided into three time periods. The first, which tells of the founders of the Jwalanagar community, extends from the last decade of the nineteenth century to 1930. The second, from 1930 to 1964, is a period of great change within the community, because during this time India gained her independence from Great Britain (in 1947) and Israel became a state (in 1948). Most of the Bene Israel immigrated to Israel, and so the community dwindled. The stories in the third part cover the years from 1965 through 2000. During these years finding a Jewish partner for marriage became increasingly difficult. The last story, "The Funeral," depicts conditions within the small Jewish communities that have remained in India in the twenty-first century.

Although the stories are fictions, all are based on the Bene Israel way of life. The Jewish community in India has for centuries lived in close proximity to both Hindus and Muslims. There has never been a Jewish ghetto or manifestations of anti-Semitism from the local population. This is a concept foreign to Western Jews, for whom it has been a constant presence. In telling my stories, I have tried to be faithful to the conditions in which I grew up and to my knowledge of the community to which I belong. I hope you enjoy reading about the Bene Israel; there has been very little fiction written about them.

1890–1930

My Friend Joseph

I FIRST MET JOSEPH on a hospital ship returning from South Africa. We had both been wounded during the early days of the Boer War and were being shipped back home to India. I had passed a restless night. The wound in my shoulder was healing, but pain made sleep difficult. I spent my time looking out of the porthole, and I watched the horizon change colors from black to gray, to streaks of pink, orange, and purple. After the sky turned a pale blue, I heard one of the other patients stir in his bed. This gave me something different to watch. I saw the dark shape of a man rise from his bed, fumble for something in his locker, and then limp toward the door. He had a crutch under one arm and a parcel under the other. He had trouble opening and closing the door, but I did not get up to help. The bloke obviously thought that he could manage by himself, so I was not going to be the one to remind him that he was incapacitated at least for the time being.

The man stood in the open doorway for a few seconds. The bundle under his arm caught my attention. He did not raise his arm or remove the parcel he held against his body, although it would have made it much easier for him to open the door if his arm could move unhindered. He placed his crutch against the bulkhead outside the door, hopped through on one leg, and then reached back to pull the door shut. I heard the sounds of the crutch on the stairs followed by creaks when each stair took his weight as he hobbled along. I wondered what made the bundle so precious that he would not let it drop. Letters from a wife or sweetheart did not normally get the amount of respect this fellow was showing for his parcel. It was also too large to contain letters, anyway.

We had been in South Africa for only a few weeks. I tried to think of other things, but my mind kept returning to the bundle under the wounded soldier's arm. Its shape was vaguely and disturbingly familiar. I did not understand the uneasy feeling of guilt that overcame me. I had not hurt the man's pride by helping him, so I had no reason to feel that at that moment I should have been doing something other than lying in bed imagining the naked bodies of the nurses who took care of us.

Eventually my curiosity got the better of me. I rose and went out on deck. Not far from the door I saw the answer to my riddle. The man stood with his back not completely to the rising sun but at a slight angle to it, so as to face northwest. He was covered with a *tallit,* or prayer shawl. His held his crutch under one arm for support, while in his free hand he held a small book. The empty bags that had held his prayer shawl and phylacteries, or tefillin, lay on a chair beside him. I did not have to look at the man's face to realize that he was one of my people. As "natives" we could not become officers in the British Army. This man had come from my ward, so he was an enlisted man, not an officer. Officers inhabited a different part of the ship. I understood the reason for my unease. I should have been praying, too. I always carried my *tallit* into battle with me so that in case I got killed my body could be wrapped in it for burial. I did not carry tefillin because I did not pray regularly. Still, I wanted a Jewish funeral if it was possible.

I waited for the man to finish his prayers and place his "holy things," as I thought them to be, into their bags before I stepped forward and introduced myself.

"*Shalom aleichem,*" I said, as it was the only Hebrew greeting I knew. "My name is Bentzion."

He took my hand in a firm clasp. "Joseph," he said.

"Could we speak for a while? Would you like to sit here or shall we go below?" I asked.

"I'd rather sit out here, but my wound hurts in the cold."

"Shall I bring up two blankets? My wound hurts, too."

"That would be nice," he replied.

This was the beginning of a friendship that lasted all our lives. I accompanied him to the deck every morning and evening during the rest of the voyage home. He allowed me to carry his prayer things, and I sat at a little distance from him until he finished praying. Not once did he ask me why I did not pray, too. The only time we spoke about it was when I brought up the subject.

"Have you always prayed three times a day?" I asked.

"Not always, but once I started I have not let off."

"How did you manage in South Africa?"

"As best I could. One time, I managed to get a little free time when we were in the jungle, or bush, as they call it. I walked toward the river in order to be some distance from the other soldiers. I found a spot I liked and I said my prayers. At the part where we step back and then forward again, I felt myself step upon something that moved. I did not let that disturb my prayers. After I finished, I looked around, and there lay a crocodile. It had not harmed me, and it made no movement toward me as I walked away, although it watched me all the time."

"Go on. You are pulling a fast one." I laughed.

To my surprise he leaned forward and caught my elbow in a viselike grip. "Don't call me a liar. I do not tell lies, and if you want to be my friend do not lie to me, either. If I tell you I stepped on a crocodile, you can be sure that I stepped on a crocodile. You can find any explanation for why it happened, but do not doubt the truth of my words." He let my arm go.

I rubbed my elbow and said, "Maybe the animal was not hungry. Just like our Indian pythons, they, too, can go without food for months once they have a bellyful of some animal."

"I will not argue with your belief. You may be right. I prefer to believe that the Lord saved me because of my daily devotions to Him."

"I wish I could believe and pray like you do," I said.

"Don't worry. When the Lord decides to grab you, you will not be able to run away. You will return to the fold quietly and willingly."

We never spoke about religion or prayer after that. We told each other everything about ourselves and our families. Then we came to the joint decision that it was time to get married. We had both had close brushes with death, so we saw the importance of having children. It would not be difficult to find brides from the villages the Bene Israel inhabited along the Konkan Coast. We had regular work, which promised a pension in old age. This was security. What else could a father want for his daughters? I was twenty-three years old, and Joseph was twenty-one. We had a future with the British Army. We considered ourselves to be suitable bridegrooms, the kind any girl would desire.

The ship docked at Bombay, but we were not free to look for girls. We had to go to a military hospital first. Army ambulances met us at the docks and took us to the big railway station called Victoria Terminus. A train waited for us there. Every wagon had a large red cross painted on both its sides. We were taken to a big military rehabilitation hospital in Deolali. This is where we met Subahdar Samuel Kolet.

Samuel Kolet was around forty-five years old. He was in charge of the medical stores. We recognized him for a fellow Bene Israel from the moment we saw him. Because Joseph wanted information about the local synagogue, we spoke to him immediately. He told us that there were very few Jewish families in the city and they had no synagogue because few of the men prayed three times a day. During festivals and on Shabbat they got together for prayers, and we were welcome to join them. He invited us to his house for kiddush and dinner on Friday night.

Dinner at Subahdar Kolet's house changed our lives forever. He had seven children, and two of his daughters were of marriageable age. Elisheva was eighteen years old, and Ketura was sixteen. I caught one glimpse of Ketura and knew that my future lay with her. She was not exactly beautiful, but she had a certain grace and charm that overpowered me. Her eyes were large, her smile shy, and her hair fell almost to her knees. She had high cheekbones and a dimple in one cheek. I watched her, and Subahdar Kolet watched me. I was not aware of this at the time. It was Joseph who brought it to my attention.

"You made an ass of yourself," he said when we were back in our hospital ward. "We will be lucky if he invites us again. Why did you have to stare as though you have never seen a woman in your life?"

"Simple," I answered, a bit annoyed at being called a donkey. "I haven't seen a girl like her before."

"She is just another ordinary-looking girl."

"That may be so, but I intend to marry her."

"Congratulations. In that case the subahdar has no reason to be angry. He cannot refuse such a good match for his daughter. You are also wise in your choice. She is familiar with the life an army family leads. The adjustment will be no adjustment at all." Joseph was sure that everything would work out for me.

I was not so sure. "You are right, Joseph, but there is a problem. Ketura is the younger of the two girls. The father will want the elder girl to be married first. I do not really want to wait," I said.

"No problem. What are friends for? I'll marry the elder one," he said. "What is she like? I was too busy watching the drama you put on to notice the other girl."

"She is small, slim, and pretty. Her hair falls only to her waist, long, but not really long like Ketura's. Her eyes are a lighter brown than her sister's, and her skin is lighter, too. Her nose is a bit upturned. She has pretty hands and feet," I replied.

"You saw a lot for a man who had eyes only for the younger girl." Joseph laughed.

The next day we searched for Subahdar Kolet during the hour we were supposed to be at the swimming pool. We found him in a storeroom counting a new consignment of red army hospital blankets. He pointed to a bench and asked us to sit there until he finished his work. We saw that he was doing nothing that he could not lay aside for a few minutes, so we assumed that he knew what we, or at least I, wanted. He was establishing his right to exert authority over us. We both took this as a positive sign.

We roasted in the Deolali sunshine. There were other benches at a distance under shady mulberry trees, but we had been asked to sit where he could watch us. It was in our interest to comply with his wishes. After about forty minutes he made his appearance and immediately took us to the veranda of the VD ward. He wanted to sit in the shade. We mopped our foreheads and necks with our handkerchiefs while he watched us with a smile. I was hesitant, but Joseph, true to his nature, came straight to the point.

"*Hum ladkaiyon ka hath manganye ayie hain.* We have come to ask for the girls' hands in marriage," he said.

"*Ladkaiyon?* Girls? You mean both?" he asked.

"Yes," Joseph said.

"Give me your home addresses and the names of your commanding officers with their addresses. I must make inquiries before I decide," Kolet said.

This was a reasonable request. It was also what custom

demanded. Joseph and I knew that sometimes a bride's father makes the groom wait for no reason at all. Our sojourn on the bench was enough for us to put Kolet in this category.

"We have only nine weeks left of our stay in the hospital here. If the answer giving and wedding are not over by then, I shall leave and look for another girl. It is not as though we are in love with the girls, and I for one cannot afford to travel back and forth," Joseph said.

"You have just returned wounded from the war in Africa. You have money."

"Not to waste it on silliness, I haven't. I come from a large family that I help support. You must realize, Subahdar sahib, that I am a man of my word. What I have said I have said. I will not spit and then lick it up. I tell you I will not waste time or money for no sensible reason."

Joseph's outspokenness made me fear that I had lost my chance to get Ketura. I cleared my throat to say something soothing, but Joseph barged in again.

"Bentzion has offered for Ketura and I for Elisheva. I am younger than he is. This should be clear before you start making inquiries. Is there something else you wish to ask us?"

Kolet had nothing to ask, so we rose and went to the swimming pool. We spent a lot of time in the pool during the next two weeks. We were not invited to the Kolet house during this period. The subahdar had disappeared from the hospital. I made inquiries about his whereabouts when Joseph was in the gymnasium with the doctors. I knew that he would not bend under any pressure Kolet tried to exert. He told me that he thought Kolet was an ass who would let a little power go to his head and make him into a tyrant. Joseph was not going to let him make things difficult for us. I was a different proposition altogether. I was nervous and anxious. I do not know how much of it was due to love, but my pride was also involved. A refusal would be a comedown in my self-image.

The man who replaced Kolet in the storeroom told me that Kolet had taken three weeks of compassionate leave to deal with family problems.

"Is something wrong?" I asked.

"No, no. He is looking into the matter of two matches offered for his daughters."

"That's nice," I said. "What does he say about the matches?" I added as casually as I could.

"He is hoping for the best, although one of them seems to be a bit of an *akadoo,* a stiff, stubborn person. Still, if you think about the size of his community, who can blame him for being anxious about his daughters?"

I had heard enough. I knew that the girls were ours. We just had to wait until Kolet returned from his visits to our homes and those of our friends. Our commanding officers would be prompt in their approvals. The officers took as much care of their men as they could, and neither of us had a blemish on his army records. They would also feel that they owed something to the men who were wounded in action.

We kept ourselves busy with exercise and visits to the recreation room, where we played cards and carom. I became quite good at darts, while Joseph made use of the library. I was not one for reading much, but he was quite a scholar. He read in Marathi, Gujarati, and English. An Irish soldier named Peters spent hours discussing books with him, while I played games of solitaire, not understanding a word of the discussions that I listened to with only half an ear.

Subahdar Kolet appeared at our breakfast table about two weeks after our last conversation with him. "You are invited to my house for dinner this evening. Be there by seven o'clock," he said before he turned on his heel and almost marched out.

Joseph and I applied to the duty officer for passes. We usually had to be back by ten o'clock, but Joseph decided that we needed more time. He told the officer that we were expecting to be given answers for offers we had made for the girls we intended to marry. The officer laughed and gave us passes until midnight. "The CO will kill me, but good luck," he said as he shook hands with both of us.

"You have some cheek," I said to Joseph when we were outside the hospital gates that evening. "You know that the doctors want us to be in bed by ten o'clock at the latest."

"Truth has its own charm," he replied with a big smile. "I had nothing to lose if he had said no, but it was worth a try. Now we will not have to hurry."

Joseph bought a packet of *pedas,* the sweetmeat that is usually distributed when an engagement is announced. He divided it into two small packets that could fit into his trouser pockets. "I don't want to insult the family by seeming overconfident," he explained. "When the answer is given, I will do the *mooh meetha.* I will sweeten their mouths. I have no intention of rushing around and trying to find a sweetmeat shop at the hour old man Kolet decides to say what he has to say to us." He suggested that I place my *pedas* in an opaque bag along with other shopping we supposedly did to vary our diet in the hospital.

At the Kolet house Joseph sat quietly while the subahdar and his wife shilly-shallied about making small conversation. He did not say more than ten words in half an hour. The girls were nowhere to be seen. Joseph watched the subahdar with a half smile on his lips. This made the older man uncomfortable. "Why are you looking at me in such a way?" The question seemed torn from him against his will.

"I want to see how long you are going to beat around the bush.

You have called to give us the answer, and we have come for it. What is it? Is it yes or no? Don't waste our time. If it is no, we shall leave immediately. If it is yes, what are you fussing around for like a clucking hen?"

Subahdar Kolet seemed shocked at the impudence of a man who hoped to be his son-in-law. His eyes narrowed as he looked at Joseph, but Joseph looked back with unabashed frankness. If Kolet was trying to establish his authority over us, Joseph was making it clear that he was not a man who could be bullied. Kolet had to understand that before he gave his answer.

"Yes. You may marry my daughters," he said.

Joseph's hand went to his pocket, and he took out a packet of slightly squashed *pedas*. He placed one in the mouth of our father-in-law-to-be and one in the mouth of our mother-in-law-to-be. I fumbled in my bag, upsetting a packet of roasted peanuts. Before I managed to take out my perfectly shaped *pedas* neatly arranged in the confectioner's box, Joseph had completed the ritual and my sweets were just a formality.

The mother called her children to set the table. All the children made their appearance with some dish or other. The family had invested a lot of time and trouble to prepare a really good meal. Joseph took out his second packet of *pedas* and gave it to Elisheva when she came in with a bowl of steaming rice in her hands.

"This is for you," he said. He looked straight into her face for the first time. He must have liked what he saw, because he gave her a smile I had never seen him give to anybody else. She blushed and looked away, pretending not to notice the touch of his hand upon hers as she took the packet from him.

We had insisted on a quick wedding, so our arrangements were hastily made. I decided to give Ketura money for the jewelry the groom is supposed to provide for the wedding. I told Joseph about this, and he agreed that it was a good idea.

"They have to wear it, so they should choose what they like," he said.

We agreed to give them an equivalent of two months' salaries. I was a lance naik, but Joseph was still a sepoy. His wages were smaller than mine, so Elisheva received less than Ketura did. Elisheva was not pleased. The first chance she got, she told Joseph that Ketura had more jewelry than she had.

"That is what I can afford," he said. "Bentzion earns more than I do. You will have to get used to the idea. It is not your father's house where all children are equal."

"Can't you get a loan?" she asked.

"I will not go into debt. You will just have to be satisfied with what I can afford."

"We sisters are getting married together. It will be embarrassing when our relatives compare what you gave with what Bentzion gave."

"Why should your true condition embarrass you? We can break off all wedding plans if you want a richer man. I can understand that, but I tell you now that I will not do things just to put on a show."

"Perhaps you have savings somewhere," she persisted.

"I will never tell you a lie, Sheba *bai,* and if you are wise you will not tell me one, either. I have told you that I do not have more money, so you'd better believe I have no money. After we marry, I will give you my entire salary with which to run the house. If you manage to save anything, you can do what you want with it. At the moment it is I and not you who know my financial condition."

Elisheva fell silent. Joseph was irritated. "A new wife is like a new mustache," he said to me later. "You have to train them both in the beginning. Later you will have no control over them." He then asked me whether Ketura wanted more than I could provide. I told him that she seemed satisfied.

"I wondered whether her father was putting ideas of a loan into her head," he said. "He is capable of it, and I do not want Elisheva to be ruled by him when it comes to matters that should be between the two of us."

We started visiting the Kolet family every evening. Although we were seldom left alone with our brides-to-be, it was a very sweet time for us. Each moment when the parents left or the other children were absent meant a smile or a touch that would not have been shared otherwise. Joseph seemed to like Elisheva more with each passing day. On Fridays he would buy flowers for her hair. I was only too willing to follow suit. Once I wanted to buy some chocolate, but he said that the younger brothers would grab the major share, leaving little for their sisters. Our gifts should be something only the girls could use. It would make them feel that they were special to us and that we cared about them. I was surprised to see him weave a basket for Elisheva to keep her thread and crochet hooks in. He had seen her crocheting lace for a sari petticoat and thought that his gift would be useful and appreciated. That is what he said, but I thought that he was slowly and surely falling in love with his "intended." He smiled without making an answer when I told him this.

Three days before the weddings our families arrived. We had rented a house not far from the Kolet house. My mother visited her daughter-in-law-to-be and made her a present of a new gold necklace with earrings of a matching design. She also gave her four gold bangles that my grandmother had sent. Joseph's mother gave Elisheva a pair of earrings and a pair of bangles that were her own. She had more children than my parents had, and she had married off a daughter the previous year, so she could not afford much. Ketura told me that Elisheva was jealous, but neither of us said anything to Joseph. He had already spoken of not marrying the girl if she made demands on him. According to Ketura, her sister was a stubborn person who liked having her own way. She did not give in easily, especially when she had her mind set on something. I thought that what he did not know could not hurt him. That was the reason I felt apprehensive when he told me that he had given Elisheva money to buy a *mangal sutra* of her choice and a wedding ring according to the size of her finger.

The day before the wedding we had the *mehndi* ceremony. This is when designs in henna are drawn upon the hands of the bride. As grooms we had our forefingers covered with henna paste, too. Then some of our relatives took a bit of henna from our fingers and went to the brides' house. The groom's henna was placed on the forefinger of the bride. We were not allowed to see our brides for ten days before the wedding, so we stayed at home and joked with the relatives who had not gone to the brides' house.

When our relatives returned, Joseph's mother immediately went up to him and asked, "Where are the *mangal sutra* and wedding ring for the bride?"

"With her. I gave her money to buy what she likes," he replied.

"That is what you think. I asked to see the *mangal sutra* and wedding ring, and she answered, as calmly as you please, that you would have to buy them because she bought a gold chain with the money you gave her."

Joseph just nodded.

"What are you going to do?" his mother insisted.

"Buy a wedding ring and a *mangal sutra*. You can return the Benarasi silk sari we bought for the *baraat* ceremony. We can use that money. She will have to come to my house in her white wedding sari."

"You foolish boy! The *baraat* sari was given to her today according to our tradition. You should have let me buy the jewelry, too. It was to accompany the sari," she grumbled.

"I'll see what I can do," Joseph said, and went to bed.

The next morning Joseph went into the city. His mother wanted to accompany him. She said that her earrings and those of his two young sisters could be sold to the jeweler in exchange for a *mangal sutra*.

"It is my problem. Let me deal with it. Nobody will have to give up anything for my sake, and my wife will have to learn to live within what I can afford if she does not want to go hungry for part of every month."

He returned after four hours. His mother asked whether he had made his purchases. He only nodded in reply.

"May I see them?"

"You will see them on the bride after I put them on her," he said.

During the wedding ceremony Joseph produced the narrowest wedding ring I have ever seen and placed it on Elisheva's finger. I remember thinking that he must have sat with the jeweler to get it made. After the ceremony was over, the elder who conducted the wedding asked Joseph to put the *mangal sutra* around the bride's neck. Joseph reached into his pocket and drew out a length of twine, the kind gunnysacks are sewn up with. It was threaded through a gold bead. He tied this around the neck of his new wife. I heard him say, "It may embarrass you, but it is all I can afford."

Joseph may sound like a hardheaded and a hard-hearted man, but I must add that his marriage worked out very well. They respected, loved, and cherished each other. They recognized that each could be as stubborn as the other. Manipulation and lies never entered their marriage. It took Elisheva more than a year to save enough money to buy a gold chain for the gold bead of her *mangal sutra*. Until that time, she wore the piece of twine as a symbol of her married status. And she found that it didn't bother her that much at all.

Shame Under the Chuppah

THE DISCOVERY OF my grandmother's diaries was a surprise to the whole family. It made us see our grandfather in a new light. We had always thought of him as a jovial, loving man who cared deeply for all of us. The grandchildren had never imagined him as a young man. His role as a husband or as a friend of people his own age was something new to us.

Grandpa had left a parcel with his lawyer and had given Uncle Immanuel instructions to read Grandma's diaries to us after his thirty-day hazkara. I had never seen the family so anxious and impatient as they were the day the diaries were read. We all crowded into the salon, dining space, and kitchen of Grandpa's apartment. Most of us sat on the floor because there was not enough space for everybody. Fans were switched on and windows and doors opened for air in an attempt to cool down the warmth generated by so many bodies packed together. Nobody wanted to miss the reading, because Grandma had died when her children were very young, and this would be their first real contact with her thoughts and feelings. My father and Uncle Immanuel remembered her, and Aunt Erusha had faint recollections. Their younger siblings had no memory of her at all. In the absence of photographs, we depended on Grandpa's stories about her. These stories were so diverse and inconsistent that none of us ever knew what was true and what was not. We all had a lot of questions that

Grandpa never answered. He did not explain why we had never met anyone from Grandma's family, or why he had no wedding pictures. I did not believe that he "lost" them, or that all of Grandma's brothers and sisters were dispersed throughout India, England, Canada, and Australia. As Jews, at least some of them must have come here to Israel. The diaries would tell us the truth at last. Diaries do not lie.

A silence fell over the family when Uncle Immanuel requested that his youngest sister read. "You have a better reading voice and will be less emotional than I, because I remember her quite well," he said. I saw his hands tremble as he gave my aunt the diaries. The stern, unemotional man was overwhelmed by memories. I gave it no thought at the time, because I was more interested in the stories we would hear from a person who had been dead a long time. I would hear about the Jwalanagar that Grandpa spoke of, but this time in the present tense and not in the past tense. Grandma's diaries would tell the truth about the place, as opposed to Grandpa's fairy tales. He had brought his family to Israel as soon as the state was declared, so we had no personal experience of the old country and life there.

Aunt Tzippora read, "First of January 1930—

"Who could believe that I am capable of such unadulterated joy? Malti, whom we affectionately call Mala, has come home for a two-month holiday. I have missed my friend desperately. She is so happy with her new home and her two children that my heart rejoices for her. We have been friends from our first day in school. She is the only person to see me as myself, behind my pock-marked face and one blind eye. Smallpox almost killed me as a baby. It left my left eye without the colored iris, so its blindness is immediately visible to other people. Hardly anybody looks me in the face when they speak to me. My white eye makes them uncomfortable.

"Most people think I'm ugly. Mrs. Jeremiah Satamkar started the nicknames Beauty and the Beast for the two of us. I was very hurt and wept when I thought that I was alone at home. Malti, however, came over for some homework and saw me crying. She coaxed the story out of me. 'Mrs. Satamkar is a foolish woman, but at least she knows that the Beast was really a prince under his skin. Beauty loved him just as he was, and I love you just as you are,' Mala said. To this day I have never had a reason to doubt her.

"Seventh of January 1930—

"Mala spent the day with us today. Mother gave me a bit of money, so I was able to buy everything needed for the sweetmeats Mala loves. We were in the kitchen, I preparing *barfi* and *rasgullas*, she making *masala dosas*—something she learned from her mother-in-law—when her father came to visit. He had a middle-aged couple with him. This was strange. Mr. Joshi never brings his guests to our house. Malti became suspicious. '*Terei leeyea rishta hai*. This is an offer of marriage for you,' she said.

" 'Don't worry. They will take one look at me and beat a hasty retreat.' I reassured her, but she was not convinced.

"We served tea accompanied by an unusual amount of savories. Mr. Joshi introduced us to his friends. 'Malti and Malka,' he said. We both bowed our heads to the guests because we were carrying trays full of food. Mr. and Mrs. Jacob Bhonker are a Bene Israel couple who want to open some sort of business in Nagpur and want to meet the Jewish people they will live among if they do come here. I don't understand Mala's suspicions. They spoke more to her than to me, anyway.

"Eleventh of January 1930—

"I cannot believe it. Mala was right. I have an offer of marriage at last. Of course I have refused. The boy has not seen me. His parents chose me because they think I cooked all the good food we offered them. They want their son to be well cared for, but he will want a girl who is pretty, if not beautiful. My parents are putting a lot of pressure on me to agree to the match. I wish I was out of their house, earning my own living and not compelled to hear their constant reproaches. I know that I am a financial burden, but what can I do? They refuse to 'eat a daughter's earnings.' I have explained time and again that the saying applies to the earnings from prostitution, not from a respectable job, but they refuse to listen. Mother keeps saying, 'Rani'—her name for me—'listen to me. What will happen to you after we die? Who will take care of you? You will not get another offer. You are already thirty years old.'

" 'Let me work and take care of myself,' I say, but they want their daughter 'honorably' married—as though the unmarried state is somehow dishonorable. I shall not give in. The boy must see me first. He must not get a cat in a bag. I do not want to be called a cheat in addition to being reproached for my looks. I have had enough of that in one house and have no desire to hear it all over again in another.

"Tenth of February 1930—

"I received a letter and photograph from Mr. Eli Jacob—he does not use the Bhonker part of his name. He says that he will accept any girl his parents choose for him. I should have no fears about that. His handwriting is neat and clear. The letters are round, well formed, and straight. They do not lean backward or forward. I like that. His photograph shows a handsome face. Although the nose is large, it is well shaped and shows character. He does not ask me to answer or send my picture. I suppose he knows what I look like, because he mentioned that his decision to marry me had nothing to do with what his parents said about my appearance.

"I showed the letter to Malti, but she seemed unhappy after reading it. 'You have not met the boy. A photograph will tell you only what he looks like. This is a studio picture that shows him at his best. The photographer has touched up his eyes and mouth in the print. You need to know more than what the shape of the nose, mouth, and eyes is supposed to show. How does he behave? What does he think? I am happily married and hope for the same for you, but you are being pushed into this marriage. I met my husband twice before I said yes. I was never alone with him, but I watched the expressions on his face, listened to the tone of his voice, and watched his movements carefully. I saw how considerate he was of others, including the servants and the animals. My parents made several inquiries. They spoke to his colleagues at work, his friends, and his neighbors. They spoke to the shopkeepers he usually buys from. Your parents did the same thing for your other sisters. Why is it so different for you? They have not met the man, either. On what basis have they decided that this is the man for you? All they speak about is the money he earns, as though that is the most important thing in a marriage. If money is so important, why do they keep you so short of it? All of a sudden they think differently? I know that you are old to be a bride, but you are more than a package to be got rid of.'

"We were quiet for a while. Malti spoke again. 'Still, you never know. It may turn out well. All marriages are a risk, anyway, and both partners have to work hard at it. I really do not know what to advise you, Malka. You will have to decide whether to risk it or not. It is your life, and the final decision is yours.'

"Fifteenth of March 1930—

"It is done. The answer has been given. Eli cannot come to Nagpur because he is still new at his job in the ordnance factory at Jwalanagar and is not entitled to leave until November. He suggested sending an engagement ring through his parents, but that means that they will have to travel all the way from Poona once again. I do not think all the fuss is necessary, anyway.

"We shall be married on the fourth of November. I am afraid that my marriage will turn out to be all wrong, but at the same time I find myself dreaming of love, a home, and babies of my own. I have never permitted myself these dreams before. It is thrilling and frightening, too. Like anybody else, I also want love and a home of my own. I do not want to end up as a servant in the home of one of my brothers. My greatest fear is becoming a 'charity case' that can be abused at the will and whim of others."

Aunt Tzippora read a lot about my grandmother's hopes and fears. Grandma had always been a dim figure in my imagination. Her diaries made her a living, breathing person with a personality. She wrote a bit about the wedding preparations and a lot about the people she knew. We had heard different versions of these stories from Grandpa when he told us about how he met and married Grandma. He had changed the characters, but the stories were basically the same. We understood at last where his inspiration came from.

Aunt Tzippora got to the wedding after about an hour of pure entertainment that showed Grandma's interest in other people and her sense of humor. We began to think that her life was full of fun and interesting things. Even Uncle Immanuel laughed. This was until we came to the description of the wedding itself.

"Fifth of November 1930," my aunt read.

"I have never been so humiliated in all my life. My parents and Mr. Joshi have deceived me. I shall never forgive or see them as long as I live. They had no right to do what they did. They shamed me in front of the whole Jewish community, our neighbors and friends.

"I got married yesterday. Eli did not want a *haldi* or a *mehnedi* ceremony. I did not want a big fuss or expense, either. The day before the wedding he sent over the usual *bari* with the bridal wreath and veil, jewelry, and a sari for the *baraat*. The bride is supposed to leave her parents' home dressed in clothes the groom provides. My mother accepted the *bari*. Mr. Joshi had arranged a party for me in his house, so I was not present. All my school friends who still live in Nagpur were invited. Malti came down from Trivandrum in spite of the fact that she is three months pregnant and suffering terribly from morning sickness. She wanted to be present for my wedding.

"I should have realized that something was terribly wrong when I began to dress for the wedding and Mala did not appear. She had promised to do my hair. My mother came in instead. She gave me shoes that were ridiculously high-heeled. I had bought a different pair. I usually wear flat shoes, but as a concession to the day I bought ones with a small heel.

" 'I can't possibly walk in those shoes,' I said.

" 'It is only for the ceremony. It will give you height. A bride should look pretty as she walks up to the chuppah. Everybody will be looking at you.'

" 'They might think that the bride is drunk when I totter up. Besides that, these shoes are tight.'

" 'It is only for an hour. You can change immediately after the wedding. The chuppah has been set up in our garden. How far do you have to walk, anyway?'

"There was no arguing with her. I dressed quietly. She insisted on piling my hair on top of my head. She claimed that it was to fix the bridal wreath. The hairpins that went into the bun on the top of my head would hold the wreath in place. I believed that it was to give me a bit of height, because I am just below what is considered average height. Mother seemed to want to make me resemble somebody else she had in mind, and I could not imagine who. I did not want to argue with her on my wedding day, so I allowed her to do what she wanted. I reasoned that as it was my last day in the house, it was not worth the trouble. I did not want to quarrel before leaving.

"The bridal veil was another story. Mother must have sat up all night with my sisters and sisters-in-law, who arrived the day before for the wedding, in order to embroider it. Eli's veil had been a simple affair. The ornate thing I was given to wear was impossible to see through. I objected. 'You ungrateful thing,' my mother almost sobbed. 'After all the trouble we took to make you look nice, you find fault with us. You don't care how you hurt us. All we want is to make you happy and to see you married with children of your own.' I sensed a strange hysteria under her words but put it down to nerves. Her Ugly Duckling, as her sister had once called me, was getting married at last. It was natural for her to be nervous, relieved, worried, and happy all at once. Besides that, I had been the only person she could talk to when things were not quite right between her and Father, so she would miss me. I had no right to make it more difficult for her than it already was. I thought about all this, and I put on the veil. I could see only my feet, but I would go to the chuppah on my father's arm. Like a blind person in a strange place, I would have to follow where I was led. They had turned their *kaani*, their one-eyed daughter, into their *andhi*, their blind daughter.

"I walked 'up the garden path' (isn't that ironic?) to where the chuppah was placed. My father took small steps to accommodate my temporary blindness. Eli sang the 'Yona Thi Si' in a clear if rather tuneless voice. A shiver went through my body. For the first time in my life somebody was singing for me. I felt my father's arm shake, too. His trembling never stopped. The man was more nervous than the occasion demanded. Something was terribly wrong. I pushed these apprehensions aside. Perhaps he had been nervous when my sisters had married as well. He was giving his daughter away to an unknown person and a life that could only be guessed at.

"At the foot of the temporary *teba,* made from wooden platforms, he placed my hand in Eli's and joined my mother in the first row of the assembled guests. I stood under the chuppah with Eli, and the wedding ceremony began. Eli read it all in a clear voice that carried to all the guests. There was the respectful silence that people keep when prayers of any sort are being read. This is what made my mother-in-law's scream so awful.

"Halfway through the ceremony Eli had to lift my veil and hold to my lips the glass of wine that he had read a blessing over so that I could drink. As soon as my face was uncovered, his mother screamed, 'Stop the wedding. This is not the girl you showed us. I insist on the pretty one with the long plait.' She repeated my hated nickname. 'I do not want a beast for my daughter-in-law.'

"I stood stunned as all hell broke loose around me. Mr. Joshi said, 'You cannot mean my daughter. She is a married woman with two children and a third on the way.'

"'*Chalbaaz. Fareibi,* you deceiver! You called your daughter by a Jewish name to deceive us. You called her Malka,' she said in the same high-pitched voice.

"'I called her Mala, which is short for Malti. Rani is the name by which the bride's family calls her.'

"'Do not make up stories,' Eli's father said. 'We told you that we were impressed by the girl's beauty. You knew very well whom we meant. Is that why she was always in her friend's house instead of at home with you? The children at your house were your grandchildren, not your daughter's friend's children as you had said. You planned it all. As our matchmaker, you knew our expectations.'

"'You will not get such a good girl as Malka Rani,' Mr. Joshi said. 'Believe me. She is just like a daughter to me. I want to see her married. That is a parent's duty. Whatever I did, I did for her good and yours. Smallpox is a visit from the Devi, and the goddess has spared Malka Rani for your son.'

"My mother collapsed in a heap upon a chair. Her body shook with sobs. 'Is it a sin to want to get one's daughter married? I did not want to lie and cheat, but there was no other way. Jewish people do not pay large dowries to get an unmarriageable daughter married.' She spread out her sari *pallo* like a beggar in the streets. 'It is a matter of our honor. Do not shame us,' she pleaded.

"Mr. Joshi took off his *pugree*, the turban he had worn only once before, for Malti's wedding, and prepared to place it at Mr. Jacob Bhonker's feet.

"I had heard enough. My people had brought shame upon me and themselves. They were making it worse by groveling. What mercy did they expect when they cheated somebody else without mercy? What honor were they talking about when they had risked it by doing such a despicable thing? The hypocritical drama on their part was shameful to me. I am not a piece of goods to be bought and sold. I turned to flee. Eli reached out and held me back with his hand. 'You are standing under the chuppah with me. Nobody should shame you here or make you unhappy. I don't care what anybody says. I will marry you,' he said.

"I tried to pull my hand away. 'I am not the biblical Leah. I will not agree to this deception.'

"'And I am not the biblical Jacob. I am not fleeing my brother, and I shall not live in my father-in-law's house, either. Unlike Jacob, I have lifted your veil before the wedding ceremony is complete,' he said.

"I managed to pull my hand loose. 'I do not need your pity. I won't marry you.' I ran to my room on my painful feet. The tight new shoes had caused them to swell. I almost fell a few times because of the stupid heels that my mother had bought in an attempt to make me seem to be Mala's height. As soon as I reached my room, I locked the door and pulled the painful things off and flung them into a corner. I tore the veil from my head and unwrapped my sari. It fell only partly on the bed. The soft silk material slipped onto the floor. The jewelry went back into the boxes that I intended to return. All this took a few minutes. My mother, sisters, and sisters-in-law banged their hands upon the door pleading to be let in, but I ignored them.

"I was combing my hair when the noise outside suddenly stopped. I heard Eli say, 'Please let me talk to her.' I heard many footsteps move off toward the chuppah, accompanied by soft whispers.

"Eli knocked gently upon the door. 'Go away,' I said as calmly as I could. 'You have no reason to talk to me. I apologize for the way my people have behaved toward you and your family. I'm too ashamed to face anybody, you most of all. Please leave me alone.'

"'I will, after I speak to you. Please let me in.'

"After a lot of persuasion on his part I let him come in on the condition that he enter alone. He sat down on the chair beside my bed. 'This is not pleasant for either of us. We were both deceived,' he said. 'I cannot promise you great happiness, but I will try to be your friend. I respect the way you stood up for yourself. Respect is the basis of love and a good marriage. Love cannot last if there is no respect. I understand the pain you are feeling at this moment. Any human being would feel the same. Trust me. We will have a satisfactory life together. It is better than unhappiness. Come on now, let's get the ceremony over and leave.'

"'You must be joking. You cannot want to marry me. Just look at my walleye and scarred skin. You would be ashamed to walk down the street with me.'

"'Beauty is of different kinds,' he said. 'The first thing I noticed about you as you walked toward me holding that bouquet of lilies is that you have pretty hands.' He came up to me and held my face in his hands. He lifted it and looked straight into my eyes without any disgust or pity in either his words or the expression on his face.

"'You have a well-shaped mouth that is a little on the wide side, and the trembling smile is most attractive. I like your small nose, and the eyes have an almond shape. You could wear dark glasses to cover the blind eye. Everybody knows what smallpox is. We will vaccinate all our children, I promise,' he added with a small laugh.

"'I shall not marry you,' I insisted.

"'After today, can you really live in this house?' he asked as he stepped back and returned to the chair.

"'No.'

"'Where will you go?'

"'I don't know.'

"'Do you have enough of an education to go out and get a job? I'll help you to find one.'

"'I got good marks in school, but my parents preferred to educate my dull brothers over me. They had to support families, whereas I was part of the parasite sex that is supported by the other if the family is to be considered respectable.' All my pent-up bitterness suddenly found expression. 'They could not spend money on a college education for all of us. Boys were the logical choice,' I added as a sign of my usual reasonableness.

"'That is not what I asked. I asked whether you have any qualifications that will help you to earn enough to live independently.'

"'No.'

"'I am offering you a way out. I was not eager for marriage, either. Still, there comes a time when one wants to settle down. I'm glad you are the one God chose for me. All this could not have happened without some plan of His. I think I can live with you. You are a strong woman, and I think that is necessary in my partner. Will you have me?'

" 'I'm very hurt and angry at the moment, but I am sure of one thing. I do not want to start a life based on pity. I cannot live under a burden of gratitude to you, either. What sort of a marriage would that be? I want to be seen as Malka, the woman I am.'

" 'Is that not what I have been saying?' He smiled, and it made him look most charming.

" 'Will you agree never to ask me to make up with my family? After I leave today, I do not want to ever return. I have been shamed before, but I have never been so degraded and humiliated. I will never see any of them again. They were all in the conspiracy together. All my life they have treated me like just so much *kachara*, like rubbish, but this has passed all limits. My only friend has been Malti, and she has been deceived, too. That is the only reason she did not come today. Her father did not want her to come for my wedding, but she came all the way from Trivandrum, anyway. He must have told her why she could not be seen among the guests by your family. She is the only contact from my past that I shall keep. Do you agree?'

" 'If it pleases you. Don't you think that you are being too hard on people who love you and only had your happiness in mind?'

" 'My happiness? Can happiness be built upon lies and deceit? It was their opportunity to get rid of me. How happy was I when I stood out there as an object of ridicule or pity, depending upon the attitude of those who looked at me? You mentioned the word "respect" in connection with love. What respect did they have for me and my feelings? I can only imagine what your parents will say and how they will treat me if I am stupid enough to consent to your proposal.'

" 'We shall not live with them, but in Jwalanagar. I promise not to take you to their house. If they want to see us, they will have to come to us. My parents will never leave their house for more than two days at a time, and Jwalanagar is fifteen hours by train. They will not come. Do you agree now?'

" 'Only if you promise that you will never tell any of the children we may have the truth about how we got married. They at least should be spared the shame. No photographs, either. I do not want to be reminded of this day, and I do not want my children to feel sorry for me.'

" 'I agree.'

" 'Then I agree.'

"Unlike in storybooks, there was no kiss or declaration of true love. All Eli said was a matter-of-fact 'Drape your sari around you and come out.'

"I had not realized that I was only in my petticoat and blouse. I felt my face burn with embarrassment, but Eli had already left. I locked the door behind him to keep out inquisitive relatives. I wrapped the white sari around myself once again. The bridal wreath and veil did not conceal my face any longer. They lay discarded on the floor. I forgot that I had on blue rubber house slippers. I went out and got married in them. The walk was more comfortable.' "

The silence was broken by a sob from one of my girl cousins. My uncles and aunts used their handkerchiefs frequently. Aunt Tzipporah closed the diary and placed it with reverence on the table. She stared at it in awe. "I cannot read any more," she said. "Let's not read her diaries in one sitting. I feel the need to digest this first."

Everybody agreed. We never again read from the diaries in their entirety when the family gathered together. Each of us pursued them alone. We read about Grandma's great love for

Grandpa and her children. She described the little things my father and his siblings did and said. Most of all, the diaries made us respect Grandpa and his inconsistent stories, instead of feeling our usual condescending tolerance of what we had considered an inexplicable quirk in his nature.

1930–1964

The Circus House

THE JEWISH COMMUNITY OF Jwalanagar was divided in its opinion about the rift between Hannah and her mother. Hannah had always resented her mother's overbearing and dictatorial attitude, but she claimed that things came to a head after the first day she spent at the house that her family disparagingly called the Circus House.

Mrs. Aaron believed that she could help her husband's career by transforming the Bene Israel community they belonged to, so she took on the role of social worker. She hoped that since Mr. Aaron was a prominent lawyer, the British authorities would promote him to a prestigious position before they left. It would be nice to be known as a social and cultural leader.

Mrs. Aaron looked as if she spent much time in serious thought about all the improvements she could make. She considered the Samuel family to be a real disgrace and decided to take them under her wing. She would teach Mrs. Samuel a thing or two about efficient housekeeping and maintaining a decent flower garden. The Samuel place was overflowing—not only with the numerous Samuel children but also with a number of animals. Mrs. Aaron believed that there should be a law to prevent people from keeping animals in towns. Villages were meant for that. She spoke to her husband about it, but he pointed out that most families kept a cow or a buffalo for milk. If she campaigned against animals, she would be known as the woman who would deny poor children a glass of milk, and that would be most unhelpful. Mrs. Aaron had to concede the point, but she did note that Mrs. Samuel kept more than the usual number. She sold the milk to supplement the family income. Mr. Aaron reminded his wife that social work was meant to help people, not to take away their livelihood.

Mrs. Aaron thought about it all and was not impressed. In her opinion, the Samuel family was a disgrace to the entire community. She was determined to reform them. The plan that seemed most feasible was to send Hannah over to their house, because one of the Samuel girls was her classmate. It would open the way for later intervention from her side. With this in mind Mrs. Aaron approached Mrs. Samuel after morning prayers on Saturday and wished her Shabbat shalom.

"I believe that one of your daughters is in my Hannah's class," she said.

"Yes—Tova."

"Hannah admires her very much but is too shy to make friends. Perhaps we should help them a little. What do you say?" She smiled.

Mrs. Samuel smiled back, and Mrs. Aaron was disconcerted. She realized that the lady saw through her. "Send her over on Sunday morning to spend the day," Mrs. Samuel said before she moved away to join her husband and sons.

"Would nine o'clock be too early?" Mrs. Aaron called out over the heads of other people who were talking to one another on their way out of the prayer hall.

"People who take care of animals have to rise before the sun rises."

Mrs. Aaron realized that the remark was not a compliment to her habits. She was also having her face rubbed in a fact that was unpleasant to her. Her fastidious cleanliness made her think of all animals as dirty. She pushed the barbed comment to the back of her mind. Mixing with these people was a sacrifice she had to make for their own good. They would be grateful to her someday.

On the day of the visit Mrs. Aaron supervised Hannah's dressing. "The lemon yellow dress; it makes you look pale and delicate," she insisted.

"How am I to play with Tova and her family if I wear that thin muslin dress over a satin petticoat that sticks when I sweat?"

"Ladies perspire; horses sweat."

Hannah ignored her. "I don't want to go, but since I have to, at least let me wear comfortable clothes." Her complaint was of no use. The mother made sure that her daughter's clothes were well pressed, the shoes well polished, and the white ankle socks spotless.

"We have to be an example to these people, so be polite and mind your manners," she said to her daughter as she walked with her to the garden gate.

Hannah said nothing. She did not even nod.

Hannah stood just inside the gate of number 7, Dalhousie Road. She clung to its bars, too afraid to move. A large brown dog was barking at her. A smaller long-haired dog stopped digging between some *mogra* bushes and added his high-pitched yips to his bigger cousin's barks. A barefoot little girl came onto the veranda and shouted, "Come here, Jimmy." She then turned and shouted to someone inside the house, "Hannah's here." She made no attempt to go to Hannah's aid; instead she jumped off the veranda and walked away, toward the back garden.

Tova came out of the house and approached the gate. The dogs stopped barking and began to wag their tails. The smaller one resumed his job of burying something under the *mogra* bush. A green parrot called out "Hello, how are you?" from his cage, which hung from a rafter on the low side of the veranda roof. His greeting was more enthusiastic than Tova's.

"Hello. Come in," she said.

Hannah left the gate and walked down the path with a faint and apprehensive "Hello."

The big dog came up to Hannah. She took a step backward. She knew that the wagging tail was a sign of friendliness, but the big mouth and large teeth unnerved her.

"Don't show your fear, or he will follow you around and even growl just to terrorize you. He enjoys frightening people. Just pat his head. He likes that."

Hannah put out her hand and touched Jimmy's head.

"Not like that. Look, I'll show you." Tova took the dog's head between both her hands and looked straight into his eyes. She scratched him between the eyes. She rubbed him behind his ears, and then applied more pressure when she rubbed his back. "Come on. Touch him and he will know that you are a friend."

Hannah had never touched a dog before. Her mother did not allow animals into the house. She could not bear the idea of dog hair on her clean floors and furniture. The thought of having to remove ticks and fleas filled her with rage against every suggestion of a household pet. Hannah bit her lip as she thought of all this, but she rubbed and scratched the dog. Jimmy's small sounds of pleasure made Hannah enjoy her first physical contact with an animal. He sounded like a baby delighting in his mother's caresses. Hannah bent down on one knee to pat him and talk to him. "Good dog," she crooned. From the corner of her eye she saw the smaller dog rush over to her for his share of attention. Before she could straighten up, he was upon her, causing her to lose her balance and fall sprawling into the mud. He licked her face and hands. His muddy paws left dark streaks over one side of her dress. His claws made two small holes in the thin material.

"Down, Badal," Tova ordered. The dog sank upon his haunches, but his tail wagged in the dirt, raising small showers of mud, part of which ended up on Hannah's shoes. Her socks resembled the dog. Both were supposed to be white but had large patches of brown mud on them.

"Bad dog," Tova said as she rubbed his head. The bad dog became even happier. His haunches rose from the ground and wagged along with his tail, showering Hannah with more mud.

The girls left the dogs and walked toward the house. Hannah sat down on the edge of the veranda and took off her socks and shoes. She shook out the mud. She rubbed her hand over her dress and droplets of moist mud landed at her feet. The parrot called out from his cage not far from her head, "Hello, how are you?"

"Dirty," Hannah replied, and laughed.

Her laugh brought a smile to Tova's lips. "You are not as stuck up as I thought you would be. Maybe it is because I've never seen you dirty before or heard you laugh. Come along, I'll show you where to wash. You could wear one of my dresses. My mother will not only wash and iron your dress before you go home, she will also mend the tear. Her work is so fine that people cannot usually tell where the clothes have been repaired."

Hannah washed herself in the bathroom. She had never been allowed to wear another person's clothes. Her mother considered it a sign of charity. The Aaron family was well-off. They could not wear another person's used clothes. Hannah dusted her clothes and rubbed off as much of the dirt as she could, but she could not bring herself to wear Tova's frock. When she was reasonably clean she joined Tova, who led her to a room where some of the Samuel children sat around a table playing carom.

"Would you like to play?" Jacob asked.

"I've never played before, but I'll try."

"What do you do in the summer, when it is too hot to go out and play?" the barefoot girl asked.

"I read."

"Yuck."

"You see, Rina, not everybody dislikes reading as much as you do."

Rina stuck out her tongue at Tova, but Tova paid no attention. Hannah was surprised by the rude behavior. She was the eldest of four children, and at her house age difference commanded respect. She looked around. The only word she could think of to describe the Samuel children was *junglee*, undisciplined. The boys sat in their undershirts, and the smallest children ran around in their underwear. An open newspaper on the floor had a pile of monkey-nut shells and orange peels on it. Hannah knew that the Samuel family had ten children. She was introduced to whoever was in the room. The boy named Benny said, "What a welcome into our home! You get covered with mud and still feel comfortable in a stained dress." Hannah smiled but made no reply. Benny added, "Don't get too comfortable here, or you will not want to go back to your stiff home."

"My home is not stiff. I love it."

"How is it that you people hardly smile, let alone have a hearty laugh?"

Hannah decided to ignore his comment. She gave her attention to David as he explained the game to her. Hannah tried to absorb all the instructions before she attempted to play. She suggested that she observe one game first, but David insisted that it was easy and that she could learn as she went along. It was not competitive. Hannah had been taught to strive for excellence in everything. This easygoing, playing-for-fun attitude appealed to her, and she consented to play.

"Ow!" she cried out, and put her finger in her mouth.

"You are using too much force," David said. "Watch me now. Align the coin with the pocket and the striker this way, and hold your fingers like this. Push rather than hit."

Hannah tried unsuccessfully. After repeated attempts, the nail on her forefinger began to throb. She wished she could get out of the game without seeming to be a sissy or a spoilsport. Benny laughed when her striker slid all over the board. The only time she got something into the pocket, it was the striker instead of a coin.

"My four-year-old brother plays better than you," Benny said.

Tova and David asked him to keep quiet. Hannah felt that Benny was insulting her, so she looked in his direction to reply, but his smile was so full of mischief that she did not want to risk another comment upon her and her inadequacies. She tried to find something else to talk about, but nothing came to mind. She glanced out of the window, hoping for some inspiration, and saw Mrs. Samuel come out of the kitchen with a pot of food. The lady went to the mulberry tree and put some food into two bowls that were at its base. Jimmy and Badal must have smelled the food, because they appeared without being called. A white cat with black patches on her back came up and began to eat from Jimmy's bowl. Hannah watched with fascination. The cat could not always get past Jimmy's big jaws, so she moved over to Badal's bowl. The smaller dog did not raise any objections, either.

"Your dogs allow a cat to eat from their bowl!" she exclaimed. "What kind of dogs are they?"

"Good dogs," Rina said.

"Dogs with their own opinions. They did not learn from other dogs," Benny said.

"It is not strange for a dog and a cat that grew up together to eat together," David explained.

"Oh, I see," Hannah said, although she did not understand. The animals seemed as strange and unconventional as their owners. She tried to concentrate on the game, but too many odd things kept happening around her. Meena, the eldest sister, came in with a pile of comics. She settled herself on the sofa and placed her feet on the coffee table before she began to read. Hannah was genuinely shocked. Feet were meant to be kept firmly on the floor or on a low footstool kept especially for that purpose. Rina had drawn her feet under her and sat like a Buddha upon her chair while she played another board game with a sister closer to her age who tended to kick her under the table if the game went badly. Legs and feet safely out of the way seemed to be good strategy. Two small boys made balls of mud in the garden and placed them on the veranda to dry in the sun. From his cage above the drying mud balls the parrot scolded them with "Naughty girl," before he changed to "Hip, hip, hurrah." Hannah heard the boys discuss how big the mud balls should be for them to dry in time for the war they and the boys who lived on the next street had planned to have on Saturday after school. The side that fled would have to treat the opposing army to ice cream. *A real circus,* Hannah thought as she tried to get a wooden coin into the pocket of the carom board.

"I have to feed the pigeons, so I'll stop playing," Benny said. "Would you like to come along?" Hannah thought that he had seen her discomfort and was offering her an escape. She accepted his invitation gratefully and followed him to a shed at the bottom of their large garden.

The walls of the shed were covered with nesting boxes, many of which had a bird inside. Other pigeons sat on top of the boxes or perched upon the rafters. The floor was covered with patches of pigeon droppings. A broom made of slender sticks stood in a corner, a silent witness to the fact that the shed was cleaned regularly. Hannah found the smell strong and pungent.

She tried to move to the open door, but Benny was too absorbed with his birds to sense her discomfort. With great pride he pointed out which birds were homing pigeons and which ones tumbled in midflight. He showed her his fantail pigeons and gave her one to hold. For the second time that day Hannah found herself enjoying contact with a nonhuman creature. She caressed the soft feathers and laughed at the way the pigeon turned its head to look at her.

"What kind are those bluish gray ones?" she asked.

"Those are ordinary *junglee* ones. There are times when we cannot afford to buy meat for the family, especially when Mother's brothers from the village come to visit and want meat all the time. My father slaughters my pigeons at those times. I give him these pigeons instead of the prize ones he used to get at before."

Hannah heard bitterness in Benny's voice. She had heard Tova make some remark to Rina at school during lunch break about their visitors who had to get the best food while their mother gave them just anything for lunch. Hannah had not realized that it could be more than dissatisfaction with the food for the day. She absorbed this new piece of information about the family while Benny took her to a wire cage that held strange long-legged cockerels.

"These are my bantams," he said.

"Bantams? I thought they were roosters."

"Bantam is a breed of fighting cocks. I make quite a bit of money on them. People pay to see cockfights. Some also place bets." He tried to sound casual, but he rose to the tips of his toes when he said this. He seemed taller.

"That's cruel."

"It is, but it is sport," Benny explained. His feet were flat on the ground once more, and he was his normal height again.

"You call that sport? A poor creature gets hurt, and one of the cocks usually dies. Can that be sport?" Hannah forgot all her good upbringing and good manners, which required that she show an interest in whatever the other person was interested in. She was angry and wanted to show her anger.

"What do you call boxing and wrestling?" Benny was also angry. His attempts to impress her were a dreadful failure.

"I call that cruel, too." Hannah sensed the disappointment in the boy, so she added, "Your pigeons are beautiful, especially the fantails. A pair of them must cover at least a square foot of floor space. I heard that you can call them to you with a whistle."

"I can." Benny smiled and demonstrated the truth of the rumor. He allowed her to feed the pigeons. Hannah was delighted when they flew down to eat from her hands. They perched on her fingers and on her head. Benny laughed and said, "You look like a clown in an advertisement for a circus."

After the visit to the pigeons, Hannah felt relaxed. She began to enjoy her time with the family. Meena gave her some comics to read. They were all from the Classics Illustrated series. Hannah realized that not all comic books fit into the category of cheap literature. This discovery startled her. Her mother was wrong about the comics and wrong about the family. She could be wrong about a host of other things as well. Hannah could read for the sheer pleasure of a good story or beautiful words without being asked "What did you learn from what you read?" All Meena said was "I have to return them tomorrow so hurry and read as many as you can."

Tova asked her mother whether they could prepare lunch. Mrs. Samuel gave her consent without any fuss or preconditions. The girls decided on a simple, easy-to-prepare meal. Boiled rice, egg curry, and a vegetable salad would be fine. They picked lettuce and tomatoes from the garden. A visit to the henhouse revealed a bad-tempered broody hen but not enough eggs. Logic demanded that each family member have at least one egg, but the girls were two eggs short. Rina warned them not to take the egg from under the basket, where she had imprisoned her black hen, because that egg belonged to her, and in a curry she would not be able to identify what was rightfully hers. Anybody could eat it. "I know that Tiggy Tiggy Touchwood is yours. I won't touch her eggs," Tova said.

"That is not her name," Rina shouted at their retreating backs.

"Do you each have a pet of your own?" Hannah asked.

"Only those who want one and can take care of one. Jacob helps us all but does not have an animal of his own. He has three beds of vegetables instead. My father says that it is no use fighting for freedom from the British if we do not make ourselves economically free, too."

"What does that mean?" Hannah asked.

"I'm not sure. He says that India must not depend on any other country for food. The country that feeds us owns us. We will be forced to do whatever they want. The result of that idea is that we have a zoo at home, and we love it. I once heard you tell your sister that ours is a circus house."

"I did not mean only the animals. You all make a lot of noise, too. Although all the houses in this area stand on large plots of land, we can hear you fighting or playing while we are still at the crossroads. Besides that, you all excel in sports. I saw your young brothers do all sorts of acrobatics on the parallel bars in the park. Rina does fantastic things with a skipping rope. Benny's pigeons and the way they obey his commands are the talk of the entire community. That is what I was referring to."

"It does not matter. You do not have to be so embarrassed. I am not angry." Tova laughed. "I think that circus people are interesting."

"Do you have a pet?" Hannah asked, trying to steer the conversation away from the embarrassing one of a circus.

"I have a lovely goat. She has not gone to the hills with the goat-herd who takes the other goats from the town to graze because she is not feeling well. My mother says that she is going to kid today. She should know. She comes from a farming family in Pali, a village near Bombay."

"Tell me about your goat," said Hannah.

"I call her Munni. I got her when she was about two weeks old. She jumped around and was fun to play with. We fed her milk out of a bottle. Now she gives us milk. She is half Barbari and half Jumnapari."

"What's that?"

"Her breed."

"In spite of all the reading I do, I seem to know nothing about the things that are really important."

"Don't worry about that. Nobody knows everything." Tova pointed to a stain on the skirt of Hannah's dress. "You've got your period. You'd better go in and wash and change."

"What have I got?"

"Your period. Didn't your mother tell you about it?"

"No."

"Come on, my mother will explain things to you."

In the bathroom Hannah took off her stained dress, petticoat, and panties. She tried to wash the blood off before Mrs. Samuel came in. Mrs. Samuel tore a soft old cotton sari into diaper-sized pieces and showed her how to fold one into a pad and then wrap it inside the second piece that was folded into a longer strip. "I do not know what your mother will give you to use, but most women cannot afford anything but this. Tie this tape around your waist and then place the cloth between your legs. The ends will go through the tape. Fold it back on itself and pin it in place. It is quite secure. Use the safety pins usually used on a baby's diapers. They have a safety cover that ensures that the pin does not open and poke you. Some women experience pain at this time. It is nothing to be afraid of, just take an aspirin." The older lady spoke as she ministered to Hannah.

"What will I do when this cloth gets full? I don't want to stain my clothes."

"Don't wait that long. Change every couple of hours. Make another pad like this one and wash out the stained one. When it is dry, you can reuse it."

"Gosh! How dirty."

"Nothing in nature is dirty. This is how God made us. It is natural for women. It also means that you are grown up now and can have a baby."

"How?"

"You will have to ask your mother that. She will not thank me for doing her job for her. She will want to put things delicately to you."

Hannah reached out and touched Mrs. Samuel's hand. "I'm glad this happened here. My mother would have made a terrible fuss." She was pleased to see the older woman smile as she handed her Tova's frock and underwear.

Hannah was delighted with the simple meal she helped prepare without any adult supervision. Mrs. Samuel offered no advice unless she was asked. Boiled rice, dal, or lentil curry, and a vegetable dish of peas and potatoes were not difficult to cook. Hannah admired Tova's confidence in the kitchen and followed all her instructions carefully. She was allowed to cut vegetables for the salad, and nobody offered sympathy when the onions made her eyes water. Hannah had to make an effort not to compare this kitchen with her mother's.

Mrs. Samuel did not gush with praise about the food. After the meal all she said was "That was nice. You are on the way to becoming quite good little cooks." Hannah thought that this was high praise. She glanced at Tova, who looked pleased as well.

After lunch one of the younger boys came in from the garden where he had been playing. "Mama," he cried out, "Munni is having her babies."

Everybody rushed out to watch. Hannah sat with the others in the shade of a tree and saw the goat deliver two kids. She watched the nanny goat lick the kids and laughed at their wobbly efforts to stand up a few minutes after birth. She had never imagined that liquid and blood accompany a birth; in fact, she had never imagined a birth at all. The only thing she had heard women talk about in connection with birth was the pain. Munni had seemed calm and in control in spite of the pain Hannah imagined she was having.

Asher, one of the small boys, went up to the goat and touched the placenta that had not emerged fully. He gave it a slight tug. "What's this?" he asked.

"Don't touch it," his mother almost screamed, but it was too late. Part of the placenta came away in Asher's hand. Jacob immediately took his bicycle and rode as fast as he could for the only vet in town. Mrs. Samuel did something that was unusual for her. She smacked Asher across the back of his hand. "Why do you have to touch everything you see? That is the afterbirth, the bag in which the babies grew when they were inside the mother. If any part of it remains inside the mother, she will die." Asher hung his head down and bit his lower lip. Tova began to weep. Hannah put an arm around her and led her into the house.

Jacob was gone for two and a half hours. He had ridden all over Jwalanagar looking for the veterinarian. The man had gone to a dairy farm on the outskirts of town. When Jacob reached the farm, the vet had already left, and nobody knew where he was. Jacob returned to the vet's office to wait for him. After some time the vet's wife told him to leave a note for her husband and go home. He would get the message as soon as he arrived.

A rather smelly veterinarian arrived just before it was time for Hannah to leave. Munni was dead, and all the children were weeping. Tova seemed inconsolable. Mrs. Samuel thanked the vet and told him that he was too late. The man demanded payment for coming. Mrs. Samuel said, "Go home, doctor. You are drunk. You did nothing and you will not get paid for doing nothing." She closed the door while he was still standing on the veranda. Bad manners or not, Hannah was glad that he had been told off.

Hannah brought her wet clothes home in a small bag. Mrs. Aaron had been waiting for her daughter's return with a lot of questions, but the first one she asked was "Why are you in somebody else's clothes?"

"They were more comfortable to play in. We can send them back after the *dhobi* washes them."

Mrs. Aaron seemed strangely satisfied with the answer. "How was your day?" she asked.

"Eventful," Hannah replied.

"What do you think needs to be changed there?"

"Nothing, Mother. They are different than your usual friends, but they are wonderful. I learned a lot today. I cooked a meal with Tova, and it was good."

"My baby in the kitchen already!"

"I'm not such a baby. I saw a goat give birth and then die. Life is not the fairy tale you want us to imagine. It begins and ends in blood and pain, and there is blood and pain in the middle, too."

"I try to protect your innocence. Children should not know too much. I'll have a word with that Mrs. Samuel about this. How did she dare to allow you to witness a birth? You are only a child."

"Not such a child, Mother, and you did not keep me innocent.

You kept me ignorant. I got my period for the first time today and did not know a thing. I stood naked in front of Mrs. Samuel as she showed me what to do. You really should have prepared me for it."

Mrs. Aaron turned to her husband with a look of horror on her face. She turned back to Hannah. "There are things I have to explain to you."

"You are a bit late. Somebody else has done your work for you."

Mr. Aaron could give his wife no comfort. "It had to happen someday," he said, and returned to his newspaper.

Hannah went to her room. She felt like a changed person. She thought that she had a precious secret deep inside her and wondered whether the Samuels' clothes that she wore were responsible for her emotions. She shrugged and laid the thought aside as absolutely ridiculous. She knew that she had been changing slowly for a long time. Now it was out in the open, both in her body and in her family.

My Son, Jude Paul

MY GREATEST SUCCESS and my greatest failure is my son, Judah Saul Gonsalves. He has changed his name to Jude Paul Gonsalves. I have no argument with this change. Perhaps it is because I am not really his father, although I could not love him more had he been my own flesh and blood.

I am the priest who found him in front of the altar of St. Andrew's Church in Allahabad. I had come in for a few moments of private prayer. The baby's cry seemed like God's personal call of reassurance to me. I was needed by somebody. This was my thought as I reached for the infant. This may also be the reason I love him more than any of the other orphans I helped raise. The boy remains special to me. He is my discovery and my son.

The baby was neither beautiful nor ugly. He was warmly dressed in hand-knitted garments. I remember that it was bitterly cold in the church. Whoever had placed the baby in an ordinary bamboo basket, the kind the sweeper women use, had placed a folded blanket under him. He was wrapped in a white woolen Kashmiri shawl embroidered with red flowers. I remember all this clearly because we kept his things for many years, until Father Francis gave them to Jude when he left the orphanage and joined the army.

My superior, Father James, was more experienced than I in abandoned babies. He immediately shook the blanket open. An envelope containing a letter and a woman's handkerchief knotted around some jewelry fell out. I was surprised.

"Payment for the child," Father James explained. "Keep it for him. It will mean a lot to him as he grows."

"Why?" I asked.

"It means that his mother was not a beggar. To his emotional side it will mean that she cared for him. It will also make our task easier. This is a sign that she tried to pay her dues. It will be a moral standard he will want to live up to."

I had not thought of all that. I watched Father James read the letter before he gave it to me. The handwriting was practiced, clear, and round. Besides requesting the name Judah Saul for her child, the mother informed us of his date of birth, time of birth, and birth weight. She enclosed a doctor's certificate attesting to the fact that the baby had received his TB and smallpox vaccinations. This was no uneducated woman, which was the usual kind who left their babies with us because they could not care for them. An unopened tin of Ostermilk baby food and some baby clothes lay at the foot of the basket. The letter was signed "Bernadette Gonsalves." I felt closer to the baby when I read his mother's name because my name is Peter Gonsalves.

Bernadette wrote that she hoped that the baby's father, Saul Korle, a Jewish man from Jwalanagar, would claim his son within a week. She said that she had written to him. In case he did not arrive, we were free to baptize the child and bring him up in his mother's Christian faith. Her jewelry was to pay for the time she expected the baby to stay with us. I looked at the hoop earrings, the kind that most schoolgirls wear, the locketless gold chain, and the two narrow gold bangles. I realized that the mother had given us all she had.

There was much argument between my Father Superior and me. I was all for baptizing the child without waiting for his father.

It meant one more soul for Jesus. Father James saw the matter differently. He was sure that the baby's father would not claim him. We would baptize him with a clear conscience after that.

"I know this community well," he said. "They never accept a child whose parents are not both Jews. These children are called Kala Israel, and although they are not prohibited from entering the synagogue, they are never allowed to read from the Torah during services or blow the ram's horn on their holy days. No Jewish parents will give their daughter in marriage to a Kala Israel. The father will know that his son has a home with us, and that will ease any feelings of guilt that may arise. We will give him a chance to claim his son so that if we are ever taken to the law courts our case will have a leg to stand on."

I was not satisfied. I knew the British deputy commissioner of police and suggested taking his advice on the matter. Surely the Christian would understand my position as a priest and a missionary. The Englishman recognized the name Korle, and he sided with Father James.

"The baby's uncle, Noah Korle, is an active member of the Congress Party," he said. "We have enough trouble with the natives and the Free India Movement. We cannot afford to be seen as forcing our religion on people who do not want it. The natives will have a field day if Korle decides to take this to court. If conversion to Christianity is your aim in life, pick up some of the abandoned beggar children whom nobody cares about. They will grow up worshipping idols without your care. The poor devil you have got will at least believe in one God. In my book that is halfway to salvation."

I was not ready to give up. "The Second Coming of Christ will take place only when all the Jews convert to Christianity," I said.

"There are too many of them for that to happen in our lifetime. Take my advice and use the little money you have to save another soul. The courts of law will give the child to his family. The mother has informed them where he is, so if you try to send him to another place we will be obliged to arrest you and find the baby."

I had sworn an oath of obedience, so I had to do what my superior decided. Father James decided to wait a month for Mr. Saul Korle to appear. Korle did not arrive, so Father James sent Father Francis, a man older and more patient than I, to Jwalanagar in search of him. Father Francis found the man but returned without him. Mr. Korle had refused to take his son into his home. He called his child "wasted seed." Francis told him that his son would be raised a Catholic, but he was not concerned. "Let him remain in his mother's religion," Francis reported him as saying. "If his mother marries, he will have a Christian father, anyway."

"Don't you feel anything for him?" Francis had asked.

"Guilt and curiosity. I am sorry that his mother is the kind of woman who does not want to care for her own child."

"Do you?"

"No. I need Jewish sons born from a Jewish mother to say Kaddish for me after I am dead."

"Who is Judah?" Francis asked.

"My father. He died last year. Why do you ask?"

"Your son will be named Judah Saul."

"I see."

So we baptized the baby with the name that connected him to his father's family, but we gave him his mother's surname. As the boy grew older, I discovered that he thought he had been named for me because I was the person who found him. It seemed like a mark of special favor from my side. I had to correct him and tell him that it was his mother's family name. He asked if he was my relative, and I informed him that I had no sisters. But it made no difference in his love and attachment to me, which were greater than his feelings for the other priests. He came to me with every small joy and sorrow of his childhood. I was the one who checked his homework and explained things he did not understand in school. He was a precious source of pride and joy for me. I ached when he ached, like the time he became tongue-tied in his first appearance in a school play.

Judah's mother had made a poor choice in a name for her Christian son. Other children in the orphanage teased him. He could be a little bully at times, and this was their way of getting even.

"Father, I want to change my name," he said to me one day.

"Why?" I asked.

"I don't want to be called Judas Iscariot or Saul the mad king," he said.

"Saul was one of the anointed. Jesus belonged to the family of Judah. David and Solomon belonged to that family, too."

"Judas betrayed Jesus."

"I am named Peter, and Peter denied his Master three times."

"Judas did it for money."

"And Christ prayed for him. He forgave him."

"I don't care. I want to be called Jude Paul," he insisted.

"Your mother chose your name. It connects you with your father's family."

"They don't want me. I don't want their name."

He started calling himself Jude Paul Gonsalves. This was the name he inscribed on all his notebooks. It was only a matter of time before everybody, including the orphanage staff and myself, called him Jude.

Jude spoke to me about his mother quite often. He was hungry for information about her. He listened to the little I could tell him with an eagerness that never abated, no matter how many times I said the same things. He claimed that he hated her for leaving him. Mothers were supposed to love their babies more than anything else in the world. Fathers could be indifferent, but mothers could not. She had cared for herself more than for her baby. I explained to him time and again that perhaps she had no alternative. She must have been unable to care for him, or she would never have given him up. Although he said that he could not believe this, I saw him look closely at every woman who came within the boundary walls of the orphanage or the school. He listened closely for each lady's name. When I asked him about this he said that he kept hoping to see a lady he bore a resemblance to, and that he always listened for the name Bernadette Gonsalves. He realized that the surname may have changed, but the Christian name would be the same.

I think that I was prouder than Jude when he graduated from high school with very good marks. The orphanage authorities agreed to send him to college, but he had other ideas. He joined the army and went away. He wrote to us regularly, and all of us in the orphanage watched his progress with pride. Each of us prayed for him, especially during World War II, when he fought in North Africa and Italy. I had always hoped that God would give him his vocation. This never happened. I was disappointed, but I accepted it. Like any father, I was happy in my child's happiness. I felt my heart tighten in my chest when I saw him in his uniform with his shining boots and gleaming medals.

The British left India in 1947. Our independence was accompanied by the Partition and by terrible atrocities. Hindus and Muslims killed one another without any pity. Helpless refugees suffered the most. Women were raped, houses burned, and property was looted. Former neighbors chopped each other into little bits. Children were not spared. Then the government decided to use the army to ensure the safety of the refugees. Soldiers who were neither Hindu nor Muslim were the first to be assigned this task. Captain Jude Paul Gonsalves was one of the officers who accompanied refugees.

Jude returned from his trips to and from the newly formed Pakistan a completely different man. We sat in the garden sipping lemonade as he told me about his experiences. I sat relaxed in my chair ready to enjoy whatever he had to say. His stories were usually rather funny, so I was unprepared for what followed.

He told me that he and his soldiers found women who had either been abducted by the other side or abandoned by their families when they fled across the border. He was speaking about the refugees created by the Partition. "The poor girls had been repeatedly raped. Many were pregnant. Most bore scars, and many had been mutilated. Few wanted to return home. It took a lot of convincing and promises of protection against enraged families to get even a few to agree to risk a journey back. I could not understand their fear, but the other officers and soldiers could. I suppose my sequestered and protected upbringing was responsible for my innocence," he said.

He remembered an exceptionally brave woman named Amarjeet. At twenty-seven, she was the oldest of a group of five women they brought back. She had three children who had managed to come to India with their father. She was left behind because she was pregnant and could not run. This pregnancy had come within a few weeks of the birth of her third child, and it was accompanied by morning sickness that had left her very weak. Her condition would have endangered the family. They fled without her. It was only for the sake of her unborn child that she was willing to try and face the family. Her example encouraged four other girls to return to India with her, but they made her promise that if their families refused to accept them she would return to Pakistan with them. These women loved and supported one another as though they were sisters.

Why did Jude tell me all this? He said that in Amarjeet's story, I would be able to see a parallel to his mother's story. I, who had always claimed that man is basically good, would be able to see and recognize man's inhumanity. His mother was an abandoned woman, the same as these women were. Her man was no different than the men these women said they belonged to. Whether they were fathers or husbands or brothers, they were all the same. That is what Jude claimed.

They found the girls' families in a refugee camp not far from Delhi. The girls bathed and tried to pretty themselves as best they could in the old clothes they had. Abraham, Jude's Jewish friend from Jwalanagar, ever the softie, bought them new slippers and *dupattas*. Shamed by his generosity, my son bought a bundle of printed cotton cloth that the girls sewed *kameezes* from. On the appointed day they took the girls to their families. The men of the families did not allow them into the squalid little room that the camp authorities had provided for the meeting. The families sat inside the room. The soldiers and two camp officials sat in the doorway. The girls stood outside in the hot sun. The *dupattas* that they had covered their heads with, as a sign of respect for their elders, offered no protection from the fierce heat. Flies buzzed around them, and the stench from the open latrines was overpowering. Nobody offered the poor things even a glass of water. Jude watched them hold each other's hands. He saw them tremble. The youngest, a child of fourteen, was visibly weeping, although it was to her credit that no sound escaped her.

Amarjeet's husband had not bound up his long black beard, as most Sikh men do. Jude recognized him as one of the men he and his friends had thrown out of a small village, where he had come to incite the locals to violence against the Muslim refugees

who were making their way to Pakistan. The woman's husband
was no innocent. He was a rapist and a murderer. When Abraham
had threatened to shoot him, he had disappeared very quickly at
the sight of the cocked pistol. Amarjeet was indeed brave to try and
face him. Her children called out to her and wept when they saw
her, but a blow from the father that sent the eldest child sprawling
silenced them all. Amarjeet bit her lips and remained silent even
as her children wept. Jude saw her body jerk when her child was
struck. Her arms reached out for a moment toward the boy before
she quickly lowered them. She was not a part of the family anymore, so she had no rights.

Her husband looked directly at her and said, "*Haraamzadi!
Maar jaana tha.* Bastard! You should have died." His hand moved
to his *kirpan,* the sword that as a Sikh he wore according to the
laws of his religion. He never removed his hand from this
weapon. Jude wondered how many people he had killed with it.

Abraham lost his temper. "*Haraamzadi* she, or *haraamzada*
you? You left her and ran away. You coward, you *gandoo,* you pas-
sive homosexual. You did not have the courage to protect her, and
now you dare to tell her that she should have killed herself. You
know that she is carrying your child. She is too far gone for it to
be anybody else's. The pregnancy started before you left. Everybody present can see that. Your children need their mother. What
kind of a *rakshas,* a monster, are you? Don't you care for your children? Your wife needs her family, too. What about your unborn
child? It is dependent upon your love and support." He was
angry, but these were questions all the soldiers accompanying the
girls wanted to ask. Perhaps they would convince the man to take
his wife back.

"I will not have, in my house, a woman who has been with a
Muslim" was the only answer to Abraham's outburst.

"How many Muslim women have you been with?" Abraham

asked. His voice had fallen low, and each word was uttered clearly and slowly. The words were a mixture of statement, question, and accusation. The effect was startling. Abraham was really angry. His eyes had become bloodshot, and he clenched his fists. His voice trembled as he tried to keep his temper under control. Jude placed his hand over Abraham's as a sign that he should be calm. Their first obligation was to the women. It was not easy to try and be reasonable in those kinds of situations, although they faced them again and again.

"That is different. I'm a man. A woman's honor lies in her chastity. A family's honor is bound up with the chastity of its women. She should have killed herself before bringing shame upon us. Take the bitch out of here before I take her life," her husband said. "I can show you men here who killed their women with their own hands before leaving so that they would not be dishonored by rape."

Mamta, the youngest girl, whom the soldiers had brought, could not control herself any longer. She burst into tears, and the girl who stood beside her put an arm around her in an attempt to comfort her. None of the other men accepted the women of their family back, either. An old woman who sat inside the room rocked back and forth wailing. "It is a curse to be born a woman," she wept. "*Hai meri bachi.* Oh, my child."

"*Chup kaar budhiya.* Be silent, old woman," one of the men shouted, but the old woman kept wailing. She tried to catch a glimpse of the five girls outside. "Same *kameezes,* like girls attending the same school," she lamented. "Schoolgirl. My *beichari,* miserable, young schoolgirl."

The soldiers took the women back to Pakistan. They tried to convince them to stay in India, but the women refused. Each had her reasons, but the one reason they had in common was that they wanted to return to the family they had set up together, even if it meant prostitution. Loyalty and love proved to be stronger than circumstance. They had nobody but one another. Since India had no rehabilitation programs for abandoned women, there was no hope for them on our side of the border, either. The soldiers had promised them their protection on the journey back, so they returned with them.

A few miles outside Meerut, Amarjeet gave birth. The emotional strain may have hastened the delivery. Anyhow, the baby was a healthy girl. When Jude went to congratulate her, her baby was dead. He found Amarjeet clutching it to her breast and weeping over it. When he took the child from her, its head fell back. There were two purple marks on either side of the neck. Some sound of horror must have escaped him, because Amarjeet looked at him and said, "It is better so. Don't be sorry for her. She is free. Save your pity for the living."

"Amarjeet!" was all he could say.

"I cannot rear a daughter in a house of prostitution. That's not the fate I want for my child."

"Stay behind in India. You can find some work," Jude pleaded.

"What work will an uneducated woman find? My parents did not want to educate me because they were afraid that nobody would marry me if I had a mind of my own. My husband did not want a wife who could get ideas from other places like books. He had to be looked upon as the source of all wisdom. How else could he be head of his family? In India, too, I would have to use my body to earn my bread. The only other thing I can do is become a servant in a rich or middle-class home. I would be at the mercy of its men once again. The wages would be starvation wages. I would have to live on the streets and be open to attack. Prostitution will be safer."

Jude cursed her husband. "I hope he dies a long, slow, lingering death," he said.

"No, sahib. Don't curse him. He is the father of my children. Three children will suffer along with him. Don't you know that a curse uttered from a truly troubled and sorrowful person against her tormentor always comes true?"

"The innocent baby! You did not have to kill the baby. Some man would have married you. You are still young and pretty. More than that, you are a good and kind woman."

"You dream, sahib." She pointed to the dead baby. "Who would have cared for that miserable creature, another man's child? I know of no orphanage where she would have stood some sort of a chance for a normal life. No, I shall return to Pakistan. I promised the girls. I am the oldest, and I must care for them. They are my children now."

Jude thought of his mother. She had faced a similar situation, and she had done what she thought was best for her baby. Jude said that he felt a great wave of love and sorrow wash over him, and he wept. He wept for Amarjeet. He wept for her dead baby and her motherless children. He wept for Mamta, the child turned woman, and for all the girls whose families had refused to accept them, although they were blameless. He wept for himself. Most of all, he wept for his mother. He realized that she must have loved him a great deal, and the parting must have been very difficult for her.

Jude fell silent, but I felt as though I was drowning in my own failure. All my teaching had been in vain. I was glad that he had finally realized that his mother loved him and that he had no more hate for her left in his heart. Still, as a Catholic and a priest I could not condone infanticide. I was sorrowful that Jude had accepted it as a sign of love and mercy instead of a lack of faith. I said that Amarjeet had played God, to which he replied that God was not interested in women, anyway.

"That's not true. Remember Magdalene. God sent his only Son to save all men." I stressed the "all."

"Son?" Jude sneered. "He had all the qualities of a woman. He suffered for men and prayed for them even when he was dying.

That is what is expected of women. Suttee is based on the same idea. A woman who is not willing to suffer is not worthy enough to be called a woman."

I was outraged. "You compare the sacrifice of Christ to pagan rites!" I almost shouted at him.

He was calm. My anger did not upset him as it used to. "All religions perpetuate the same myths," he said with a smile.

"Christ is not a myth."

"Perhaps. Let's not argue about it."

Jude had never believed completely. He always had some reservations. As a priest I rebuked him. As a father I tried to find excuses for my son. I put everything down to the shock of his experience, but there was worse to follow.

"I told you that my friend Abraham is a Jew from Jwalanagar."

"Yes, you did," I said. My skin prickled all over with apprehension. Jude's smile of satisfaction meant that he had bad news about the father he hated.

"Guess what? I'm my father's only son, although nobody knows that he has a son."

"Perhaps he has only daughters." I saw from his smile that this was not the case, so I said, "I see. He did not marry."

"Oh, but he did. Twice. His first wife had some medical complications soon after she became pregnant. Her womb had to be removed. He made her miserable as long as she lived because she couldn't have any children for him. When she fell ill she did not go to the doctor, and he never even noticed her condition. Eventually another Jewish woman brought the doctor to the home. He couldn't do much, and the lady died. My father, Mr. Saul Korle, as a fairly religious Jew, observed a year of mourning. Yet within a fortnight of the one-year ceremony for his wife, he got married once again." Jude smiled his new, cruel smile. "The story gets better," he added.

"Worse, you mean."

"Of course. Worse for him. He married a girl from Bombay. The wedding took place in the morning so that he could take the evening train back to Jwalanagar. They arrived early in the afternoon. He took his new wife home by tonga. When he was paying the tonga driver, a dog attacked the horse, and it began prancing and jumping around in an attempt to avoid the dog. The dog ran behind my father. The end result was that the horse knocked Mr. Korle down, and its front legs came down upon the man's back. He has been in a wheelchair ever since. No babies and no Kaddish for him."

"You sound happy," I cried. "You revel in another man's pain. Where is the kind, loving, and caring boy I knew? Where is the Jude who would do anything for other people?"

"He is still here, Father," Jude said, placing a hand over his heart. "I'll still do anything for anybody. It is only natural that I should be glad when my enemies suffer."

"It is not natural or right to be glad when anybody suffers. Besides, that man is your father. He cannot be your enemy. I am sure that in some corner of his heart he thinks of you and loves you."

"Then why hasn't he come in search of me?"

I had no answer to this. Instead I said, "You are giving your own sorrows more importance than those of others. Where is your pity, Jude? What about the poor woman he married? Has she not suffered, too?"

"Like the old woman in the refugee camp said, 'It is a curse to be born a woman,' " he replied.

I had leaned forward during my attempts to make the boy see sense, and I fell back in my chair at his last remark. I looked closely at my son's face. The expression of defiance told me very clearly that Jude had done something he was ashamed of but was not yet ready to apologize for.

"What have you done, my son?" I asked as gently as I could. Jude's face crumbled. "Bless me, Father, for I have sinned."

This phrase from the confessional registered in my mind. Perhaps not all was lost. "Go on. Tell me the rest," I said.

"I went to Jwalanagar. Abraham showed me my father's house without knowing that I am Mr. Korle's son. Later, I went to see him. I told his wife that I had to speak to her husband alone. I introduced myself as Judah Saul. As soon as he heard my name, my father told his wife to go to the pictures with the servant girl. The two women seemed glad to be given an outing, but it increased their curiosity about me."

I noticed the different ways Jude referred to his father. His feelings about him were mixed. There was hope for my son. He still thought that what he had done was a sin. He would learn to understand and forgive. I kept hoping for the best as I listened to Jude speak.

"After they had gone, I asked him about my mother," he said. "I had no intention of hurting him either physically or with words. I just wanted to know about her. He gave me two pictures. One was a snapshot taken on a picnic, and the other was in an old school magazine that he had kept. By the way, in both pictures she is wearing the earrings and chain you gave me. She had been a primary school teacher when Mr. Korle knew her in Jwalanagar. My mother came to Allahabad to take her teacher's training at St. Mary's. She had said that she was married, so nobody questioned her pregnancy. She gave me up only when she had to return home. Korle did not know what happened to her after she left Jwalanagar for a job she had found in Delhi.

"So far everything was fine. I got angry only when he began to speak against my mother. He called her an unnatural woman for leaving me. He had no remorse whatsoever for the part he played in my being born and then being turned into an abandoned child.

I managed to hold my tongue not because of whatever you have taught me but because I wanted to hear what the man had to say. He then used abusive language against my mother. He blamed her for his condition. He said that she had written to him and asked him to at least take care of me even though he could not marry her. She wrote that I was his responsibility and that if he did not take me he would be cursed all his life. He would have no children if he refused to recognize me as his son. Mr. Korle wanted to know what kind of a woman would curse the man she loved.

"'A woman who is deeply hurt,' I said, but he did not even hear me. He just kept on blaming her curse for his being a cripple and in a wheelchair. He had to depend on other people for many things. The joy had gone out of his life. It was an effort, but I kept my temper under control. I made tea for him and listened to everything he had to say. Then we heard his wife return, so I rose to leave. The man who had made no attempt to touch me during the entire time I had spent with him and who had not once called me son or acknowledged our relationship in any way suddenly put out a hand to stop me. 'Judah, remember my Kaddish. Will you say it for me after I am gone?'

"I knew that this was important to him, so in my anger I used this knowledge to hurt him. 'I don't think that it will be possible,' I said, 'and my name is not Judah Saul. I changed it to Jude Paul long ago. You see, I am only wasted seed and not Jewish.' I saw him flinch at my quoting the words he had used for me long ago. It gave me a strange pleasure that he remembered. 'I am not connected to anybody,' I said. 'I am not a religious man who prays the prescribed number of times every day, either. I could say a rosary for the peace of your soul if and when I hear of your demise. That's all I can do.'

"I knew that I had been very cruel, but I was not sorry. I wanted to hurt the man who had hurt both my mother and me. I did not feel any different when Mrs. Korle sent for me later that evening. She had found her husband unconscious on the bathroom floor. He had slashed his wrists, and she thought that I might know the reason. I donated blood for my father because I have the same blood type. A private doctor conducted the whole operation at home; had he taken his patient to the hospital, it would have been reported to the police as an attempted suicide. Nobody wanted a public scandal.

"My feelings did not change, even when he recovered consciousness and thanked me for saving his life. 'I was only returning the favor,' I said. I saw him wince. This should have made me feel bad, but it did not. I twisted the knife a bit further. 'It is all right. Don't give it a thought. I'd have done it for anybody. The good fathers taught us orphans the importance of Christian charity,' I said, and left. I took the first train out of Jwalanagar."

Jude looked at me for the comfort which I was unable to give. I told him to try and understand his father's situation, his beliefs, his upbringing, and his expectations in life. The man must be lonely, afraid, and bitter in his wheelchair. He must have repented for his sins. Jude had to be the better man of the two by being magnanimous, but my son thought that I was talking sanctimonious nonsense.

"People should pay for whatever they do," he said. "It is only right," he declared with full conviction.

After this incident Jude became more and more irreligious and heretical. I wanted him to forgive his father and ask for his father's forgiveness in return. To date, Jude has not been able to bring himself to do either. I have pointed out the Fifth Commandment to him, but he maintains that a parent has to be worthy of the honor the commandment demands. He claims that duty is different from love, and nobody can be commanded to love. I have failed the boy. My love and acceptance of him have not sufficed. He has come to understand his mother's situation, but he still hurts over his father's rejection. He has succeeded in life, but success is nothing without peace of mind. I have not been able to teach him the secret of that, either. My love could not replace the love of the natural parents he longs for. I have not been able to implant in him a love and belief in God, either. So far my love's labor has borne scanty fruit. I will remain a failure until the time Jude Paul, my son, attains happiness and tranquillity.

Nathoo

THE ARMY CAPTAIN STOOD in an open field and looked at the scene around him in horror and despair. He had traveled all night in the company of other soldiers from the Indian Army in the hope that they would catch up with a group of refugees and take them safely across the border. They had found them, but it was too late. The light of early dawn was enough to show them that the earth was covered with dark patches where human blood had soaked in. The captain thought that it was worse than any charnel house he had ever seen. In slaughterhouses animals were killed for a purpose and with every thought for a quick death with the least amount of suffering involved. The field he stood in had been a place of senseless slaughter and mutilation. The earth was strewn with severed heads, chopped-off limbs, and decapitated bodies. Some bodies had just a slashed throat or a stab wound, while others were beyond recognition. The bodies of the women had gaping wounds where their breasts should have been. Their genitals were burned and mutilated. The bodies of babies and children were in a horrible condition, too. Nobody had cared about their innocence and helplessness in a world of crazy adults. Their only crime was that they were born into a religion different from that of their killers.

This is the glorious beginning of Indian independence, the captain thought. "Nothing I saw in Burma, Malaya, or Indonesia was anything compared with this. Here it is neighbor killing neighbor and brother betraying brother. These are my people. I always believed that we are a kind and loving people who are incapable of brutal behavior." He thought of the girl he had married five months ago. He was glad that he had been posted out of Quetta, a city in the north of the new country called Pakistan. His transfer to Kalyaan had come before independence and Partition. His gentle wife had been spared these horrible sights.

The captain had been chosen to accompany the refugees because he was Jewish. Although there were Hindus in the group, most of the other soldiers were either Christian or Zoroastrian so that they did not feel partial to either the Muslims or the Hindus. The Muslim refugees traveling from India to Pakistan were in exactly the same position as Hindu refugees who traveled from Pakistan to India. All were equally miserable and vulnerable to attack from anybody who decided to loot and murder them. After the first attack on refugees, revenge became the excuse for more murder. After Partition, people who found themselves on the wrong side of the border took their few belongings and made their way to the country of their choice as best they could. Some used bullock carts, some used horse-drawn tongas, but the majority went on foot. All were open to attack. Trains, the fastest means of travel, were stopped on their tracks, and not a single passenger was allowed to escape death. Slaughter and rape were perpetrated by both sides with equal ferocity and cruelty.

The soldiers built funeral pyres with whatever combustible material they could find. Broken carts and dead branches from trees in the area were gathered. The bodies were laid on top and drenched with petrol before somebody set a match to it all. The captain wept openly without any sense of shame. Many of the other men in uniform wept, too. Some cursed the perpetrators while others questioned God. The captain walked some distance away from the pyres and sat in the shade of an acacia tree. The sun had climbed quite high, and he needed shade. He folded his legs into the position sadhus use for meditation, but his mind was not fixed upon any one point. He could not block out the sight of dead bodies or the smell of burning flesh. He rocked back and forth, mourning the deaths of his countrymen and -women. He hated the madness that seemed to have overtaken his people and felt an impotent rage at his inability to stop it. Most of the soldiers with him had confessed to similar feelings.

Suddenly the captain stopped rocking back and forth as he mourned. His body stiffened. He thought that he had heard somebody moving up behind him. His hand flew to his service revolver, and he spun around to look before he rose slowly from the ground. *I hope it is one of the bastards responsible for this. I'll personally beat him into something even his mother won't recognize,* he thought as he looked around. The sounds came from some low bushes not far from where he stood. The person making the noise seemed to stumble, fall, and then rise again. The footsteps had a broken rhythm resembling that of a wounded person. The captain took no chances. He waited for whoever was in the bushes to emerge.

"Raise your hands over your head and come out," he called in a fierce voice.

"*Muth maaro.* Don't kill me," a child's voice called back, before a young boy made his stumbling way out of the bushes. His torn clothes and staring eyes were enough to tell the officer that the boy belonged to the group of refugees and that he had seen the atrocities committed against his own family.

He returned his revolver to its holster and took the water canteen that hung from a buckle on his web belt.

"*Pani. Pani chahiyae?*" The boy stretched out one arm toward the figure in uniform before his knees buckled and he collapsed in a shapeless heap. The captain ran toward the boy and shouted over his shoulder, "Doctor! There is one alive." He heard some soldiers run toward him, but he did not stop to look. He reached the boy and sprinkled water over his face. The young survivor recovered slowly. His hands shook as he placed them over the hands that held the canteen to his lips. He drank greedily before he sank back upon the earth. His eyes were fixed on the young officer.

"*Shukriya.* Thank you," he whispered. "*Fauji?* Army?"

The captain nodded. He noticed the relief in the boy's eyes and on his face. "What is your name?" he asked.

"Nathoo."

"Where is your family?"

Nathoo pointed to the bushes. He rose and started to stumble back toward them. The doctor and two other soldiers had reached them, and the doctor asked one of the soldiers to stay behind with the boy. The older men would investigate. "*Sab ko maara,* they killed everybody," the boy mumbled. "*Maa aur didiya vahaa,* Mother and my elder sisters there." He pointed to the bushes. "*Pita aur bhai vahaa,* Father and my brothers there." He pointed toward the burning pyres. "I hid in a bush. Nobody saw me. They found the other children, but I do not know why they did not find me." He shed no tears. The boy was in shock.

The doctor, the captain, and another officer named Jude Paul set off in the direction that the boy had pointed to. Behind the bushes there was a depression in the ground. A hillock rose beyond it. The side of the hillock was covered with various articles of women's clothing. In some places the clothes were strewn around, and in other places they were in orderly piles. The captain felt his stomach tighten. He knew what he would see on the other side of the mound. Jude Paul made the sign of the cross. "Please, Jesus," he kept repeating, "please, Jesus, let them be alive. Oh, Jesus, please, please."

The three men climbed the hillock and looked down upon a scene none of them had ever seen, even in their recent grisly experiences. They would never know how many girls and women were raped and killed there because the heap they found was made up of pieces of flesh the size women use to make curries, goulashes, and stews. The ground was soaked with blood. Ants were carrying off the smaller pieces of flesh. Vultures were sitting in the trees waiting for the funeral pyres to burn out and the men to move away so that they could descend to the feast that other men had provided for them. Jude Paul used the vilest words in the dictionary as he cursed the vultures, the murderers, the government, and anybody he could think of. He then started to recite the Hail Mary and went to the trucks for petrol with which to douse the remains. The other two men stood beside the remains and tried not to look at them or imagine who these pieces once were.

"Rajan, I'm taking Nathoo home with me," the captain said to the doctor. "A refugee camp is no place for him. He will only hear more horror stories, and his hate will grow. Do you think that he will agree to come with me?"

"His family was killed by Muslims. What do you think will happen when he hears that your name is Abraham? He will think that it is Ibrahim. You will have to explain to him what a Jew is. Not many Indians know what Jews are. I have only met three in the army, where all kinds of people meet. This boy's village could not have had more than Hindus, Sikhs, and Muslims. Even the Parsis live farther to the south."

"I will speak to him," Abraham said.

The boy sat under the acacia tree and watched the funeral pyres with an impassive face. He answered questions but volunteered no information. He said that his mother called him Nathoo Ram and the soldiers could call him that. His village was in the province of Sind, and when that had been given to Pakistan, his family had decided to go to India. All his relatives were from his village and another village not far from his. The Muslims from his village had accompanied them for a full day in order to protect them. They had camped for a night and then walked for another day. They were attacked just after nightfall. No, he had no relatives in India. His people all lived in Sind.

Abraham approached the boy and said, "My name is Abraham. I am the first *fauji* that you saw today. I have a question for you."

"What?"

"Will you come and live with me in my house?"

"Why?" the boy asked. He sounded curious, not angry or skeptical.

"I haven't been able to stop the suffering, but maybe I can help one person to suffer less. A refugee camp or an orphanage is not the best place for you."

"*Thik hai.* It is all right. I'll go with you. I have nobody left in this world, anyway." It seemed that he was resigned to whatever might happen to him. He did not even want to know the reason it was happening.

"My wife will be happy to welcome you." Abraham wanted to make sure that the boy knew his name and religion, so he repeated, "My name is Abraham. It is not Ibrahim. I am not a Muslim. I am a Jew. You do not have to feel that you are betraying your family by staying in my house."

"I am glad that you are not a Mohammedan," Nathoo replied.

For the next week Nathoo followed Abraham wherever he went. They met a few officials in Pakistan and established a camp to hold the people who wanted to cross over. Here the army would protect them from those who wanted to harm them. Nathoo was surprised to find that the Muslims had suffered the same atrocities at the hands of the Hindus as the Hindus of his group had suffered. He could not believe that all men were cruel. The more refugees he met, the more disillusioned he became with life. Abraham realized that he could not leave the boy with anybody because he was not sure what the child was capable of doing. Abraham asked to be relieved from making more trips across the border and explained the situation to his commanding officer, who sent another officer to replace him.

Abraham took Nathoo to Kalyaan, the place to which the army had transferred him. Abraham thought that perhaps there he could feel young once again. He felt much older than his twenty-four years. He hoped his eighteen-year-old wife would make life seem beautiful again. They lived in a big house with a large garden, and Abraham hoped that Nathoo could learn to be happy there, with a room of his own and a school to attend. He would make friends with children his own age. Abraham told Nathoo about his dreams for him and asked him to tell him everything that he thought about his new home and new life. Nathoo agreed.

Nathoo said he liked Dina, Abraham's wife. She did not have the hard hands and body of the women who worked on farms in his village, and she wore a sari, not a *salwar kameez,* but she was okay for a city-bred memsahib. He decided to call her *didi,* elder sister. He liked the clothes and shoes she brought for him from the bazaar. Nathoo saw through her trick of making him feel important and knowledgeable when she asked him about plants and animals. She actually wanted him to learn Hindi and English. He told her that she could teach him to read in these languages if she would let him teach her to read in Urdu. They struck a bargain, but she was a poor student. Abraham laughed when he heard this and told Nathoo that he would find a school that taught in the language he had learned to read in.

Abraham found a school that taught in the Urdu language and registered him there. Nathoo was a bit disappointed when he was told that he had to repeat class 7. The Partition of India had cost him a year of education. Abraham took Nathoo to a tailor to get three sets of school uniforms. They bought the required books and a new schoolbag. Abraham and Dina saw the boy smile for the first time when he dressed for school. He ran a clean, soft rag over his well-polished shoes. He repeatedly looked into his bag to make sure that he had all the necessary books. Dina had prepared sandwiches for his lunch, and Nathoo asked that she place them in a well-fastened toffee box so that nothing would stain his books. Abraham was as pleased as the boy was.

School, however, did not prove to be a success. Two hours after leaving the boy in school, Abraham received a phone call from the headmaster asking him to come and take Nathoo home. The boy had lost all control and had tried to beat up any child who came within reach. Abraham mounted his bicycle and rode as fast as he could. A journey of five minutes seemed to take an hour. He found Nathoo tied to a chair in the headmaster's office. He was thrashing about as much as he could. His eyes bulged, and words of invective poured from his lips. Abraham was surprised at the vocabulary of abuse Nathoo possessed.

"Why did you have to tie him up?" Abraham asked. "I can understand his reason for saying what he is saying. If I had been tied to a chair I would scream and use abusive language, too." He knew that he was trying to find excuses for the boy. Nathoo was not being punished. He was only being restrained. He must have done something terrible.

"I am sorry," the headmaster said. "We tried everything, but the boy seemed to have gone crazy. He bit the hands of the teacher who tried to hold him away from the boys he was fighting with. We had to bandage two boys and send one to the hospital to have his arm set."

"What started it?" Abraham asked.

"A prayer. A boy said, *Allah hu akbar.*"

"I am sorry, but for Nathoo it is not a prayer of praise. It is the cry of a murderer. His entire family was killed in front of his eyes when they tried to cross over from Pakistan. The words brought back terrible memories for him. These are the words he heard over the cries of his people as they were being slaughtered."

The headmaster's eyes filled with tears. "Poor God," he murmured. "What evil is done in your name!"

The sight of Abraham had a calming effect on Nathoo. "*Bhai* sahib, elder brother, please take me home," he said.

"I am sorry about the boy, and I will explain to any parent who comes here with complaints, but I think that Nathoo should not return to school. We cannot stop teaching our religion or our prayers because of one child," the headmaster said.

Abraham untied Nathoo but held his arm in a firm grip. He was afraid that the boy would try to get at the headmaster. His eyes returned to their normal size, but they still flashed hatred at everything around him. Abraham made him sit on the bicycle bar in front of him. The headmaster gave Nathoo's schoolbag to Abraham, who, being afraid of freeing Nathoo, hung the bag around his own neck before cycling home. A few small children pointed at him and laughed, but he was too worried about the boy to realize how ridiculous he looked.

Life did not become easier for Nathoo. He had bouts of depression that bordered on madness. He dreamed about the horrible day in early September 1947 when he had lost his entire family and all the Hindu inhabitants of his village. He would get up screaming, and Abraham and Dina always rushed in from their room. Abraham held him in his arms until he calmed down. His voice soothed the boy and spoke to him through all his hallucinations and nightmares. Nathoo tried to focus on Abraham's voice when his tortured mind dragged him toward his dead family. As long as he had something to read or some work in the garden, his memories stayed away. Kalyaan was not as cold as his village in Sind, but he thought of asking Dina to teach him to knit. It would be something to do.

As the months passed Nathoo's condition improved. Then, in January, the Quadri family came to live with Abraham and Dina. Khaleel, the third son, had been Abraham's classmate. Because they were to embark from Bombay on their way to Karachi, they asked if they could stay with Abraham until their ship sailed. They did not know anybody in Bombay, and Kalyaan was only one hour by train from Bombay. Abraham's father and Mr. Quadri had worked for many years in the same textile mill and were good friends. There was nothing unusual in the arrangement. Abraham had stayed with them quite often when he was a child. They were almost family.

Nathoo took one look at Mr. Quadri's pointed beard and large crocheted skullcap and went into hysterics. Abraham carried the screaming boy into his room and tried to speak to him. Nathoo took about twenty minutes to calm down. He then told Abraham that one of the rapists had a beard and a white crocheted cap like Mr. Quadri's. Mr. Quadri changed his cap for a furry Russian-style hat, but Nathoo still had fits of madness. He refused to eat with the guests. At times he stood behind the door, where Abraham could not see him, and showed a broom or a slipper, both signs of insult, to any member of the Muslim family who could see him. At other times he made threatening signs with a kitchen knife. He cursed them in Urdu that was too pure for Abraham to understand. Abraham or Dina would realize from the sad expression on Mr. Quadri's face that Nathoo was up to something. They spoke to the boy and sometimes sent him on errands that took him out of the house and gave him time to think. Nathoo always went to Mr. Quadri later with tears of regret and begged his forgiveness. "You are not the people who did these terrible things. I am sorry. Your people have suffered exactly the same as mine. Please forgive me." Mr. Quadri held the boy and wept, too. He had lost his eldest son, daughter-in-law, and two grandchildren as they made their way to Pakistan. He understood the boy's pain.

Mr. Quadri saw Nathoo struggling to read a book in the Devanagari script, so he offered him some books in Urdu. The boy was delighted. He read all the books that the old man could give him and spent time discussing them with him. Nathoo was the most tearful person when the family departed. His blessing for them was "May you have a garden with apricot and cherry trees. Sind is beautiful in springtime. May Allah always protect you." Abraham was surprised at Nathoo's use of the Muslim word for God. He hoped that it was a sign of improvement in the boy's mental condition.

Spring came to Kalyaan, but Nathoo thought the season could not really be called spring. The trees did not lose their leaves in the winter and renew them when it became warmer. Some trees did lose their leaves, but none ever became bare. By the time the last leaves had fallen the first buds had already opened. Everything was different. He was glad when he noticed that Dina was pregnant. She told him that the baby would be born in late summer. He looked forward to the new arrival. He pestered Abraham for classes in carpentry. He wanted to make a crib. Nathoo began to think more about the baby and less about past events. He would be an uncle soon. He made a new friend named Anthony, who lived four houses away from Abraham's house. The two boys played hockey with the boys from Anthony's school. Abraham hoped that Nathoo was turning into a normal twelve- or thirteen-year-old.

Learning had been put off for a while because it proved difficult for Nathoo, although he read Urdu fluently. He said that he never had any difficulty at school in Sind. The Devanagari script was hard, and English was impossible. He could read and write in one language and that was enough. His brain had plenty to cope with without forcing new symbols and signs into it.

Abraham spoke to him about returning to school. "The neighbors will think that I do not want to educate you. Soon they will think that you are not my younger brother but my servant."

"They can think whatever they wish as long as we know what we are."

"Do you remember how happy you were to go to school? Perhaps we could try it again. I'll register you in a different school this time," Abraham said.

"I don't want to go. Maybe in a few years my devils will leave me. That's the time I'll be ready for school."

"What if you are an old man by then?"

"Then I'll be a man with only seven years of education. I'll learn some trade and earn an honest living."

Abraham realized that he would have to wait a bit longer. He agreed to apprentice Nathoo to a carpenter for a few months. A lot of love and support could still prove to be the cure for the boy's mind.

The Indian custom was that a girl went to her parents' home for the delivery of her first child because she needed the help of a more experienced woman at that time. Since Dina's mother was herself expecting a baby, Abraham suggested that Dina stay with her cousin in Bombay, where he and Nathoo could visit her every day.

One day in May, Abraham and Dina decided to go to Bombay and make the arrangements for a room in the hospital where the baby was to be born. Dina told Nathoo that they would be home late in the evening. She had arranged for him to have his dinner with Captain Gupta and his family next door. He could also invite Anthony over after Anthony had finished his homework. Nathoo wished them a safe journey before they left, which was rather early in the morning.

Abraham and his wife returned late that evening. They were surprised to find a policeman sitting on the culvert near their gate. Another policeman stood on their doorstep. All the lights in Captain Gupta's house were blazing. A few people had gathered outside the gate.

Abraham and Dina opened the gate and approached their house. "What's the matter?" Abraham asked the policeman on his doorstep.

"I am Deputy Inspector Rehman. Are you the person Nathoo Ram lived with?"

"Yes."

"I am sorry, sir. Nathoo is dead."

"It cannot be. He left for carpentry classes this morning. He liked it there. He was not sick. Was it an accident?" Dina asked.

"No. Please come into the house. I'll explain," the deputy inspector said, leading the way. "I've not touched anything, sir, except the body. We have sent it to the morgue."

They entered the dining room and looked around. A chair lay upon its side on the floor, and a rough, coir rope lay coiled on the table. Besides that nothing seemed changed.

"Look at the tablecloth, sir. There is a note pinned to it. Shall I read it to you?" Rehman asked.

"You will have to. Neither I nor my wife can read Urdu," Abraham replied.

"Whoever finds this," the policeman read, "please do not

blame my *bhai* sahib, my elder brother Abraham, or my *didi*, his wife. I cannot go on living anymore, so I am going to join my family. Today two men reminded me of this. They said that I was a shame to all Hindus because I live with a Muslim family. They stuffed a cloth into my mouth so that I could not cry out when they beat me.

"I have decided to stop living. The world is too cruel and my memories are too much for me.

"Nathoo Ram, who was once also called Ramchandar Natraj."

Abraham and his wife looked at the rope. The deputy inspector pointed to the ceiling fan. "We found the body dangling from there. The boy did not like the roughness of the coir rope, so he took one of your handkerchiefs and put it around his neck under the rope. You will have to come to the morgue to identify the body. I must warn you that it is covered with bruises. I will also have to take the letter to the police station as evidence."

Two days later Abraham sat upon a stone bench on the banks of a river and looked at the water. As the only "relative" of Nathoo, he had set fire to the funeral pyre and collected the ashes, which he had scattered on the surface of the water a few minutes earlier. He had thrown the earthenware *chatti* that had held the ashes into the river, too. He regretted what he had said to the pundit who officiated over Nathoo's funeral. The man had asked for money, which Abraham had given him without saying a single word. The pundit then advised him "for the good of the soul of the departed person" to feed as many people as he could and give charity to the temple. Abraham refused. "I shall give charity when, where, and to whom I wish, if I wish."

The first rays of the sun turned the rosy streaks in the clouds into a glowing golden color. Abraham watched men bathe in the river where he had scattered Nathoo's ashes. An old man caught his attention. The man immersed himself several times in the water. He took water in his hands that were joined in the shape of a small bowl, and he poured a libation to the sun as it began to rise. He did this three times. Then he made his way up the bank and changed into dry clothes. The heat of summer had dried the river to a fraction of its usual flow. The stairs that normally led to the river stood several yards away from the water. As the old man made his way toward the spot where Abraham was sitting, he stumbled against an exposed stone. He picked it up and examined it carefully. The river had worn it into a smooth oval shape. The old man looked around. He found a flat stone with a depression in the center. He stood the oval stone in the flat stone and joined his hands together in silent prayer.

Does this man worship Indra or Shiva? Abraham wondered. *He worshipped the sun for Indra and then the forces of creation for Shiva.*

The man passed very close to Abraham. He sensed that Abraham was staring at him, so he looked at him and smiled.

"Do you really believe in God?" Abraham asked.

The old man put an arm around Abraham's shoulders. "It does not matter, my son, whether I believe in God or not. What matters is whether God believes in me and all men after what we have done to His world."

The man smiled at him once again before he turned and made his way slowly away from the river, carrying his wet clothes in one hand. He held both arms straight out for balance against the uneven ground and as an aid against stumbling.

Rats and Cobras

PEOPLE WHO MAINTAIN THAT village life is superior to life in the city have usually not experienced the difficult conditions in a village for a significant length of time. A two-week visit to the village in which my mother grew up was enough to change my romantic views of rural life forever. The other person in our family who was similarly affected by this visit was Meena, my eldest sister, also called Michal. After we returned home she would fly into a rage if any of us said "rat" or "cobra" to her. This visit also made us fashion-conscious as far as our underwear was concerned.

It all started with my maternal uncles' visits. Mother's brothers often visited us and stayed for a month at a time. Our parents always gave them the best of everything we had. They got the best parts of the chicken or goat for dinner. The only mangoes offered to them were the big fleshy ones of the *langra* or *kalmi* variety. The woman who came to help Mother with the housework was ordered around by them all the time, and they never gave her any extra money when they left. Before leaving they always invited us to their home, even though we never took them up on their offer. They would act as though they were the offended party and would insinuate that my father was too stingy to spend money on a holiday for his family. Then one day, Father, in a mischievous mood, accepted the invitation. Uncle Joel, as usual, had asked Father to

allow him to exercise his hospitality for a change. Father smiled
his innocent smile that warned us, who knew him well, to expect
some trick or mischief.

"You are right, Joel," he said. "It is time I gave my family a holiday. Since we are a large family we shall not stay a month, as you
have so generously invited us to. Two weeks will be enough. You
can expect us on the fourteenth of next month."

Uncle Joel managed a weak smile. Mother looked at Dad in
surprise but said nothing in front of us. Uncle Joel climbed into a
waiting tonga, which was drawn by a beautiful black horse, and
was driven away to the railway station.

We were not a rich family, and my father was the only working
member. My mother's little economies included sewing as many
of our clothes as she could. The shirts that the boys wore and all
our frocks were her handiwork. Her expertise, or her patience,
stopped with our underwear. We all wore boxer shorts because
these were easy to cut and fast to sew. Some of these shorts had
longer legs than other ones. If nothing else, as girls we learned to
keep our rather long dresses carefully drawn over our knees each
time we sat and rose. We were not ashamed of our knickers as
much as it was considered shameful, indecent, and immodest to
show the tiniest bit of them. Most girls we knew wore boxer
shorts as well and had the same problem.

Mother sat at her sewing machine for hours in order to give
each of her ten children at least two sets of new clothes for the
visit. I do not know how our parents controlled the lot of us on
the train journey. It was also the first time that any of us had left
home, so everything was new and exciting. We saw coolies dressed
in red shirts carrying heavy suitcases on their heads as they
rushed about in every direction. There were hawkers selling fruit,
sweetmeats, peanuts, and cooked vegetables with puri. The best
thing I saw was a bookstand that could be wheeled around the

platform. Father was extravagant and bought us a children's magazine to read on the journey. He knew that because Mother's village was such a distance away, in a different state, in fact, we would have to spend about fifteen hours on the train. The excitement wore off after a few hours. When we reached our destination we were cranky and dirty. I expected Uncle Joel to take us to his home in a tonga or rickshaw, but he met us with two bullock carts. I felt sorry for the miserable beasts having to pull the lot of us and our luggage, but when I saw other overladen carts on the road, I realized that our bullocks were really quite lucky. The village animals pulled carts overloaded with whatever they were carrying. Sometimes the driver had no place in the cart and he actually sat upon the yoke across the necks of the poor beasts. It all seemed very cruel to dumb animals.

Life in the village was hard. We helped wherever and whenever we could. We did not really mind the work; it was the attitude that angered us. The sorghum crop had been harvested a day or two before our arrival. We helped mix the grain with leaves from the neem tree, which serve as a strong, natural insecticide, and then put the mixture into sacks that were sewn shut. The boys helped with the animals. We girls drew water from the well for the family and did our laundry on a flat rock not far from the well. We took turns at the hand mill to grind the day's flour. In spite of all this we did not feel welcome. The food was plain and the portions served to us were pretty meager. We were never given a piece of fruit. We never had milk or yogurt, either, in spite of the number of cows and buffalo the family owned. Eggs appeared on the table only in the form of omelets to which plenty of onions had been added. This made fewer eggs serve more people than they would have had they been poached or boiled. Everything produced on the farm was for sale. We were too young to realize that food was part of their income, which was needed for things like education and weddings. Our hosts ate exactly what they offered us, but we children thought that they were being mean.

The nights were only a bit cooler than the days. We sprinkled water on the earth to cool it about an hour or two before we brought out our beds. The beds were simple bamboo and rope constructions that we stored in an empty room every morning along with our bedding and took out to place under the trees every evening. The children were sent to bed early, while the adults sat up talking, smoking, and drinking toddy, an alcoholic drink made from the sap of palm trees.

On our third night in the village, Meena announced to us that she smelled mangoes and intended to find them.

"Oh, shut up and go to sleep. There are no mangoes here," my brother David said.

"I tell you there are," Meena replied. She got out of bed and literally followed her nose as she walked away sniffing the air. She returned within ten minutes. "Come on. I've found a godown fairly bursting with sacks filled with sucking mangoes," she whispered in excitement.

We followed her to the godown. We smelled the sacks and felt the lumps inside. These were definitely mangoes. Meena took Joel's penknife and cut the jute string that was used to sew the sacks shut. She chose a sack that was in the row farthest from the door. David fetched a pail of water, and we washed the small mangoes in it in order to remove the sap from the tree or the fruit juice that had dried upon the skin. They could cause boils on our lips or the area surrounding the mouth. This was also the reason we discarded the first few drops of juice we squeezed out of the fruit. We pressed the mangoes in our hands and rolled them between our palms. This freed the seed from the pulp and turned the pulp into a thick liquid. We then sucked the juice out. Because we had to hide the skins and the seeds, we simply put them back into the sack from which we had taken them. During the ten nights that followed our discovery we devoured almost two sacks of mangoes, leaving only the empty skins with their seeds within them.

Two days before we left, the sorghum sacks were removed from the godowns and loaded onto a string of bullock carts. They were taken to an auction to be sold to some wholesale dealer. After the sacks were removed, we armed ourselves with pieces of firewood, bamboo staves, or hockey sticks and had an actual rat hunt in the godown. We killed many rats. The frightened creatures ran around in confusion as we hit them with whatever we had. They ran over our feet, they tried to climb the walls, they tried everything possible to get away, but we had no mercy. A big, fat, gray rat ran straight at Meena. The unflappable Meena jumped around screaming. Surprised, we turned to look at her and saw the rat run down one of her legs. Meena vengefully whacked him with the broken chair leg that she had.

"That's for thinking you could do what you did," she spat out at the poor creature as he expired.

"What happened?" I asked.

Meena was too angry and unnerved to think straight. "He ran up one leg and down the other," she said, shaking her skirt and brushing her legs with her hands. Before we had time to react to this piece of information she moved very quickly to a hole in the wall. She bent down and caught something with one hand while in the other she held her chair leg poised over the hole. As we watched, she drew out a cobra with one swift motion and smashed him on the head the moment it came through the hole and before it had the chance to turn around and strike her.

We just stood around foolishly looking at what she had done. Meena delivered another resounding whack upon its head which stilled the last twitches of the snake. No queen carried herself more regally or held her head higher than Meena did as she walked out carrying her chair leg scepter before our admiring gazes. We were left to dispose of our kills and hers.

A woman who worked on Uncle Joel's farm came into the godown. She was horrified to see the dead cobra. Being a worshipper of the god Shiva she believed cobras to be holy. "It was only there to kill the rats. How did it harm you? You have offended the god Shiva." These were some of the many things she said to us. Very reverentially she picked up the dead snake and went out. A few of us followed her out of curiosity. I saw her remove a silver ring from one of her fingers and place it within the mouth of the dead cobra. She called to her husband, who built a funeral pyre and put the snake upon it. He placed more wood on top of the snake and poured melted butter over the whole construction before he set fire to it. Throughout the ceremony they muttered prayers and asked for forgiveness.

Meena was sweeping the floor when I told her what I had seen and heard in connection with the dead snake. "She said that snakes keep the place free of mice," I related.

"Keeping cats would be safer," Meena replied.

David was standing by the window. "What if a cat had chased the rat up your skirts?" he asked with an air of innocence.

He started to slide away toward the door, keeping at a safe distance from her all the time. Meena continued sweeping. She never paid the slightest attention to any of our brothers when they tried to tease her. They usually got tired after a while and left her alone. This occasion proved to be different.

"What did it feel like when the rat brushed past you, *there*?" David paused a little before saying the word "there," and he raised his eyebrows as he said it. Meena stiffened and bit her lips but continued sweeping silently.

Jacob and Benjamin came in from the next room but stood

close to the door, too. "A cat is bigger. It may feel better," Benny said. Meena's movements became jerky, and her lips disappeared within her clenched teeth, but she still continued sweeping without making any answer.

"Do you know why she went for that snake?" Jacob asked.

"No," David said. "Tell us why."

"She wanted the snake to follow the rat. You know the cobra is sacred to Shiva." He edged farther away. "You know which part of Shiva is worshipped—"

He never finished what he was saying. Meena let out an angry bellow that seemed to come not from her throat but all the way from her belly. The boys scattered in all directions. I was the poor innocent who had no idea what the boys were talking about, so I stayed fixed to the spot and received several blows delivered with the broom across my back and shoulders. Luckily, the broom was made of soft grasses so the blows were completely harmless. Meena calmed down, but the boys kept their distance from her for the remaining two days on the farm.

Finally, it was time to leave. We were all loaded onto two bullock carts. We were impatient to be gone, not only because we did not like the place but because what seemed like a caravan of bullock carts was being loaded with sacks of mangoes from the godown where we had feasted. Father noticed our impatience and realized that something fishy was going on. He said nothing, but we knew that we would have to answer questions later. We were already moving toward the gate when we heard the surprised voice of one of the workers.

"Sahib, these sacks are open."

After a short pause we heard Uncle Joel's angry voice. "Horrid children! Little thieves! They have caused me to lose money. Twelve people came to stay and I fed them. Now this!" He said more angry things about the ingratitude, laziness, and bad habits of city people. I remember thinking that we were not city people, just people from a small town that was visited every night by jackals from the hills nearby.

Mother looked at Father, but he did not look at her. "Two rupees if you can get us to the railway station within fifteen minutes, and an extra one to the driver of the cart that reaches first," he said to the men. The drivers cracked their whips and we practically galloped out of Mother's village, never to return. After this none of our maternal uncles visited us in our little town ever again. Perhaps they were afraid that we would all visit them in return.

Our vacation, if it can be called that, had other long-lasting effects. Whenever the word "rat" or "cobra" was used, we had to be careful not to look in Meena's direction, or we would be struck by some flying missile. She continued killing rats and snakes that were foolish enough to try and mark their territory in our house or garden, but nobody dared joke about it with her. We kept our trite remarks about rats and cobras to ourselves. The other effect was upon our underwear. The next time Mother sewed us shorts, Meena ran lengths of elastic through the hems of both legs for all of them. "How do you like your new bloomers?" she asked, holding up the newest pair. We all agreed that it was an improvement.

Hannah and Benjamin

HANNAH AND BENJAMIN'S WEDDING caused much controversy in Jwalanagar. Nobody except Hannah's parents was surprised when the two decided to get married. Her parents believed that their daughter was marrying beneath her class and status. Hannah pointed out that Benny had a regular job as a lecturer in Hindi literature at a local college, which carried a pension plan and compulsory life insurance. These explanations had no effect on them. They were sure that she could make a better match within the community if she would only wait. Her mother tried all the arguments she could think of to dissuade Hannah from the marriage.

"You will not have a comfortable life. People in the educational profession earn hardly anything. It will be a constant struggle to make two ends meet."

"I can always work," Hannah said. "Did you not have it hard during the early years of your marriage? Dad was not always a successful lawyer."

"That's the reason I can say this. I have the experience."

"No, Mother. That's not the reason. You really look down upon Benny's family, and you do not want to be related to them. You are afraid that I'll have a big brood of children like his parents do, and then what will your sophisticated friends, in the society you aspire to, say? Isn't that the true reason?"

Mrs. Aaron shook her head, but Hannah remained unconvinced. "You cannot think even one good thought about him because you will not allow yourself to think of him as a human being. Come on, Ma, I challenge you to say one good thing about Benny."

"He is Jewish," Mrs. Aaron said.

"Is that the only thing in his favor? You disappoint me, Ma. You do not even see him as a person. All you see is his family and his financial status."

Mr. Aaron also refused to give his permission, but his daughter pointed out that she was over twenty-one and an adult. She did not need his permission. He flew into a rage at what he described as "insubordinate, undaughterly behavior." He dragged her upstairs to the room that had once served as a nursery. Its windows were high and barred. Hannah would be locked up in this room until she decided to be reasonable and do what her parents wished. Hannah refused to give in, so she was imprisoned there. The advocate and his wife did not think that their delicate daughter, brought up to be a lady, could do so unladylike a thing as escaping. If she did try, she was bound to make a noise that would be noticed by the family or the servants, all of whom were ready to defend the family honor.

Hannah, however, broke out. She took off her shoes and climbed out of a rather small and high bathroom window. She got onto the tiled roof without making a sound. With the sewage pipe from the toilet for support, she climbed down to the ground. Hannah was glad that her mother had an aversion to dogs. A dog's barks would have been a dead giveaway of her escape. She made her way to the fence around the garden. Her sari ripped on the barbed wire when she crawled under it. She went straight to Benjamin's house, bursting in on the Samuel family as they sat around the table for dinner.

"Once again you come to my house in dirty clothes and no shoes," Benny said when he saw her. She did not give a flippant reply as he expected, but burst into tears. Mrs. Samuel rose and went to her. She put an arm around Hannah and led her to a chair. After she narrated all that had happened to her, David, Benjamin's brother, offered Hannah and Benny his motorcycle. "Go into the next town and get a civil marriage immediately," he said. "Stay the night out of town. Your parents will not want to annul the marriage after that. We can have the religious wedding later." This was his advice.

"Are you out of your mind?" Benjamin said. He turned to Hannah. "You are going home this minute. We will marry, but not like this. We just have to prove to your parents that we will have nobody else but each other."

"I am surprised at how ruthless you can be, David," Mrs. Samuel reproved her son. "Mr. and Mrs. Aaron must have their reasons for being against this match. You have to convince them of your commitment to each other. Although they are wrong in the way they are handling this affair—at least I think so—eloping is no answer. It is not as romantic as it sounds. The whole community will treat Hannah as a stubborn, willful girl and Benjamin as a man with no principles. Go on, Son," she addressed Benjamin, "take her home. Good luck, and God bless you both."

Mr. and Mrs. Aaron were surprised to see Benjamin ride up their driveway on his bicycle with Hannah perched behind on the carrier.

"What's the meaning of this, young man?" Mr. Aaron thundered.

"I have every intention of marrying your daughter, sir," Benjamin said. "Nobody, not even you, will prevent that from happening. But I'll come in the respectable and honorable way for my bride. I shall not elope with her, so there is no need to imprison her. You have my word." He held out his hand.

Mr. Aaron thought this was effrontery. He ignored the proffered hand. Shaking hands was equivalent to sealing a bargain, and he had no intention of demeaning himself by bargaining for his rights with the cheeky young man in front of him. "She is my daughter and she'll marry whom I tell her to. It is my right as a parent."

"You are wrong, sir. You cannot force her against her will. She will tell the boy you try to force on her that she is in love with me, and he will refuse the match."

"Don't be so sure," the indignant father replied.

"If he is stupid enough not to break the engagement, I will walk out of the wedding ceremony," Hannah said. "I will declare in front of the assembled guests that the wedding is taking place against my will. The Jewish wedding ceremony does include the question—"

She did not finish the sentence because a slap from her father left her holding her cheek. A second slap never landed because Benjamin held Mr. Aaron's hand in a powerful grip. Hannah turned and fled to the bedroom she had been locked in earlier. The difference was that this time the room was locked from inside.

Hannah remained in the bedroom for almost a year. She came down only for her meals. Her father called her to come downstairs when he returned from work, and she did not disobey. She entered no conversation. When the rest of the family asked questions, she gave the shortest possible answers. Benjamin made no attempt to enter the house and try to speak to her. Every evening, exactly at five, he rode past on his bicycle whistling her favorite song. Hannah waited at the front door and waved to him. He raised his hand in silent salutation. Her parents realized that they either had to give in or have an unhappy old maid on their hands for the rest of their lives.

The father broke down before the mother did. He sent for Benjamin over his wife's protests and agreed to the wedding. He pointed out to Benjamin that the Bene Israel community knew about his objections to the wedding. They would never stop ridiculing him. Hannah had defeated him. She had destroyed everything he had worked for. He swore that he would never forgive either her or Benjamin. She had proved her father to be ineffective in controlling the women of his family. His masculine pride had been offended.

The most experienced cooks among the Jewish women arrived to help Mrs. Aaron with the wedding feast. They tried to control their smiles while they koshered the mutton and chicken. Mrs. Aaron kept telling everybody how parents must give in to their children's wishes because it is their happiness that is of paramount importance. The couple loved each other, and what is marriage if there is no love?

Benny's youngest sister had inadvertently spilled the beans to her friend, a young Bene Israel girl, whom she told of Hannah's imprisonment and initial escape. She had meant this as an explanation of her hero worship of her wonderful big brother. This friend, however, repeated it all to her parents. The story spread. An imprisonment was too unusual and exciting an event not to be big news in the community. An elopement would have been better. People had been irritated by the high and mighty ways of the advocate and his wife. They felt compassion for the parents' plight but could not help reveling, at least a little in their hearts, at what they considered to be the downfall of the Aaron family. Hannah had rubbed her parents' noses in the dirt.

"That's what comes from giving girls too much freedom and too much education. They think they know everything, and that their elders are fools," Mrs. Jacob said. "The utter shamelessness of it all! A love marriage! What is the Bene Israel community coming to? We are behaving like the Britishers. They are spoiling our children with Western ideas."

"I'll never allow a son of mine to marry any daughter born to that willful and stubborn girl," Mrs. Penkar said.

"No respect for her elders. Keep your daughters and daughters-in-law far from her. She will be a bad influence," Mrs. David said.

"Oh, come on! She is a good girl with a fine spirit. She did not give in but fought for what she believed in," Mrs. Abigail Samson, the oldest lady present, said.

"Spirit and fighting for what we believe in will lead to no amount of unhappiness in marriages," Mrs. Penkar insisted. "Imagine your daughter-in-law wanting her way in everything. This girl is not coming near my daughters and daughters-in-law."

"That's your business," said Mrs. Samson. "Look into your heart and accept the truth. We all envy her a little. I know I do. I'll not allow any mudslinging in this kitchen while I am around. Now let's cook up a great feast and make this wedding a memorable event."

The ladies held their tongues in the presence of the older lady. They did some soul-searching, too. A couple so much in love was a wonderful thing. Everybody pitched in to make the wedding a grand success. It was spoken about for generations in Jwalanagar as the best wedding held at the shortest possible notice.

Rakhi

SHALOM SAT IN HIS SHOP watching the men and boys in the street. He counted the number of *rakhi*s each wore around his wrist. This signified the number of sisters the man or boy had. Shalom felt waves of sorrow mixed with envy pass over him. He once had a sister who tied a *rakhi* on his wrist, put a vermilion *tilak* upon his forehead, and placed in his mouth something sweet that she had prepared on this festival dedicated to love between brothers and sisters. He always had a gift ready for her. He usually took her and her family to a movie and a restaurant in the evening.

As a young boy of fifteen, Shalom had developed a crush on his neighbor's daughter. Although he suffered in silence for almost a year, he could never gather enough courage to do something about it. The opportunity to ease his pain presented itself one evening, when his mother asked him to take some food to the neighbor's house—the house of his beautiful Leela.

"Poor Mrs. Mehera can't bear the smell of cooking these days. She also has the urge for something sweet," his mother explained to his father. In his room, Shalom scribbled a quick note to Leela expressing his love for her.

"Shalom! Come here. What's keeping you so long? I want you to deliver this carrot halvah while it is still hot," his mother called out.

"I'm coming, Mama," Shalom replied as he crumpled the note and pushed it into his trouser pocket. He took the hot tiffin carrier from the kitchen table and walked to the house next door, whistling a jaunty tune. Shalom was lucky. Leela answered the door, and he hurriedly thrust the note into her hand. "It's for you. Don't show it to anybody," he whispered as he walked past her into the house. "My mother has sent something especially for you, Auntie," he announced to Mrs. Mehera. Shalom left her exclaiming over the fact that there were hot puri included with the halvah that she had unthinkingly expressed a desire for. On his way out Shalom promised to convey Mrs. Mehera's thanks to his mother. Leela came to close the door, but she avoided looking at his face. *She has read my note and is feeling shy. After all, she is a modest girl,* he thought triumphantly.

Shalom did not see Leela for the whole month that followed. She was always either at home or surrounded by a group of silly, giggly girlfriends. Then one day the Mehera family invited his family over for lunch. Shalom dressed carefully. He thought that perhaps he would be able to get a few minutes alone with Leela. All he wanted was her yes or no. It made no difference to him that he was Jewish and she was Hindu. He just did not think ahead or clearly in those youthful days. All he saw was a girl with large eyes, a friendly smile, and a ponytail. She laughed in excitement when she played Kho-kho, or seven tiles, with her friends on Sundays and school holidays. He thought her laugh was the happiest sound in the world.

Shalom and his family had hardly settled down upon the sofas when Leela entered carrying a *thali* with a *diya*, a lighted oil lamp, upon it. She made her way straight to Shalom and moved the *thali* in a circle around his face. He felt his heart fall all the way to his carefully polished shoes. He knew what this meant. He had not given a thought to the fact that today was a holiday—the festival of Raksha Bandhan. Shalom stood up as Leela placed the *thali* and its contents upon the coffee table. She picked up a *rakhi* and tied it around his right wrist. She then took a pinch of vermilion-colored powder and made a long mark on his forehead, between his brows and up to his hairline. He opened his mouth and received the sweet *laddu* she had prepared for the purpose. Since he was the elder of the two, she bent and touched his feet. Shalom raised her and placed his hand upon her head in blessing. He knew that he was expected to give her a gift, but he had no money on his person, and so he looked to his father. His father took out two ten-rupee notes from his wallet and passed them to him. Shalom placed them in Leela's *thali*. The cotton string attached to a ball of fluff that was surrounded by a few strands of tinsel had smashed all his dreams of romance and placed upon him the responsibilities of an elder brother. Leela had made a claim to friendship and affection but had refused romantic love. This was a declaration of love of a different kind, not what he had imagined for hours every night before finally falling asleep.

Shalom took his new responsibility as seriously as any blood brother would. Leela had been an only child until the grand age of fourteen, when a new sister arrived. Shalom ran all the way to Mr. Mehera's office to inform him that his mother had taken Mrs. Mehera to the hospital. He accompanied Leela on her visits to and from the hospital, and also helped her prepare a room for the new baby.

Unfortunately, the baby was born with a defective heart. Shalom helped the family as though he were their natural-born son. He went to the weekly market and did their shopping. He purchased the medicines from the pharmacy when baby Gita was ill. He sat up nights in the hospital so that her parents could get a little rest. Shalom had three brothers, but after the *rakhi* cere-mony he had two sisters as well. When Gita died at the age of three, Shalom felt as though his heart had been wrenched out. He remembered the hours he had spent carrying the sick infant in his arms and wept at the thought of never being able to carry her again. Shalom had prayed for the success of the operations the little girl underwent, but he had not been able to change God's decision for the baby. His parents were unsuccessful in their attempts to comfort him. Then Leela spoke to him. He remembered her words very clearly. "We are all on a journey, Shalom," she had said. "Gita's journey is over. Be glad that she is not suffering any longer. She was too young to have sinned, so she should be spared the pains of rebirth." Shalom had different religious beliefs, but he drew comfort from the fact that the baby he loved would not suffer any longer.

The years passed uneventfully. Shalom did not get a college education. He became a cloth merchant. He opened a small store where he sold saris and material for dresses and trousers. As he became more successful, he bought a larger store and started selling ready-made clothes as well. Leela went to college and received degrees in history, economics, and political science, but she was not allowed to work. Her parents found her a husband, and, as a good and dutiful daughter, she married the boy they chose without asking any questions. She moved to Lucknow but came home every year for Raksha Bandhan. Shalom looked forward to her visits.

A few years later Shalom met Bathsheva and fell in love with her. Leela was the first to know about the romance. She and her family were present at his wedding. She introduced herself to Bathsheva as "Shalom's only sister." Shalom realized that a simple cotton thread had bound two people in a beautiful and lasting relationship.

Shalom sat in his shop reminiscing. He had watched both his and Leela's children grow up, get married, and have children of their own. Two years ago Leela had been diagnosed with cancer. Shalom and his wife spent days and nights in the hospital with her. He had been present when she died, and she held his hand to the last. Even when she was in a deep coma he had sat there holding her hand. He left only when a nurse covered Leela's face with a sheet.

"I wanted to take a tiny bit of her ashes and make a *tilak* on my forehead the way she always did for me on Raksha Bandhan," he told his wife after Leela's cremation.

"Thank goodness you did not do it!" she exclaimed.

"Why?"

"You don't know what it means, do you? Just like among us, we make sure that every little piece of the body is buried, the Hindus also want the whole body to return to the elements. Keeping a bit of it behind is considered hindering the soul. It does not give it its full freedom. The soul must wait till the body is properly disposed of. Only an enemy would have done what you felt like doing."

"Oh, I see! It makes sense. Do you know, my dear, how my relationship with Leela started?" he asked, turning to face his wife.

"Yes, I do. She used a piece of string to turn romantic love into fraternal love. She left you free for me, and I'm grateful. She was a wonderful person. I loved her, and I'm glad we had her in our lives. I'll miss her most at *rakhi* time. We always looked forward to the movies and dinner you took both families to on that day."

"So will I. So will I." He sighed. "Of all the Hindu festivals, I like this one the best."

"I agree," his wife said. "It celebrates family ties and love in its purest form."

Shalom sighed once again as he remembered all this. "Thirty percent reduction on gifts for Raksha Bandhan," he announced, and directed a young sales assistant to put up a notice in the shop-window to that effect.

Hephzibah

"DID YOU KNOW YOUR GRANDFATHER the way we know you?" my cousin Danny asked our grandfather one day.

"Of course I did," Grandpa replied. "I grew up in a big joint family. I not only knew my grandparents, I even knew my great-grandmother Hephzibah."

"She must have been a very old woman," Danny said.

"Not really. She had married as a very young girl. I'll tell you about her and about something that happened shortly after my tenth birthday. Her birthday was two days before mine. She had just turned eighty-four," Grandpa said.

Hephzibah was born to a Bene Israel family in the city of Sholapur. Each of her siblings was born in a different town. This was because her father worked for the railways and he got transferred from place to place. One day he came to Jwalanagar to visit a cousin. The two men went around the whole town and the areas surrounding it. Hephzibah's father liked the place so much that he decided to bring his family to live there permanently. He found a four-room house with a garden around it. He then visited the local schools, and when he returned to Sholapur he spoke to his wife about the intended move. She was glad to move to a town that had a few Jews.

Hephzibah was always proud of the five years of schooling that her mother permitted her to have. Her mother had been brought up to believe that a girl's education should be confined to the kitchen and the house. Schooling gave girls ideas that led to their wanting more than society was willing to give them.

Her father insisted that his daughters know how to read and write. "They must be able to write a letter and inform us that they are well. That is the bare minimum no girl should be made to do without," he said to his wife, who did not agree but considered it disloyal to oppose his wishes.

"Just until they can write a letter," she said.

Hephzibah's father agreed. Even after five years of Hephzibah doing exceptionally well in school, her mother did not change her mind. She insisted that her daughter stay home and not be exposed to the corruption of outside ideas. Money paid as school fees was needed more urgently in the house. It was wasted on girls who did not have to go out and find jobs to support their families. That was a man's duty. Hephzibah's father consented. His financial situation was rather tight, and his sons would need an education more than his daughters would. Hephzibah never forgave this discrimination and promised herself that her children would all have at least a matriculation certificate, irrespective of the sex they were born into.

A Jewish bridegroom was found before Hephzibah's eleventh birthday. She was married three months after she had her first menstruation. Her first son was born before her fourteenth birthday. Hephzibah did not have as many children as most girls in her situation did. She tried to induce a miscarriage when she became pregnant shortly after the birth of her sixth child. The *dai*, the local midwife, did the best she could, and the fetus was successfully aborted. But the bleeding was so bad that Hepzhibah's husband took her to the hospital run by Scottish missionary doctors. Here it was determined that her uterus had to be removed to save her life. Hephzibah was relieved when her husband consented without a second thought. *He does love me,* she thought. The loss of her womb meant no more babies. That was a welcome thought to Hephzibah. She did not want to end up with sixteen or eighteen children like her mother and aunts had. Six were more than enough. She would take care of them and educate them in the best way she could.

Hephzibah's daughters married good Jewish boys whom their parents and grandparents had chosen for them, and they left her home forever. They did visit for a couple of years but stopped as their own families grew in size, and money could not be spared for nonessentials. Holidays were an unaffordable luxury, and loyalty to the husband's family took priority over love for the home they were born in. This was the accepted way of the world. Hephzibah was proud that her girls lived according to the traditions. The natural result was that her sons' children knew one another very well. Her daughters' children were acknowledged as relatives but they remained almost strangers.

Hephzibah was called Eppie by her husband, and that was the name by which the Jwalanagar Jews knew her. She was one of the grand old ladies of the community. As soon as she arrived at the prayer hall, the women rose and gave her the best seat in the front row of the women's section. A special armchair was kept there especially for her, the way comfortable armchairs were kept for the oldest men in the men's section. Two little girls were given palm-leaf fans and ordered to fan her. After a while other little girls replaced them. Hephizibah was "Granny Eppie" to the whole community. She was the first person the local Jews visited each year after Yom Kippur. No wedding took place without her pronouncing it a suitable match. The young couples visited her for a blessing once the wedding was over. Each returned with a coconut, the sign of fertility, and two silver rupees, the symbol of prosperity.

Granny Eppie should have been happy in her old age, but she wasn't. The cause of her sorrow was the quarrel between her two sons, Nathaniel and Reuben. Nobody could remember what the fight was over. But the details of all that was said and done during the quarrel were remembered and increased the anger on both sides. The two brothers refused to forgive each other. They would not even look in each other's direction if they happened to be in the same place at the same time. Reuben had worked as a clerk in the local law courts and lived in a rented house in the center of town. After he retired, he and his wife moved in with one of his sons, who, as an employee of the local textile mill, lived in a house at the very outskirts of the town, in the quarters that the mill provided for its staff.

Nathaniel thought the move was made as an affront to the rest of the family. He believed that Reuben was moving as far away from everyone as he could. He did, after all, have another son who lived in town. The worst part of it was the problem Reuben was now causing for the minyan in their synagogue. Nathaniel was religious. The synagogue was an important part of his life. He constantly worried about the difficulty in obtaining a minyan, the ten men required for a religious service to be complete. Reuben came on his bicycle for all the services. This did not please Nathaniel. The physical exertion of cycling was a desecration of Shabbat. Even worse, Reuben smoked a cigarette as he rode, in spite of the religious prohibition against lighting a fire on the holy day. Nathaniel did not want a person who did not keep Shabbat to be called up to the Torah to read the portion of the week. In a community with not many readers, Reuben was sure to be called up. Once, when this happened, Nathaniel objected, and Reuben stepped down.

"Stop this nonsense," Mr. Samson said. "There are seven *aliyot*. Do you have another person who can read Hebrew as well as your brother does?" The other men supported Mr. Samson's stand on the matter, and Reuben was asked to go ahead and read the portion.

"He should live closer to the prayer hall," Nathaniel insisted. "We should not be expected to stand and pray behind a person who desecrates Shabbat."

"Be reasonable, Nathaniel," Bentzion Moses said. "The man is on a pension. He cannot afford to pay rent any longer. Perhaps you would prefer that he insist on his half of your parents' home while your mother is still alive?"

"If you are concentrating on prayer, what does it matter who stands in front of you and who behind you?" Mr. Joseph asked. "Your mind should be with God and on your prayer, not on other things. His prayer and his way of life are his business, not yours."

Nathaniel had no answer for this, and Reuben did not deign to say a single word in his own defense. The men present nodded to Mr. Joseph and then to one another. Nathaniel felt humiliated. It seemed to him that his brother smiled with satisfaction at his discomfort.

Things went from bad to worse between the two men that year, but their wives remained good friends. Nathaniel's wife, Yael, said to her husband, "You may quarrel with your brother but that is no reason for me to stop seeing my brother-in-law and sister-in-law. Your mother wants to see her son and his family, too. You do not want to go there, so I will accompany her. This bitterness must not spill over to the children. The cousins must know one another. After all, they are family."

Nathaniel had no argument against this line of reasoning, so he said, "Do what you want. Who listens to me in this house anyway?"

Sunday was market day in Jwalanagar. Farmers from the surrounding villages brought their produce to sell in the temporary stalls set up there. Everybody went to the Sunday market to buy vegetables and live poultry. It was cheaper than purchasing provisions in the shops of the town. On one Sunday, during the eight days of Succot, Nathaniel noticed his brother pushing his bicycle. Two bags full of vegetables hung from the handlebars. A closed straw basket containing two live ducks was tied onto the carrier over the back wheel. Suddenly there was a screech of brakes. Nathaniel saw a truck careening out of control, heading straight in Reuben's direction. Without another thought he threw his own bicycle aside and ran to his brother. He pushed Reuben hard with both hands. Both men fell against some *ghadas*, earthenware pots. The truck went over the front wheel of Reuben's bicycle, crushing it out of shape. The vegetables were completely ruined. The ducks in the basket sent up a terrified quacking, and people gathered to see what had happened. Nathaniel quietly paid the stall keeper for the broken *ghadas* and left without looking in his brother's direction.

The next day was Shmini Atzeret. The Jewish community gathered for prayers. Reuben said the Birchat Ha'gomel, a prayer recited by religious Jews who have been saved from a disaster. Before the service ended, Hephzibah sent one of her small great-granddaughters to Nathaniel with some instructions. The little girl went up to him and pulled at his shirtsleeve. He bent down, heard what she had to say, looked back at his mother, nodded, and went over to Bentzion Moses, who was the main reader for the day. Bentzion began to read a Mi Shebeirach for Reuben.

Reuben exploded with anger. "I don't want a blessing from you," he said to his brother. "Who do you think you are?"

The whole prayer hall fell silent. Nobody had dared to fight in the place of worship before. Everyone's breathing became audible. "It was not I but your mother who asked for the blessing," Nathaniel said with a sneer.

Either Reuben did not hear, or he did not care about what his brother had said. "You hypocrite! You pretend to care when in reality you don't care two figs for anybody. You want people to think that you saved my life, but you did that without knowing that it was I the truck was heading toward. Once you saw whom you had saved, you did not even have the courtesy to ask if I was all right. You were sorry that I was not dead. Go on, admit it."

Now it was Nathaniel's turn to be angry. "You ungrateful swine," he said in a low, controlled voice. "I knew it was you."

"Is that so?" Reuben used the tone he adopted when he wanted to be sarcastic. "Was it me or your precious minyan you were worried about? Who will be the tenth man whose presence will ensure that your prayers will reach heaven? Wasn't that your main worry?"

Nathaniel felt his hackles rise. "I just wanted to save you the embarrassment of having to thank me. You are a shame to the family. You are like the *aravot* in the *lulav*." He pointed to the bundle of willow branches, myrtle sprigs, and a palm leaf in his brother's hand. "You do not study the law or keep it. You will be smashed to little pieces and trodden underfoot like the willow branches after Shmini Atzeret prayers."

Reuben went red in the face as he tried to control his voice. "You have no business looking down on other people," he said in a low voice that carried to the corners of the prayer hall because of the silence. "If you consider yourself to be the *etrog*, just remember that the other three elements are from the outset tied together as a group. It is the conceited citron that has to be forcibly brought together with the rest so that the blessing can be made."

At this point everybody heard Hephzibah knock on the floor three or four times with her walking stick. Her voice did not quaver as it sometimes did because of her age or when she was excited. Everybody heard her chastise her two sons who were already grandfathers. "Even the Lord does not bless Israel until all her children, worthy and unworthy, are together," she said. "The willow will be smashed to pieces and will enter the earth, but what will happen to the citron? It is too holy to be thrown away. It will be cut up and fed to the family or made into jam. After passing through twenty-one feet of intestine it, too, will end up in the earth—that is, if a pig does not get it and force it to undergo the whole process once again. At least the willow will enter the earth as it always was, but the citron will become a smelly mess. Don't be so proud. Both of you are my sons, so I can say this to you. I don't know what you think of yourselves. I just know that you are both absolute idiots. I have tried to reason with you for over a year. Don't think that you are so big that I can't give you both a pasting. Stop this stupidity right now." She raised her voice a little as she addressed Mr. Bentzion Moses. "Benny, please continue with the Mi Shebeirach," she said. The blessing was read, and the community filed out of the prayer hall one by one after the service.

The next day was Simchat Torah, and the Jewish community of Jwalanagar watched the two brothers dance together, first with their arms wrapped around the Torah scroll and then with their arms around each other. Bentzion's wife, Ketura, who was sitting beside Hephzibah, leaned toward her and said, "Today is the day we complete one reading of the Torah and start another. It seems that your sons have a new beginning to their relationship, too."

"I hope so," Granny Eppie said. Her wishes were surely granted, because Mr. Arava and Mr. Etrog became firm friends once again.

"Grandpa, why did your grandfather and his brother make up after they fought for so long?" Danny asked.

"Everybody had a different opinion about that. Granny Eppie never spoke about it. The elders in the community held it up as an example of parental authority and filial obedience. My grandpa was more honest. He said that his mother had made him feel like a shit in front of the whole community. My father agreed with him. He thought that Granny Eppie's words had made the two men see sense. Everybody had their own theory."

"What do you believe, Grandpa?" Danny asked.

"We children knew that Granny Eppie was not a woman who made idle threats. We were all convinced that the two brothers were afraid of the thrashing she said she could still administer if they did not stop quarreling."

The Horoscope Never Lies

SUBAHDAR MAJOR HERMAN KILEKAR walked up to the orderly on duty outside Colonel Gonsalves's office. He said that he wished to speak to the colonel and watched through the open window as the orderly went into the office. Colonel Jude Gonsalves looked up as the orderly stood at attention and executed a smart salute.

"Subahdar Major Herman Kilekar requests a meeting with you, sir."

"Is he here?"

"Yes, sir."

"Send him in."

The colonel put the papers he was reading into the in-tray. He would deal with them later. He had not seen Herman Kilekar for years, but he could guess what Herman wanted to see him about. The interview would be painful for both of them and fraught with memories. In spite of it all, if not because of it all, Herman was selfishly glad to have somebody with whom to share the heaviness of his heart. He watched the colonel run a hand through his hair, unconsciously neatening himself for the critical gaze of the JCO. Herman had been his weapons training instructor when he took an advanced course in officers' training school. The student still showed respect for his old *ustaad*. Herman also took such pride in his uniform that it inspired neatness and discipline in others.

The orderly returned and told Herman to go in. The subahdar major marched in, snapped to attention, and saluted. The colonel rose and went around the desk with his hand extended.

"Salaam, sahib. I have not seen you for years. How are you?" The men shook hands warmly. The colonel would have liked to thump the JCO upon the back in welcome, but he could not show such familiarity with his teacher. The distance of rank did not allow much closeness, either. "How long has it been, sahib?" he asked.

"About fifteen years, sir. You got promoted and left us. How have you been? How is the family? The children must be quite big now."

Gonsalves pointed to a chair and seated himself in the one beside it. He did not want a desk in between, dividing them. Herman took off his beret and held it in his hand so that Gonsalves would realize that this would be a long interview. Herman would not have removed his beret if he intended to leave quickly. He wanted to impress upon Gonsalves that he had something to say and intended to get what he had come for. His body language said it all. His lips were pursed so tightly that the ends of his big mustache actually quivered. Gonsalves realized that at another time he would have thought it funny. He would even have made jokes about it, but this was not the time for humor.

"Yes, sahib?" Gonsalves asked.

"It is about the condemned man, Manohar Sanga. If you grant permission, I would like to spend his last night with him—that is, if he agrees to have me, of course." Herman was not really making a request. He was making a declaration. He was going to see Sanga with or without permission. The request was just a formality.

"You are both from the same village, I remember."

"Yes, sir."

"Permission granted." Normally Herman would be expected to

leave at this point, but each man understood that the other needed him. They had both served with Sanga, and both loved him. Each had different memories of him and also a few that they shared. They could talk to nobody but each other about him.

Herman's mind went back to an incident when Gonsalves was a young major in command of his first unit. Herman was a havildar at the time and Sanga a sepoy. This was the first time Herman saw the unofficial, softer side of his new commanding officer. They had been on an exercise for two weeks in a hilly jungle area around Jwalanagar, not far from Herman's village. One evening he overheard Major Gonsalves telling his second-in-command that he had been called back to headquarters for a briefing, so he would take the jeep and driver. He would be back early in the morning before maneuvers began.

Herman stepped forward and requested permission to spend the night in the village. "I have not seen my wife for six months, sir, and you will be driving through. It is only twenty miles from here."

Before the second-in-command could say anything, Gonsalves laughed. "Make sure that you get enough sleep to be fit for duty tomorrow. Come along. Hop into the jeep. Captain Battiwalla," he called out, "please inform the subahdar major that I have taken Herman Kilekar with me."

They drove through the jungle as dusk was falling. Herman remembered thinking that perhaps the major was afraid of wild animals and that was why he talked so much. He was full of questions about the village, the crops, the villagers, the headman, and everything else. Herman was not talkative by nature and did not want to fraternize with the officers. His short, curt answers did not deter his commander in any way. Even as a cadet Gonsalves had behaved as though he had ants in his pants. Finally, just in order to make conversation and not to seem rude, Herman had pointed to a small mud-and-brick house with a courtyard around it and said, "That's where Sanga lives." He did not expect what happened next.

"Come on, let's visit him. He is on leave now. Boy! Won't he be surprised? Driver, drive to that house. We will not stop for more than fifteen minutes." Gonsalves was full of enthusiasm for what he no doubt thought was a gesture of friendship between comrades.

Herman was horrified by this turn of events. Sanga's family would be embarrassed because of their poverty. The uncouth, city-bred commander would not even have the sense to leave his shoes outside the door. How would he greet Sanga's parents? Would he show the proper respect to which older people are entitled? Herman tried to say something to dissuade him, but Gonsalves was too full of his own idea to listen. Herman remembered thinking that the major resembled a pigeon with its chest puffed up, cooing and strutting around in small circles as though it were the only creature in the world with something to say.

They reached the house and stopped. Herman sprang out of the jeep and ran to the courtyard door. He intended to warn the person who opened it that the visitor was Sanga's commanding officer. He knocked and knocked, but nobody answered. Major Gonsalves walked around the house. He looked at the tops of the papaya trees that showed over the courtyard wall. He looked at the bottle-gourd creeper that spread its leaves over the roof tiles. He inhaled deeply and declared that the mustard crop would flower soon. A cow lowed from inside the courtyard. "That animal is in distress and should be milked soon," he said. *Okay, so you know something about farming, you condescending bastard,* Herman recalled having thought. He also recalled being relieved that nobody in Sanga's family was at home.

They returned to the jeep and drove slowly around the fields, careful to avoid potholes in the mud paths that served as roads. "You can leave me at the crossroads under the big pipal tree in the center of the village," Herman said, not really wanting the officer in his house when they were not prepared for him. Gonsalves might have thought that he was honoring them, but if there was nothing in the house to offer him, Herman's father would think that they were guilty of inhospitality. His mother would have to go to the neighbor and borrow sugar for the tea. Officers did not sweeten their tea with jaggery. It was never right to borrow when the person concerned could do without it. At least that was what Herman had always believed.

"My house is on the other side of the village, and I do not want to inconvenience you. I will be under the tree by five o'clock in the morning," he said. It did not seem to work.

"No inconvenience. I want to meet your family. Since we missed Sanga, let me say salaam to your *mata* and *pita.*"

Herman hoped that there would be something to offer this determined, high-ranking, unexpected guest. They usually managed something, but it was always for villagers who knew one another. The sahib was used to better fare than the poor villager who supported not only a wife and children but old parents and younger siblings, too. Herman smothered these thoughts and smiled at the idea of seeing his parents, wife, and children. He stopped daydreaming when he heard a woman's voice calling to them. *"Ruk jaao. Ruk jaao bete. Ruk jaao.* Stop. Stop, sons."

The jeep stopped with a screech of brakes, and Herman watched the major jump down from his seat beside the driver and run toward the old lady advancing across the fields. *"Kiya baat hai, Mataji? Aap theek to hain?* What has happened, Mother? Are you all right?"

Herman recognized Sanga's mother. Horrified, he watched

her take the end of her sari *pallo* in her hand, open a knot, take out a crumpled rupee note, and give it to the major sahib. Herman stood up in the jeep, waving his hands madly around his head. The lady did not even glance in his direction. He saw the major place both his hands together and bow low in front of her. *Why so low, do you want to touch her feet like a dutiful son?* Herman remembered thinking. The old lady placed her hand on the major's head in blessing. She then turned and made her way slowly across the fields, unaware that the major had not moved an inch. He stood motionless and watched her straight back until she disappeared. Her shapely figure and majestic walk radiated dignity through her tattered sari, graying hair, and bare feet. It was really beautiful to watch her. Before she rounded the corner of the first house she looked back and the major raised his hand and waved to her. She waved back.

Major Gonsalves moved rather slowly as he returned to the jeep. He sat quietly for a few moments before Herman broke the silence. "She is only an old and ignorant woman, sir. Please forgive her. She does not know the difference between stripes on the sleeve and pips on the shoulder." Herman felt embarrassed for her and the family. How would Sanga feel when he heard about it? The rich folk really had no business going around slumming just to feel righteous. Who needed favors of this kind, anyway?

Herman was surprised to hear the major choke over his next words. "Don't ever apologize for a mother. You do not know how fortunate you are to be blessed with such simple, pure love. This lady told me that she had heard from her neighbor about some of her son's army friends coming to visit when nobody was at home. His mother was sorry that Sanga has gone to the next village to buy a new plow. She thought that we had journeyed far and would be hungry and tired. She felt guilty that she was not there to draw water from the well for us to wash and to give us something to eat. Anyhow, she gave me a rupee for all of us chaps to have a cup of tea at the village tea shop. This is the first time a woman has called me son and given me money to go out with my friends. Come on, sahib, please show us the way to the tea shop."

Herman noticed with surprise the tears in the officer's eyes as he gave the required directions. The driver, Gonsalves, and Herman had samosas with their tea so that they spent a little more than a rupee. Gonsalves told them a bit about his life over that cup of tea. He had grown up in an orphanage in Allahabad. That was all the major knew about where he came from. He grew up full of longing for a family. It was his dream to have a woman call him son. The priests who ran the orphanage always called the young boys son, but Gonsalves had never heard it addressed to him in a woman's voice. When he heard this, Herman wished he could take the major home to meet his mother, but time was short and they had dallied over their tea. The major left Herman at the tea shop and promised to pick him up there at five o'clock the next morning. Herman's parents and the major never met, and Herman still regretted it.

Subahdar Major Herman Kilekar looked at the man who sat facing him. The colonel's hair had grayed a lot. He had thickened around the waist and had bags under his eyes, which to Herman seemed to be the result of immoderate drinking. The eyes that were usually full of mischief were glazed and full of tears.

"What are you thinking, sir?" Herman asked.

"I am thinking of Jaanki and the letter she wrote to me. I am sure that you have thought of it very often this week. What can I say to her? How can I hurt her and the woman who called me son and gave me money to have tea with my friends?"

"I have thought of it all," Herman said. "You will not have to tell a single lie. We will speak to Sanga and he will agree, I am sure."

Gonsalves bowed his head between his hands, and Herman said nothing for a few minutes. He remembered the letter, too. Sanga had been missing for four months before he turned up at the unit gate and asked to be taken into custody as a deserter. The major made him sit for a week in the quarter guard before he held a court of inquiry. Depending on the findings of this court, Sanga could possibly face a court-martial. Gonsalves was very angry that Sanga could bring such pain and disgrace upon his family.

Then, on the fifth day of Sanga's imprisonment, Gonsalves received a letter in Arabic script. He decided to visit the officers' mess in the evening. The bachelor officers and those without their families lived and dined there. Captain Osman was a Muslim, and he had learned to read and write Hindi and Urdu in spite of his education in an English school. He was able to read the letter to Gonsalves. This is what he read:

Respected Major Sahib,

May my presumption in writing to you be forgiven. It is a matter of life or death, or I would not be so impudent.

Manohar Sanga, your soldier, came home on Monday. He had been kidnapped by dacoits who took him into the hills. They sent a messenger asking for money, but we could not pay. They threatened to kill him if by the next crop season we did not raise the money. We have only one cow, and there would never be enough money even if we sold everything. Then Sanga managed to escape. He made his way back to the village and his home, but the family would not let him into the house. His eldest brother stood in front of the door with an ax in his hands, and his father stood near the courtyard door with a *laathi*. "Go back to the army," my father-in-law shouted. "This is a Rajput house. We live by the Rajput code of honor. Remember, *Jaan jaye pun vachan na jaye*. Life may depart, but we will keep our promises. You swore to serve your country. Go away. We have no place for you." I wept and pleaded that they at least give him a piece of bread to eat, but they called him traitor and coward. They would not give him anything. I then asked how he could possibly return to his unit if he had no money for a railway ticket. "If you have any money you can give it to him," my eldest brother-in-law said. I ran out and gave him the two gold bangles my parents had given me for my *gauna* last year. I asked him for your name. I hope I remembered it correctly.

Sahibji, the soldiers say that their commanding officer is their *maai-baap*, their mother and father. Hear the plea of your daughter, and do not snatch away my *suhag* from me. The people in his family will kill him if you send him home in disgrace. Give him the harshest punishment, but keep him alive. He is my life and my love. I have nothing in the world besides him, and he is not to blame. He is a brave and a good man. He would never hesitate in doing his duty. Please listen to the prayer of

Your daughter,

Jaanki

When Gonsalves returned home he found Herman waiting for him. Herman drew out a letter from his shirt pocket when he saw his officer. Gonsalves did not seem to want to see anybody in the emotional state he was in, but he could not turn the havildar away. He was rude enough to say no word of welcome and let Herman begin his speech out on the veranda instead of inviting him inside. Herman was not deterred. He was on an important mission.

"My father has sent me a letter about Sanga. You must hear it, sir," Herman said, preparing to read.

"Yes. He was abducted by dacoits. I've heard that story," Gonsalves said. All his irritation showed in his voice. Herman misunderstood and thought that the major did not believe the story.

"But it is true, sir. The whole village knows it. They saw it all,

and Sanga's wife came to my father. She is illiterate and needed
somebody to write the letter for her. My father reads and writes
the letters for the whole village. Besides this, Sanga had told his
wife that we serve in the same unit, so if she had some message
or parcel to send when I was on leave she could give it to me. She
had your name but not the address. My father filled that in."

"So that is why the letter was in Urdu, not Sanga's native
Hindi. Why don't you people teach your children to read and
write?" Gonsalves asked.

"We have a school now, sir, but nobody would ask a child to
write such a letter."

Herman let the major fret and fume until he calmed down. He
then took his leave and went back to the barracks. Once there, he
walked to the quarter guard and spoke to the havildar on duty. A
sentry was sent inside with a message for Sanga. Soon Herman
saw a hand wave behind the barred window, and he realized that
Sanga knew there was hope for him.

The next day was Thursday, the day Major Gonsalves held *dur-
bar*. This was the time when all the men assembled together and
had the opportunity to air their views and grievances without
going through the proper channels, as prescribed by army regulations. Even the prisoners attended. It always ended with a speech
by the commanding officer. On this particular day Gonsalves
said, "A father can refuse his sons anything they ask for, but he
can never refuse his daughter a single thing. There is a man present here who should go to the *mandir* with two coconuts as offer-
ings. One coconut as thanks for being saved from punishment
and the second as thanks that God has given him such a wonderful wife to love and care for him." He watched Sanga straighten
up and smile broadly at everybody around him.

That was the end of that story. Captain Battiwalla and a young lieutenant called Mustafa went to Sanga's village and recorded the evidence given by the villagers. Sanga was released from quarter guard. A year later Gonsalves was promoted and posted out. Herman took a course for JCOs before he left the unit, too. The men had not seen each other until the recent war with China; in fact, they hardly ever thought about each other or the old unit. It was only when they met an old comrade that memories came flooding back and found expression in their speech. During the war, Sanga had been the havildar in charge of a platoon of men. For some reason he abandoned his post for a little less than twenty minutes when it came under fire. Sanga returned to his post and fought bravely, but his lapse had cost the division the lives of thirteen men. His men thought that their platoon leader had advanced, and they tried to move forward, too. The enemy had been waiting.

Sanga took full responsibility. He stated that he had abandoned his post in the face of the enemy. There were too many witnesses for the defending officer to be able to do much to save him. The court-martial was brief, and Sanga had nothing to say about the verdict except that it was fair and what he deserved. The verdict was execution by firing squad.

All Sanga's friends were horrified. He had always been a good friend and a brave soldier. They could not understand what had happened, and Sanga never told anybody what had gone through his mind. He said that it was unimportant. What really mattered was that he was responsible for thirteen women becoming widows and he did not know how many children becoming orphans. Herman knew that Gonsalves had been granted permission to be with Sanga on the night before the execution. He also knew that Gonsalves had asked for permission for another two men to be there as well, thinking that perhaps Sanga had a friend he would like to be with. He did not even know that Herman was in the area. When the subahdar requested permission to join him, Gonsalves said, "It is only appropriate that Sanga should spend his last day with a face familiar to him from his early childhood. It may be some comfort to him, and he may want to send some message to his loved ones at home. He may even open up and finally speak about those terrible twenty minutes. If nothing else, it may bring a measure of peace to him. You know him well from childhood," Gonsalves said.

"Not really, sir. He is younger than I, so he had a younger group of friends."

"You always watched out for him, though."

"That was a favor to his mother. She came to our house when Sanga told her that he and I served in the same unit. She was worried. You see, sir, his horoscope said that he would be very harshly punished for breaking laws. It also foretold that he would die with his hands behind his back before the age of thirty-four. Hands behind the back and punishment by the law meant only one thing to his mother. She thought that poverty would drive him into a life of crime, and that he would be hanged in some jail. She was happy when he joined the army because she imagined that a steady income would keep crime away. She came to our house and requested that I make sure no army rules were broken. The poor woman was terrified during the dacoit business, but Manohar's new bride, Jaanki, pulled them through that. I did not have to work hard to keep my word, sir. Sanga never broke a single law in his entire life."

"I can't understand what happened. Why did he do nothing to defend himself?" Gonsalves muttered.

"He thinks that he is a coward. Thirteen men died because he gave in to his fear. He cannot live with that," Herman explained.

"How will his family live now? I don't understand him. He could at least have tried to save himself."

"You have to be a Rajput to understand, sir. Nobody will associate with him. Nobody will want to be connected to him through blood, marriage, or friendship. That is why I have a request, sir. His daughter is engaged. The boy's family will break off the match if they hear. Please don't inform the family, sir. We can cremate the body here. I can carry the ashes home, and his family will perform the ceremony of scattering the ashes on the river. I'll write the letter for you—"

Herman realized that Gonsalves was annoyed with him. He could imagine him thinking, *This stern, taciturn man has suddenly become verbose. Who does he think he is? Does he think that I am incompetent and incapable of performing my duties?* Herman knew that Gonsalves had asked the brigadier if he could write the letter informing the family of Sanga's death, because he knew them. Moreover, he had always taken an interest in Jaanki. Herman sensed the discomfort Gonsalves felt on being read so easily by him. Gonsalves knew that Herman had guessed that he would try to be the one to contact the family and make sure that there was a human touch in the letter, and he was disconcerted at being so well understood. "Do you think I cannot write a letter with sensitivity and tact?" Gonsalves asked.

"You can't write in Urdu, and that is all my father, the village reader of letters, can read," Herman answered in his most matter-of-fact manner.

"Your children are still uneducated?" Gonsalves smiled. He realized that he had been outmaneuverd.

"Such letters are not given to children to read," Herman answered.

The men sat together for more than an hour and composed a letter that covered just one side of a sheet of paper. It sounded spontaneous in spite of the extreme care put into it. They took the letter with them when they visited Sanga in his cell. The condemned man listened as the letter informing his family about his death was read out to him. He then nodded and shook hands with both Gonsalves and Herman. "Thank you," he said. "May God reward you in this life itself." They were non-Hindus, so they did not believe in reincarnation. Their reward had to be within this lifetime.

They spent the rest of the night sharing memories, smoking, and playing cards. Gonsalves had brought in a bottle of good whiskey. "Forgive me tonight, *ustaadji*," he said, "but perhaps this may help." Herman had sworn off strong drink many years ago. Sanga did not want to be drunk the next day and make any mistakes. He had never touched liquor and did not feel the need to do so now. Tea and cigarettes would suffice. Nobody spoke of the afterlife or tried to guess what the others were thinking. Sanga could not dictate any letters because his family was not to be told of his execution, but he sent loving messages to his wife and children, which Herman promised to deliver. Gonsalves couldn't bear it any longer. "Tell us, Sanga, what happened during those twenty minutes?" he asked.

Sanga smiled sadly. "Nobody has a right to know what I don't want to tell. My shame and my guilt must die with me. You will try and make excuses that I don't make for myself. Just let that matter rest and stay with me until my time comes. I'm glad to be among friends. Thank you for everything you are doing."

"But what about Jaanki?" Gonsalves persisted. Herman aimed and delivered a hard kick at the colonel's foot under the table, not realizing that this was the first time he had not been conscious of the barrier of rank between them. Sanga rose to go to the toilet without catching the look of surprise on Gonsalves's face.

"*Bayvakoof,*" Herman hissed angrily. "Are you completely stupid? You are here for one person and one person only. That person is Sanga. Jaanki is something precious he holds close to his heart. Perhaps he does not want to talk about her. His heart must be aching for her without us adding to his misery. We are here to listen, and to talk only about those things he wants to talk about. Remember that." Herman had once again turned into the weapons instructor who ordered the cadets around.

"*Maaf karo ustaadji*. Please forgive me," a completely contrite Gonsalves said. Then, true to his nature, he smiled and saw humor in what had just happened. "How many times do I have to run around the parade ground holding my rifle above my head?"

Herman laughed. At this point Sanga returned. "What did I miss?" he asked.

"We were remembering the time our colonel was a cadet and I was his teacher. You should have seen this little pipsqueak of an officer-cadet. He was the smallest little fellow in the class, but he made the biggest noise. He got punished the most but never stopped laughing. One of the instructors, a British sergeant, said of him, 'That bloke is like a kettle, up to his neck in hot water but still whistling.' Pretty small kettle, if you look at him."

Gonsalves drew himself up to his full height of five foot five. "I'm not so little. Not everybody can be over six feet tall like you, *ustaadji*," he said, causing everybody to laugh.

The rest of the night was passed like any ordinary night among friends. Herman noticed that Sanga visited the toilet rather often. Perhaps it was the result of the quantity of tea he had drunk, perhaps it was his body reacting to the fear that his mind was trying to suppress. It may also have been that his emotions got unruly and he needed a moment of privacy to indulge in them before he brought them under control. Twice already he had washed his face before returning. He must have shed a few tears for Jaanki and the children.

At dawn the guard called out to them. Each man washed and straightened his uniform. Herman watched Sanga comb his hair and carefully part it on one side. *He seems to be getting ready to go on duty,* Herman thought. They walked out together and exchanged quick hugs. Gonsalves spoke to the officer in charge of the firing squad. This man had been given the worst duty a soldier can be called upon to perform, and he tried to oblige the condemned man in any way he could. The six soldiers of the firing squad looked sick. Herman heard one soldier say *"Hey, Ram,"* and saw another close his eyes in what he thought was a moment of prayer. Herman knew that each man was hoping that he did not pick up the rifle with the bullet in it. Five men would fire blanks and only one would have a live bullet.

Sanga walked to the post driven into the earth against the brick wall. Herman was grateful that the wall was of rough brick without whitewash. The bloodstain would be horrible to see. Sanga refused the blindfold, and Gonsalves did not allow the soldiers of the firing squad to tie Sanga's hands behind him. He took a rifle and removed the bullets. He then took it to Sanga and placed it behind the post that Sanga stood against. Sanga smiled and held the empty rifle behind his back. He looked at the duty officer and nodded. At the order of "Aim," Herman saw Sanga's hands tighten on the rifle he was holding. Perhaps the last thing Sanga heard was the word "fire." The sound of the gunshot was short and sharp. Sanga fell first to his knees. He then toppled over sideways. Blood spurted from his back and splattered the wall behind him. One of the soldiers who fired said, *"Baap re,"* and clutched his stomach. He was probably the one who felt the kick of the rifle as the live bullet left it. Herman noticed all this as if in a dream. He rushed to Sanga. By the time Gonsalves and Herman reached him he was already dead. Herman covered Sanga's eyes with his hands and said the Shema and the short *bracha* he had been taught to say on hearing news of a death. Then he picked up the body of his comrade and carried it into the quarter guard with the help of Gonsalves, who was muttering a Hail Mary.

———

The war was over a few days later, and Herman returned to his village on the outskirts of Jwalanagar. He made his way to Manohar Sanga's house. Sanga's entire extended family had collected together. They expected news of their loved one. If one soldier had returned others would be on their way, too. Herman was dressed in his uniform, which had been carefully starched and pressed. His boots and belt were well polished and all his medals shone. People sat upon the floor, which had been plastered with cow-dung paste that had dried and become hard. Everything was clean and tidy. Herman smiled at everybody, hoping that his father would hurry. The whole village was used to this man reading their letters out to them. News became news to them only when it was heard in his voice.

Herman's father entered with an earthenware pot in his hands. There was a sharp intake of breath. Herman took the *chatti* and placed it in the hands of Sanga's eldest son, who was about twelve years of age. The boy placed it on the floor very carefully and looked up at Herman with fear in his eyes. He knew what this meant. Herman then opened the button on the pocket on the left side of his shirt and removed a letter, which he gave to his father to read. He snapped to attention and smartly saluted the *chatti* containing Manohar Sanga's ashes. This little bit of army ceremony and show of respect for the dead soldier would be a source of comfort and pride to the bereaved family in the years to come. Herman then went to sit cross-legged on the floor beside Sanga's eldest brother. All eyes turned to Herman's father as he began to read.

Respected parents, beloved wife, dear children, and loved brothers and sisters of Manohar Sanga,
     It is my sad duty to inform you all about the death of your dear

husband, father, son, and brother. He died a soldier's death with a gun in his hands. He did not flinch or move from the post, although his rifle had no bullets in it. He smiled as he faced the bullet that killed him. This bullet went straight through his heart so there was no suffering involved. Like a true Rajput, he had his wounds in his chest and not in his back.

I am the same officer who received his wife's letter many years ago. I am sorry, my daughter, that this time I could not save your *suhag*. You must be strong and live for the sake of the children you had together. They must grow up strong, honest, and truthful like their father. A respectful *namaste* to Mataji and Pitaji. The country owes thanks to the parents of such upright and valiant men as Manohar Sanga was.

I salute you in your grief and pray that God gives us all strength to bear this loss.

Yours most sincerely,
Colonel Jude Paul Gonsalves

The silence lasted a few minutes as the family absorbed the news. Then the crying and lamenting began.

"He would have been thirty-four this Deshera festival." His mother wept.

"The horoscope never lies," his eldest sister-in-law said.

"You and your superstitions," her husband replied. "Hands behind his back, indeed! His officer writes that he had a gun in his hands."

"He must have fought until he was out of ammunition," another brother said.

Herman heard no more. He watched Jaanki. She sat quietly without moving or weeping. Slowly, she raised her hands and then brought them down hard upon the stone hand mill. She broke all her glass bangles. A sharp piece remained stuck in her flesh, and blood began to flow from the cuts in her skin. With one hand she wiped off the big red *bindi* she always wore on her forehead. She then rose and went to the mirror that stood on the windowsill. She picked up the old-fashioned straight-edge razor that the men used for shaving, and she began to shave off the hair from her head. Herman looked at the long braid that reached well below her hips. Soon it would be gone. Her rough leather slippers lay discarded by the hand mill. She would remain barefoot for the rest of her life. Jaanki had become a widow.

Although he was a big, strong, and battle-hardened man, Herman could not bear to see the pain and misery involved in the ceremony of a woman's widowhood. He knew that her life was over. Herman ran out of the house and leaned against the wall as heaving sobs tore through his body.

Under twenty minutes of weakness and look at the cost. Fourteen such living dead! Manohar Sanga, what have you done? Herman thought, but not one word found its way past his lips. He just lifted up his voice to heaven and wept.

Hunting and Fishing

THE BOYS OF THE Jewish community of Jwalanagar disliked Mr. Rajpurkar, the man who had been employed by their parents to teach them Hebrew. His presence in their town meant that their summer vacation was ruined. They were expected to spend hours in the prayer hall, which was really a part of the Samson family's house, which in turn meant that somebody was watching them all the time. Misbehavior or absence from a lesson would be reported to their parents. Old Mrs. Samson gave them cold lemonade and home-baked *naankhati* to encourage them to study. She believed that education was difficult to acquire on an empty stomach. This was wonderful for those who liked sweet stuff. Those who did not had to pretend that they did in order to avoid a lecture on gratitude to God for all that He gives human beings.

The month of May oppressed the residents of Jwalanagar with its searing heat. One morning tempers were particularly short among the group of boys who hung around the compound waiting for their teacher to appear. The man was late as usual.

"I'm fed up with this fellow. Yesterday he asked us to be here at nine o'clock, and then he arrived at three," Reuben said.

"He said that he forgot," Gabriel sneered.

"How long does he expect us to hang around here? He is having a holiday on our expense. My mother placed ten rupees aside every month to pay for this chap to come from Bombay and teach us. It is an utter waste. We are learning nothing," Rahamim said.

"He is not from Bombay but from Panvel, a village outside Bombay."

"Who cares? It is all the same to us," Reuben remarked with a shrug.

Rahamim drew a pack of cards from his pocket. "I brought this along to pass the time," he explained. "I knew that the teacher would be late, and my grandfather insists that I wait until he comes, no matter how late he is."

"Let us forget the teacher today. We could do something else," Moses said.

"Our parents will punish us," one of the smaller boys said.

"If we all run off together they will have to realize that we do not like the Hebrew master. We might get punished a few times, but Mr. Rajpurkar uses the cane much more than they ever do," Reuben said.

"I am tired of his *aleph patta ah beth patta bah* and then getting the cane for looking out of the window and dreaming," another small boy said.

"He never has a good word for anybody. He finds something or the other to make fun of. Gabriel is our best reader, but our *masterji* calls him a frog because he cannot sing well. Remember when he said that God listened to King David's prayers and requests because he sang them so well?" Hannoch said.

"Yes, but Samuel had something to say on behalf of his brother and got caned for it."

"What did he say?" Judah asked.

"He said, 'Is that so? I thought that God listened because the prayers were sincere. If God is offended by harsh voices, why does He give them to us?' "

The boys discussed the event at some length before Gabriel spoke up. "Forget the stupid old *masterji* for now. I suggest that we go into the jungle for *shikar*."

"*Shikar?* Like fun! Where are the guns to go hunting with? I see no bow and arrows, either." Samuel, his younger brother, laughed.

"The problem with you is that you have no imagination. We have our catapults. We will shoot birds. Uncle Simon gave me an air gun. I'll take that," Gabriel said.

"What will you do with the birds after you shoot them?" Samuel wanted to know.

"Cut them up, cook them over an open fire, and eat them."

"And will that be kosher?"

"I'll pinch the knife Uncle Abie uses for *shichita*. I'll use a skullcap and say the *bracha,* too. You know that I have learned it by heart. Is that good enough for you?" Gabriel asked.

"No. That will still not make the meat kosher. You cannot cut an animal that is wounded or hurt."

"Come on! You don't have to be holier than the pope."

"The pope does not interest me. He is not my model of piety. I am a Jew. Remember? Anyhow, I cannot be as cruel to animals as you are. I'm going fishing."

"Oh! And fishing is not cruel? You stick a hook into a living thing and drag it out of the water. You pretend that the hook does not hurt, and the fish flopping around gasping for breath is a kinder death than a slit throat or a bullet through the head."

"You are right, Gabi. It is cruel, too. Anyhow, I am going fishing. Let Mr. Rajpurkar have our share of lemonade and *naankhati*. Take your bicycle, whoever wants to come with me." Samuel walked out from under the shade of the jackfruit tree and went toward the veranda, where all the bicycles were. "If you are so adept at pinching stuff, I suggest that you don't forget the spices and salt," he called over his shoulder.

"We will meet here, but outside the gate, at six o'clock. In that way we will all go home together. The punishment will be shared

and will not fall upon only one person at a time," Samuel added
as he pulled his bicycle off its stand.

"I must say that Samuel is a practical chap. He knows exactly
what we need," Reuben said.

Samuel was joined by three other boys—Hannoch, David, and
Judah. Gabriel was joined by Moses, Reuben, Jerry, Hayim, and
Michael. The rest of the boys went home. The older ones wanted
to go to the pictures because they had heard some college girls
make plans to be there for a matinee show. The younger ones
were more interested in a game of marbles or *gilli-danda*. Everybody left. Hannoch heard one of the Samson daughters-in-law
remark, "Serves that man right. He should learn to be on time
and to keep appointments when he makes them."

A group of boys on bicycles headed toward the hills. Nobody
expected to find a tiger, or even a deer. The animals had fled
deeper into the jungle as the city had grown in size. The boys
hoped to return with peacocks, partridge, and quail. They filled a
canvas bag with stones. This was ammunition for their catties.
Gabriel had rejected a cloth bag. He said that hunters used canvas
bags. It kept the blood of the birds they would kill and carry home
from dripping all over the place. Reuben had ground green chillies and garlic on his mother's grindstone while Jerry kept watch
for her return. They were able to wash the grindstone and place it
in its former position before his mother returned with the vegetables she had gone to market for. He related all this to his friends
as they rode along. Soon they broke into song. Later Hayim whis-
tled the tunes of popular songs from different Hindi movies.
They felt that at last they were on holiday.

The happy mood did not last long. After strenuous cycling up
the hills they found nothing to shoot. The birds had more common sense than the boys had. They kept out of the sun. The boys
searched everywhere, but no peacocks or partridges were to be

seen. Even common crows and sparrows were absent. A group of parrots flew screeching over their heads when something disturbed them, but this was of no use. Nobody ate parrots. Those birds were not kosher. Hunger began to gnaw at the boys' insides. Jerry had placed an earthenware pitcher full of water in the cloth bag that had been rejected by Gabriel. This bag was placed in the little basket attached to the handlebars in which people usually carried small children. The cold water did not last long in the blistering heat of May. Six thirsty boys emptied the *surahi* and then suffered in the heat.

"I would not mind a few of Mrs. Samson's *naankhatis*," one of the boys sighed.

"Her cold lemonade would be even better," another boy said.

"I'm hungry. Let's go home," Hayim said.

"Not before we do what we came to do. We will eat wildfowl today," Reuben insisted.

"We promised to meet the others at six o'clock. We cannot return before then," Moses pointed out.

"Samuel and his party must be sitting on the banks of the river, under the shade of some trees. They do not have to go in search of their game. The fish will come to their bait. The river is full of water, too," Reuben said.

"Don't envy them so much. The water is too dirty to drink. Our mothers boil even the water the municipality provides after treating it. My father says that it must boil for at least twenty minutes," Michael said.

"Yes, we know that. Still, they can swim and cool off. My whole body is itching from the salt of my sweat. I am sure that my neck and back will be covered with prickly heat. I hate it."

The boys grumbled about their misery and spent much time envying the other group of boys. They wished that they had gone with them. Moses even suggested going and joining them, but this was turned down. It was just too far to ride in the heat of the day. Most important of all, it would be an admission of defeat in a task they had set themselves. They did not want to face the ridicule of the others.

Around one o'clock, Michael spotted a pair of pigeons in a tree. He pointed them out to the others. Very silently each boy took his catapult out of his pocket and fitted it with a stone. They were hunters at last. Gabriel imagined that he was Robinson Crusoe on a desert island hunting for his dinner. Six stones flew from the catapults into the tree. Two struck branches and fell to the ground. One stone flew wide and at a completely different angle than was intended by its marksman. Three stones reached the pigeons. The birds must have heard the stones whizzing through the air because they left their perches in a hurry. One pigeon flew off and the other fell to the ground. It was wounded in the wing. Reuben put it into the canvas bag. "Let's get some more before we cut it," he explained. An hour later they shot a dove. The boys decided that it was time to eat. They were too hungry to wait any longer.

Gabriel found that he was not very brave when it came to slaughtering the birds. His hands trembled, and his stomach seemed to turn over. Shooting from a distance was different from holding a trembling creature in his hand and then killing it. Everybody looked at him because he was the one who had pinched Uncle Abie's knife and promised to do the part they considered a religious necessity.

"I am not yet bar mitzvah," Jerry said. "I cannot do it. The meat will not be kosher."

"It won't be kosher, anyway. The birds are hurt," Gabriel said.

"You are just searching for excuses. Why don't you admit that you are a sissy and that the sight of blood upsets you," Moses said.

"Have you ever seen me cry or faint when I get hurt?" Gabriel was offended.

"That happens when you are not expecting it. Say that you cannot do it, and I'll do it for you," Moses said, watching him closely.

"You are challenging my manhood and my leadership of this gang. Give me the dove and see. I'll do a better job than my uncle Abie."

The dove was handed to Gabriel, who placed a skullcap on his head with complete seriousness. *Shichita* was not a joke. The animal had to be dispatched as swiftly and as painlessly as possible. He said the prayer. Silently he added a prayer for strength and a steady hand to do the required task, as well as to defend his honor. He bent the dove's neck over its back and held it all together in one hand along with one wing and one leg. He then drew the knife very swiftly and as deeply as he could over the thin neck. Blood spurted over his hand, but he held the dove steady, its neck bent back and the blood pouring into the earth at his feet, until its quivering stopped. He then covered the blood on the earth with mud and put his hand out for the pigeon. The performance was repeated.

"That was very neatly done," Moses said. "You must have watched Uncle Abie closely."

"Thank you." Gabriel hardly got the words out of his mouth before his stomach heaved and a stream of vomit spurted out from his lips.

"You are a sissy," Hayim said.

"It is just the heat. He did not have breakfast this morning, either," Jerry defended him.

"How do you know?"

Gabriel did not hear any more. He was too busy bringing up what little food and water was left in his stomach after his hours of abstinence. He forced himself to recover as soon as he could.

His reputation was at stake. He picked up the pigeon and began to pluck its feathers while the others talked.

"There is no water to wash the flesh," Jerry said.

"We can't eat it full of blood." Gabriel stood up. The hunting trip had been a complete waste of time for him. He spotted a jackal under a bush. He threw one of the birds at it. The jackal ran off a short distance and then stopped. He turned around and looked back. The second bird was thrown in his direction. This time he recognized the object. He ran back and picked up the second bird. His mate had jumped out of hiding and made off with the first.

"The whole day has been a complete disaster. Let's go back," Michael said.

The boys returned to Jwalanagar. Samuel and his party did not return at six o'clock as promised. It was seven before they returned. An angry Gabriel confronted his brother at the cross-road before the Samson house.

"You said six o'clock. Has Mr. Rajpurkar infected you with his sense of punctuality?"

"Don't shout without giving me a chance to explain. You sound like our father does when he is angry."

Gabriel did not care for the comparison. "Okay, explain it to me."

"Judah does not have a bicycle. David carried him on the bar of his bike. We had to cycle many miles. Judah's bum and leg got numb sitting on that bar. One of his slippers fell off when we were halfway home. He did not even feel it, and nobody else realized it, either. Suddenly he looked down and began to cry. 'What will my mother say? She will beat me. She will say that money does not grow on trees.' We all know how harsh his mother is, so we consoled him as best we could and rode back till we found it. Now let's go in and see what our parents have to say."

All the parents had gathered in the Samson house. They had come there in search of their sons when the boys did not return home in time for evening tea. Their voices carried up to the gate. To their truant sons they all seemed to be more angry than concerned about the children. The Samson daughters-in-law were trying to cool off their tempers by giving them glasses of cold lemonade.

"You cannot really blame the boys," Mr. Bentzion said. "Mr. Rajpurkar is to blame. I wonder where he is."

It was a relief to the boys that the blame would not land squarely on their shoulders. They exchanged quick glances. Judah could not contain himself. "I saw him sitting in a rickshaw and talking to some woman who was sitting on her balcony. This was in Chelipura."

"What were you doing there?" his father thundered. Chelipura was the red-light district of Jwalanagar. He caught Judah by the ear and gave him a solid smack across the cheek.

"I went there to buy fishing material," Judah wailed. "It is cheaper there."

"Everything is cheaper there, my son. You just be careful," Mr. Joseph said as he pried Judah's father's hand loose from Judah's ear.

"I did not want to say anything until I was sure, but Mr. Rajpurkar has been seen in that area by many people. He is not a fit teacher for our children. What sort of an example is he?" Mr. Samuel said.

In the presence of a more exciting scandal, the children's truancy was forgotten. They were ordered home while their parents stayed behind to discuss the new situation. Mr. Rajpurkar's services had to be terminated. The children would be free for this vacation at least.

"I had an awful time," Gabriel confessed to his brother on their way home. "You were right. Hunted meat cannot be kosher."

"Except for Esau, which hunter does the Bible mention? Then you should remember that Esau was not a Jew. He sold his rights."

"I hate to admit it, but you were right. I should have gone fishing. You at least had a good time."

"We did not. We did not catch a single fish. Not far from us there were some boys who did not even have fishing rods. They opened safety pins and shaped them into hooks. These fellows caught one fish after the other. We fished in different parts of the river but had no success. I was afraid that you would make fun of me, so I paid one boy a full rupee for two small fish. They would be worth about two annas in the local fish market. Then, when we went back for Judah's slipper, I dropped the fish somewhere along the road and did not miss them until later. Nobody was going to go back for that, not even I."

"I can tell you something. I'll remember this hunting and fishing idea of ours as long as I live," Gabriel said.

"So will the rest of the Jews of Jwalanagar, especially when they go hunting and fishing for a new Hebrew teacher." Samuel laughed.

1965–2000

Dreams

ENOCH SAT IN AN ALCOVE just off the kitchen, trying to write a letter to one of his daughters in Israel. It always annoyed him that he had nothing to say that would interest his children or grandchildren. He felt cut off from them. Perhaps Miriam, his wife, should not have encouraged them to follow their dreams. She should have been more anxious about Enoch's dreams instead. Everything he had hoped for depended heavily on his children remaining with him and inheriting all that he had worked very hard to build. He had left his hometown of Jwalanagar and come to Bombay as a young man. After years of thrift and hard work he had managed to establish a workshop that had a few lathe machines. He took orders from bigger businesses to make small spare parts for motors and engines. Enoch dreamed that his sons would build a factory and take orders from no one. They would work for themselves, not for somebody else. This did not happen.

The three girls married and moved away, as was expected. It was the boys who disappointed him. Gabriel, the eldest, moved to Israel in spite of everything Enoch said against it. Gabriel had said that he dreamed of helping to build a home for the Jewish people. Menashe, the middle son, had moved to Jamshedpur on the east coast of India, to work in one of the steel mills owned by the Tata family. At the time Enoch had felt like banging Miriam's head against a wall. Her support for the children was unbearable. She should have stood by him.

Instead of agreeing with him, she had said, "They have a right to their own lives and their own dreams."

"What about my dreams?" he had demanded angrily.

"You have accomplished what you set out to do. You cannot expect your sons to sacrifice their ambitions for yours."

"Why not?" he asked. Did the woman understand nothing of how important it was to him? Of course there was no reason she should put his happiness before that of her children, he reasoned bitterly. He was only a ceremony relative, whereas they were connected to her by blood. His ire had risen at these thoughts, and the answer she gave did not help in the least bit.

"It is not natural," she had said. She then added insult to injury by asking, "Did you stay with your parents? You also left to build a life of your own. They are doing the same thing."

In the face of this logic he kept silent, but he never forgave her. It seemed to him that she did not really care for him, not enough to put him above everything else in her life. Enoch could never understand her support of their youngest son, Ephraim. Effie had decided to learn fashion design and interior decoration. What kind of profession was that for a man? People would think that he was a pansy. Effie had announced that he did not care about what anybody said. "That's right," Enoch had exploded. "Live up to your name. F.E. Fuck everybody."

Effie had laughed at this interpretation of his name, and Enoch nursed a grudge against the fleeting smile he thought he saw on Miriam's face. It was no consolation to him that his son was earning well and that he had been sent abroad on several occasions by the company he worked for. Enoch still thought that his sons had betrayed him and that Miriam had helped in all three cases.

A knock on the door announced the arrival of Mr. and Mrs. Gupta, who occupied the flat across the hallway. It was rare for the couple to arrive together. Mrs. Gupta usually dropped in during the day, when her children were in school. She would chat with Miriam and ask for advice about children or for cooking tips.

Mr. Gupta sometimes stopped by after he returned from work for a quiet hour with Enoch. The fact that the couple came together and was formally dressed made Enoch and Miriam immediately aware that this was a special occasion. The lady had changed from the cotton sari and rubber slippers that she wore at home to a silk sari with matching leather slippers, which were reserved for going out. Her husband wore a long-sleeved shirt and closed shoes, instead of the usual slippers and short-sleeved shirts he wore on informal visits to his neighbors.

After a bit of polite conversation Mr. Gupta stated the purpose of their visit. "Uncle-*ji* and Auntie-*ji*, we have come to invite you to the wedding of our daughter Sunita. The date the pundit has given us as auspicious is the twenty-fourth of June. We expect to see you with family and friends." He gave Enoch a red envelope containing the invitation.

"Congratulations," Enoch said.

"That is wonderful," Miriam said. She then rose and went into the kitchen and returned with some sugar in a saucer. She covered her head with the end of her sari and went up to Mrs. Gupta. "Here is something sweet. It is a Bene Israel custom to put something sweet into the mouths of people who bring good news." Mrs. Gupta opened her mouth and received a teaspoonful of sugar. Mr. Gupta suffered from diabetes, so he took just a pinch of sugar in honor of his neighbors' tradition.

"That's a nice custom," Mrs. Gupta said, "but it must be hard on the people who have to hand out invitations."

"Oh yes, it is. I could not stand the sight of anything sweet for months after the weddings of our children," Enoch said. "In each Jewish house we had to ask which side faced west so that we would be facing Jerusalem when we presented the invitations and swallowed a sweetmeat or a bit of sugar. The older people and relatives who live in the city would have been insulted if the invitations were not delivered personally. The postal service was only for those who live far away. Well! We have finished with that part of our lives. Now it is your turn."

Mr. and Mrs. Gupta left after about half an hour. Enoch and Miriam promised to help with the wedding arrangements. Mrs. Gupta's request was that Miriam teach Sunita how to cook a few simple dishes. The bride-to-be had shown an aversion to the kitchen, and her parents were worried. Miriam said that she would do what she could.

Two days later Sunita appeared in Miriam's kitchen. Enoch was in his favorite chair in the alcove, trying to read a book that he found uninteresting. Glad of an interruption, he listened to the conversation in the kitchen. He had always been too busy with his work to watch Miriam train his daughters. This was a chance to see her at work.

"I don't want to cook and clean," Sunita said. "I want to study. Why can't I have a career like my brothers do? I want to stand on my own two feet and earn my living, instead of depending on some man my father buys with a dowry to support me all my life."

"That's a tradition that will be broken when women like you do not demand dowries for their sons. In the meantime, you have to adjust to your circumstances and learn a few simple things that you will need even if you live alone." Miriam's voice was even and completely matter-of-fact. As if to reinforce this impression, she added, "Peel those potatoes and then chop two onions as fine as you can."

"Auntie-*ji*, you don't understand. I have dreams, too," the girl complained. "You have always stayed at home. You cannot understand what I am saying."

"Is that so?" Miriam countered. "I, too, was young once upon a time. I had a dream that was very precious to me, although my parents could never understand it. I wanted to sing and dance. I wanted to learn the Bharatanatyam."

This was news to Enoch. Miriam had never mentioned any of this to him. He waited for her to continue. She, however, needed to be prodded by Sunita before she picked up the story.

"What was wrong with that?" Sunita asked.

"Nothing, as I understood it. For my parents it was different. Song and dance were connected to prostitution as far as they were concerned, and nothing anybody said could make them change their minds. The Bharatanatyam was a dance performed by devdasis, temple prostitutes, in front of idols. It was not something nice girls, especially Jewish ones, should aspire to. My parents did not see it as a form of art."

"Didn't you try and learn it anyway?"

"Of course I did. I am human, too. My friend Nalini went to a special school to learn classical Indian music and dance during the evenings. At home I was not even allowed to sing songs from the Hindi films. Nobody knew that I could sing a few ragas and play simple tunes on Nalini's sitar."

"You couldn't get what you wanted, but my dream is so close. A few years more and I can be something. It's so close," Sunita repeated, stressing the words "so close."

"Perhaps your husband will allow you to study. Ask him," Miriam advised. "Dreams have a habit of seeming very close. You feel that you can just reach out and touch them. They can make you very unhappy. You just have to learn to give priority to what is important and forget what is not. One dream can be replaced by another one, but people cannot. Those you love must always come first. I'll give you an example from my life. I always wanted to live in a house with a garden where I could sit on hot summer evenings. I wanted each child to have a separate room, or at most

share it with one other child. We couldn't have that. We came to
Bombay where people sleep on the footpaths because there are
not enough houses for everybody. We were very lucky to get this
house. So I forgot that dream. I had a more important one. I simply wanted my family to be happy. I still do. It would be nice if
they were all within visiting distance, but if their happiness lies
elsewhere, I have to accept it. There are times when I feel like a
complete failure, and other times when I think I have succeeded.
That's enough chitchat for now. Let's get to work."

The next day Enoch watched Miriam carefully in whatever she
did. He realized that all the things that were familiar and that he
had taken for granted were really quite new to him. He had never
realized how much effort she put into preparing a meal for him.
He watched her go through his shirts in search of buttons that
had become loose. He had always felt that she took better care of
the children and neglected him. Yet he could not remember missing a button on his shirts or trousers even once. He had never
taken an unironed handkerchief out of the drawer before he left
for work. This woman was a stranger to him in many ways. He
did not know what she thought about many subjects that interested him, and he did not like that. Enoch decided to court his
wife once again and come to know her better than he did.

Later that night, Enoch followed his usual custom of reading in
bed for about an hour. He put his book down and watched his wife
as she undressed. He compared the aging woman he saw with the
bride who came into his life forty years ago. She still folded her
sari carefully and placed it on a clothes hanger with its matching
blouse over it. Her petticoat still went onto the same shelf in the
cupboard that she had chosen the first time she had placed her
clothes there. Her underwear went straight into the laundry bas-

ket for the next day's wash. She reached for her nightdress, and Enoch said, "No need for that yet. Come to bed without it."

Miriam smiled and came to him. She placed the nightdress on a chair beside her side of the bed. He looked at her body, causing her to blush. Her skin had wrinkled in some places and dimpled in others. Her once-firm breasts had begun to sag. The flatness of her abdomen had been replaced by a belly that was covered with stretch marks, a result of her pregnancies. The two parts of her body that symbolized her maternity seemed to want to meet; the belly rose and the breasts pointed down. She seemed to have shrunk a little in height, too. It was not a bad body for a sixty-year-old mother of six, but it was not the body of the bride he remembered.

Miriam got under the bedcovers. She turned to kiss him. He kissed her upon lips that offered little resistance because her dentures rested in a small bowl of water beside the bathroom sink. He cupped her face between his hands and looked into her eyes. "I love you, Miriam," he said. It was true. He loved her with all his heart. They were growing old together. He wondered what she thought of the effect of age on him.

"Miriam, have I become an old man?" he asked.

"Just as much as I have become an old woman," she replied.

That was not much of an answer. He wanted to know what she really thought. Of late he had become unsure of her thoughts, and her reactions sometimes surprised him. "I mean, have I changed much since the early days of our marriage?" he asked.

"Everybody changes with time."

"Yes, I know. But what changes do you see in me?"

"There is less hair on your head, for one thing," she said, ruffling his thinning hair. "You need glasses to read, and you must admit that you have a bit of a paunch. Besides that nothing much has changed."

"Do you mean that time has brought no other changes?" he insisted.

"You have become more crabby and impatient during the day and a better lover at night." She laughed.

"Do you mean it, especially the last part?" He was flattered and curious.

"There is something to be said for experience. Now put your book away and switch off the light. I am getting old and may fall asleep while waiting for you to finish the chapter. That wouldn't be fair after the condition you've got me in."

Enoch laughed and did as she requested before he reached for her.

Dropped from Heaven

MRS. SOLOMON STOOD OVER a pile of saris that lay spread out on her bed. She had to choose three for her three daughters to wear for the picnic that everyone from the Jewish community of Jwalanagar would be going to on that day. The choice of clothes was usually left to the girls, but this time there was more at stake. A family with two grown, unmarried sons had come down from Bombay in search of Jewish brides, and the competition was going to be stiff. There were a dozen girls of marriageable age in Jwalanagar, and Mrs. Solomon hoped that at least one of her daughters would be chosen. She would inquire about the particulars of the boys and their family later. Her first duty was to make sure that her girls were dressed in an appropriate way.

Mrs. Solomon gave much thought to what would be regarded as an appropriate sari. It must be neither too expensive nor too cheap. She did not want the boys to think that her daughters were spendthrifts who spent too much on themselves without thinking of the other needs of their family. On the other hand, she did not want to give the impression that the girls dressed without taste or that the family was poor. Silk saris were rejected as too expensive, and cotton ones were rejected, too—not because they were made of the cheapest material but because they would get crushed and crumpled. Her daughters must look fresh and attractive at all times. That left full voile and nylon georgette as the appropriate materials because they would not wrinkle.

She called her daughters to her. "Girls," she said, when they arrived, "choose a sari each to wear to the picnic today." Lily picked a white one that was printed with bunches of red, purple, and yellow flowers. "That's nice," Mrs. Solomon said. "Any color blouse will go with that one."

Because a sari is just a six-yard piece of material that is unstitched, women of different sizes can wear the same sari. The petticoat worn under the sari has a drawstring, so the sisters could borrow one another's clothes very easily. But blouses are a different matter. They are stitched to size. Lily's choice was very convenient for Mrs. Solomon.

Shoshanna also picked a print, but this time their mother objected. "No, child. You should choose a solid color. You are on the plump side. A print will make you look fat. And if the blouse is of a different color, it will cut you in two pieces—to the person who looks, I mean. A single color for everything will give you a sleek one-piece appearance." The words had hardly left her mouth before Mrs. Solomon realized she had made a mistake.

Yocheved, the eldest of her daughters, reacted immediately. "Who is going to be there? Who are you intending to show us off to like animals in a cattle show?"

"What do you mean by 'cattle show'? Did I not also get married this way? Your father saw me at my cousin's wedding. You have to make an effort, too. Do you think that a bridegroom will be dropped from heaven right onto your doorstep?"

"I expect nothing, and I am not going on the picnic," Yocheved said. Shoshanna placed the sari she had chosen back upon the bed. She did not pick up another. Lily stood indecisively with her sari still in her hand.

"Danny," Mrs. Solomon called out to her husband. "Please come here and speak to your girls."

Mr. Solomon put down the book he was reading and went into

the bedroom to come to his wife's aid. He had warned her that this could happen. He had said that it would be better if the girls did not suspect anything and dressed as they normally did. He did not relish the ongoing debate that all the Jewish parents they knew would be having with their daughters. In the end he would have to give an unfair order and expect it to be obeyed.

"What's going on here?" he asked, pretending that he did not know.

"Your girls refuse to go on the picnic. Now you explain to them why they should," his wife said.

"Why don't you want to go?" he asked dutifully.

"From all the preparations Mama is making, we are sure that some unattached boys are around," Yochi said.

"And so?" he asked.

"We don't want to be like dogs in a dog show." This was Yochi again.

"There is a difference," he said.

"How much of a difference?" she countered. "They get a ribbon and become studs; we get a ring and start reproducing, too."

"I'm not going to argue with you. These are the norms of the society we live in. It can't be helped. Get dressed. We leave in an hour." He walked out of the bedroom and resumed reading his book. Nobody was going to worry about his clothes, so he could read a few more pages before they left.

Both parents realized that the girls were in a humiliating position. They understood their anger and sympathized with the girls, but like all parents they wanted their daughters married and settled in homes of their own. Lily was young and pretty. She should not be too much of a problem to get married off. Shoshanna was a bit plump, but she had the ability to make everybody around her laugh after being in her company for only a few minutes. Of course the boys would have to speak first, and she had to be unself-conscious enough to be her natural self. The parents hoped that at some wedding or function where she was not aware of a strange male presence she would make a catch that would turn into a match.

It was Yocheved that they were worried about. She was the oldest of their daughters. She was headstrong and set in her ways. Mrs. Solomon felt like kicking herself for making such a fuss over the saris. Both of the prospective bridegrooms were younger than Yocheved. She did not stand a chance, anyway. The problem was that Shoshanna followed Yochi in everything. If Shoshanna did not get married soon, she would become an old maid just like her elder sister.

The girls continued to argue with their mother until a compromise was reached. They would accompany their parents with a smile if they could wear what they wanted. Yochi appeared in a cotton handloomed sari of green with a black border. Her hair was pulled tightly into a knot at the nape of her neck. She looked like the schoolteacher she was. The uplifted head and straight back made Mrs. Solomon feel a bit sorry for the child who had not completed the day's homework. She found herself wondering what her daughter would look like if she held a cane in her hand.

Shoshanna wore a pink sari with magenta polka dots, just to spite her mother. Her blouse was magenta-colored, too. Mrs. Solomon thought that she was trying to look like a birthday cake, but she wouldn't succeed because her long loosely plaited braid and the dimples that appeared whenever she smiled were most attractive. Lily wore her own clothes to please her sisters, but in a material that pleased her mother. Mrs. Solomon had to be satisfied with this. She was proud of her girls, but the daughters of the Daniels family and the Isaac family were equally, if not more, attractive. They were all good daughters, and although she wished all the girls the best, her natural instinct was to make sure of her daughters' future.

The families collected near one of the local high schools, where a bus awaited them. The women greeted one another in falsely excited voices.

"Hello, Dolly! So nice to see you," Mrs. Solomon said, wishing Mrs. Isaac well but eyeing her daughter Yael, who stood at a little distance from her family. She was her usual pretty self, and she had made no attempt to dress for anybody. Soon the younger of the two visiting boys went up to her with the lamest of excuses.

"Is this the bus that goes to the caves?" he asked.

"Yes," Yael answered, and looked away.

"At what time does it leave?" he continued.

"In a few minutes," she replied.

"Thank you," he said, and moved off.

On the bus he managed to sit behind Yael and her mother. He listened to their conversation and paid little attention to anybody else. *Yael is going to be the one he offers for*, Mrs. Solomon thought. She began to watch the elder boy closely. He seemed to be bored and disinterested. The scenery was different from that of Bombay, but the boy did not even glance out of the bus window. He sat next to his father and read a copy of *Reader's Digest*. He walked beside him from the time they left the bus until they returned to it, not leaving his father's side to see anything the guide pointed out in the caves. He made no comment about anything. The only time he did anything that showed his personality was when a group of tourists arrived, and a foreign lady missed her footing and fell against him. He tried to steady her but lost his balance, too. The boy and the lady both landed in a sitting position with their legs stretched out in front of them. The young man helped the lady up. "It is inappropriate for the Jew and the Gentile to be flat on their backsides in front of the Lord Buddha," he said in a mock-serious voice. The foreign lady laughed as she thanked him and rejoined her group.

This boy probably has a girl from another religious community on his mind, and his parents are trying to get him hitched to a Jewish girl, Mrs. Solomon thought. *He is not going to like any of the Jwalanagar girls. He has not looked at a single one of them. It is a pity, because he has a nice sense of humor.* She reached into her bag and took out *Pride and Prejudice*, the book that she wanted to finish reading. She couldn't help smiling when she compared herself to Mrs. Bennet. Mrs. Solomon hoped that, like her, she would succeed in getting all her daughters married—even if she had to make herself a bit ridiculous to do it. It was horribly humiliating to be put on show, but it was equally humiliating to watch the girls, who were the pride of one's life, being rejected. Yochi was already thirty years old. She was not beautiful, but she certainly was not ugly. Her stiff bearing was a bit intimidating, but only if one did not know her. There was warmth and understanding for others in all she said and did. *She has missed the boat through no fault of her own,* Mrs. Solomon thought. *What will happen to her when she grows old? Who will care for her when she is helpless? Her brothers' and sisters' children will not want to be bothered with an old aunt. She must marry and have her own children.*

Mrs. Solomon remembered the time she had asked her eldest son, Joel, who worked in Poona, where there was a sizable Jewish community, to take Yochi into his house. She had hoped that her daughter would get married and settle down there. The girl lived with her brother for five years. She cooked and cleaned and took care of his wife and the children as they arrived. Joel's wife had declared herself sick as long as her sister-in-law stayed with them. Then one day they quarreled. Yochi accused her brother of being ungrateful. Joel answered, "What did you do in my house that I cannot put a monetary value on? I could have paid a servant much less than I have spent on you for the same work." Yochi packed her bags and took the first train home. She found a job with a primary school and studied for her BA privately. Later, she was offered a position as a high school teacher with St. Mary's Girls' School, although she still taught in the primary section, too. As for Joel, he never employed the servant he had bragged of being able to spend so little on. And his wife promptly got well.

Mrs. Solomon watched the proceedings around her. The girls were nervous at first and hung back. They stayed behind the group and lingered in each cave after the others had left. But anxious mothers made sure that their daughters were always in sight so that the boys and their parents could watch them and make their choice. The younger boy had eyes only for Yael, and he directed his small talk and feeble jokes at her. She blushed but responded after a while. The prospective bridegroom smiled. Everybody realized that Yael Isaac was the chosen one. The girls relaxed and began the usual banter they made when they got together. Mrs. Isaac, however, was under pressure. She wanted to impress the visiting family. She offered them some sweetmeats with the declaration that Yael had prepared them. Mrs. Jirad was standing beside her at the time, so she turned to her for confirmation. "Oh, yes," Mrs. Jirad said, "everybody loves Yael's *barfi*. It is indistinguishable from her mother's." Hearing this Mrs. Solomon thought, *Sour grapes.*

Mrs. Solomon looked at Nina Jirad. The poor girl wore high-heeled slippers to make up for her short stature and could hardly walk on the rough and uneven paths around the caves. The Buddhist monks who had excavated the caves out of the rocky hillsides and then painted pictures and built statues had all walked barefoot. They could not have imagined that somebody would come to their hermitage prancing about on her toes. Nina looked flushed and embarrassed. Mrs. Solomon wondered whose idea it had been—the mother's, the father's, or the daughter's.

By the time the families returned to their houses after the picnic, it was around six o'clock. Mrs. Solomon was disappointed. She was glad that one of the local girls would soon be settled but was sorry that it was not one of her daughters. Her daughters did not seem to mind too much, though. Lily took her books to study, and Shoshanna sat at the sewing machine stitching a new *kameez*, which she preferred to a sari as more practical for the purpose of cycling to college. Yochi took a pile of notebooks and started correcting the geography homework of class 7.

Around seven-thirty, there was a knock on the door. Mr. Solomon opened it to a strange man who held a little girl by the hand.

"Is this where Miss Solomon lives?" the man inquired.

"Yes," Yochi said as she rose from her chair. "Please come in, Eliza. You must be her father. I thought that we were to meet at school tomorrow."

Eliza and her father came in. Mrs. Solomon saw a middle-aged man whose hair had begun to thin. There was a definite bald spot at the back of his head. He was tall, but he did not have the stooping walk that most tall men adopt to seem shorter. "I'm sorry I cannot come to the school tomorrow, so I have taken the liberty of calling on you at home," he said.

"That's all right," Yochi said.

Mrs. Solomon went into the kitchen to prepare a pot of tea. She had some sweetmeats and spicy tidbits left from the picnic. Soon everything was ready and arranged on a tray. She lifted it and carried it into the drawing room. When she entered she was surprised by the smile on her husband's face. Shoshanna and Lily had put down their work and were sitting with the visitors.

"Come, Sarah," Mr. Solomon said. "Meet Mr. Simon Divekar. He is a new Jew in town, and his daughter is in Yochi's class. He has been asking about the synagogue and the other activities of the community."

Mrs. Solomon put down the tray and shook hands with Mr. Divekar. "When did you come to our town?" she asked.

"Only last week. My daughter has had to change schools in the middle of the year, and I was hoping that Miss Solomon would consent to tutor her and help her catch up to the rest of the class. Eliza can stay for an extra hour after school ends or can come here."

"Whatever is convenient for you," Yochi said.

"I would prefer her to come here. Since I do not live far from here, it would be easier for me to pick her up after work."

"That's fine with me," Yochi said. "To whom do I address my notes? Who helps her with the schoolwork she does not understand?"

"I do, but she has to wait a long time until I return home every evening."

"Doesn't your wife help her?" Mrs. Solomon asked in perfect innocence. None of her daughters could accuse her of plotting or planning this time.

"No, Auntie," he said. "I am a widower, and there is nobody else to help her or her brother."

Mrs. Solomon's heart jerked to a halt before it started beating again. She looked at Mr. Divekar more closely. He seemed to be around forty years old. A button was loose on one of his shirt cuffs. His trousers were not properly pressed. The man needed a wife, and he knew it. Maybe there was hope for Yocheved after all.

"Why don't you bring the boy, too?" she asked in order to make conversation and distract attention from Yochi's flushed face. Mr. Divekar seemed a bit too observant of his daughter's new teacher. Mrs. Solomon wondered whether she was imagining it. She would ask her husband later. She handed around the cups and kept quiet. They had to settle things like tuition fees and the hours that would be convenient. Mrs. Solomon collected the tea things, headed for the kitchen, and realized that her heart was singing.

Monsoon

THE WAR WITH CHINA IN late 1962 did not affect Jwalanagar directly because it was situated far from the area of the fighting. In fact, the inhabitants had to remind themselves that there was a war going on. Life in town continued as usual for most people. But the war did have a long-lasting effect on student life, due to the introduction of the National Cadet Corps in schools and colleges. Summer camp had become the holiday most students could no longer afford to take, and NCC camps gave young people the opportunity to spend time away from home with friends. Rank in the NCC became a mark of prestige among the student population. The Corps also offered a source of additional income to poorly paid college lecturers and professors.

Benjamin Samuel, a lecturer who taught Hindi literature at a local college, decided to join the Corps. Besides his patriotism and his natural sense of adventure that longed for something new, he and his wife found it difficult to manage on his small salary. They had four little children. Hannah did all the housework, and Benjamin longed to give her a bit of the material comfort she gave up when she married him. He spoke to her about his desire to join the NCC. He would have a hand in training the future soldiers of the country and make some money in the process.

"It will be good for you to have something different from just teaching and worrying about us." She placed her hand on his belly. "All this will disappear after the runaround they will give you during the training. You will become the strong, muscular Benny I married."

Benjamin quickly earned the right to be called lieutenant. The extra money made it possible for the family to rent a house on the south bank of the River Murli. Hannah soon had both a vegetable and a flower garden. She was proud of her success in growing things. Benjamin bought the children a dog. He was pleased with life. His wife seemed happy with the house and the children. Although she was always busy, she was content.

The family had been living in the house by the river for three years when Benjamin and the other college teachers in the NCC had to attend a special camp for a brush-up course during their summer vacation. Tents were pitched on the north side of the river, just across from his house. He could watch his family from the tent that served as the infirmary. Hannah could not identify his figure among the other uniformed men across the river, but he did not have the same disadvantage. She wore her usual clothes, and no other women appeared in their garden to confuse him. Benjamin watched Hannah water the garden in the early hours of the morning before it became too hot to stay outside. She came out to hang the wash and then to take it in. The elder children helped her while the younger ones played with the dog. In the heat their figures would become hazy, but Benjamin watched them every opportunity he got. He began missing them more than he had in the previous camps he had attended, when he did not see them at all. The six weeks had always seemed to fly, but this time they dragged. Route marches and weapons training classes did not leave him so tired that he could not haul himself to the infirmary and watch his family.

The weather did nothing to cheer Benjamin. The heat increased his feeling of dissatisfaction. Sweat caused the prickly heat rash on his skin to itch. He looked at the parched earth and sighed. He reread a letter from Hannah. "My dearest," she wrote. "Just look at the parched earth around you and think of me. It has cracked open in its longing for rain. I long for you the same way. Don't you be like the monsoon, though. It comes and satisfies the earth for a while before it disappears for another year and leaves the earth to manage as best she can." His answer to this had been "Your lover shall be home with you before the rains arrive to satisfy the earth's desire. The monsoon season has always been the season of love and renewal. We shall take up our lives once again and renew old promises. I shall not leave you or the children—unless it is for another NCC camp. Unlike the monsoon, I am always with you. The rains come once a year for a few weeks, and I leave once a year for a few weeks."

Benjamin's prediction that he would return before the rains did not prove to be correct. The monsoon arrived early that year. The sky darkened. Peacocks cried out from the hills and forests around Jwalanagar, announcing the arrival of rain. The air became almost too heavy to breathe. Then the hot winds suddenly became cooler, and flashes of lightning appeared, followed by thunder that rolled around the hills like the sound of drums accompanying kathakali dancers. The rain came down in big drops. Dry dust flew into the air where the rain hit the earth. A heavy, musky smell rose from the ground. People rushed outdoors to welcome the rain. Benjamin watched his children dance in the garden, their hands outstretched to catch the drops. Little Eva was in only her underwear. Steam rose from the earth as it began to cool down a bit. Benjamin hoped that it would rain for a good while before it stopped. If the rain was insufficient, the heat would become insufferable, and everybody would wait for the next shower covered with sweat and full of irritation.

As the rain became heavier, visibility decreased. Benjamin watched the figures of his children grow dimmer before he lost them altogether. He followed the general belief that rain was good for prickly heat, and so he stripped down to his underwear to have a bath in the rain like his children across the river before he went into his tent to change.

The rain fell with a vengeance. Water collected in puddles, and small streams flowed down the hills to join the river. Benjamin knew that rats would leave their burrows in the fields to find shelter in houses that people built. Snakes would follow them in search of a sure meal. He hoped that Hannah would remember to block any unneeded holes in the walls and floors of their house. Drains from the bathrooms could not be helped. For the first time he regretted leaving the small flat they had occupied on the third floor in a poor section of town. An upper-story flat was more difficult for snakes to enter than a house built on the ground. *Come on, Benny,* he said to himself, *you are going crazy. Hannah is an efficient woman who like you grew up in a house with a garden. You are imagining things that may never happen. You are what your wife calls a crackpot. Your mind has cracked a bit. You want Hannah like the earth wants the monsoon rain. Think of something else now.* He watched the people disappear into their houses as the downpour grew more intense. Bullfrogs began to croak as advertisement of their mating readiness. Benjamin listened to the thunder and the sound of the rain.

"Benny, we will not have the sport period this evening," Lieutenant Malik said. "I'm glad. I am teaching a course in magnetism and electricity next semester, and so far I have taught only a course in heat and light. I must go over the material so that some clever student does not make a fool of me with his questions."

"I'll read *Shakuntala*. Kali Das and his Sanskrit are a bit difficult for my brain, which is more used to Hindi."

"Of course you will write to your wife first. The post leaves in the morning," Malik teased.

"Of course."

The rain let up for a few hours but then resumed. Lightning and thunder became fainter and then vanished altogether. The clouds seemed to have stopped quarreling with one another and made a combined effort to soak the earth. Trees offered no shelter from the rain. Water dripped off the leaves onto any person or animal below. Women laborers hurried to work, their wet saris clinging to their bodies, revealing every line and curve of their figures. Those who could afford a mackintosh or a piece of rubber sheeting used it as best they could. Modesty was the luxury of those who had the means and wherewithal to protect it. Benjamin watched the world go by from the flap of his tent. There was little anybody could do outside because of the downpour. He listened to the river that had stopped murmuring and had started to roar. *Two and a half weeks more,* he thought, *and I shall be home.*

Three days later there was a dry spell for a few hours. The sun came out, and a small group of ragged children gathered to look up at the rainbow. People appeared in the streets on the south side of the river. On the north side the camp commander decided to drill his men. Benjamin lined up with his squad. He looked toward his house. He saw his children squatting in the garden over something they saw in the grass. Soon they rose and began to run all over the garden. Naomi, his eldest, brought out an old cardboard shoe box. Benjamin smiled. They must be collecting *lal buchi*s, the big, red ground spiders that are as soft as velvet to touch. He had done the same with his brothers and sisters. He smiled to think that his daughter Eliza would retreat as soon as she came across the bunch of wriggling millipedes that appeared during the season. She had once told him that she thought of them as a revolting mess. They also made a horrible crunching sound when they came underfoot. He saw Naomi suddenly slip on the slushy ground. Eliza tried to help her to rise but drew back when Naomi held out her hands to ward her off. Benjamin imagined that she screamed at her sister's touch. He saw Hannah come out of the house and lift Naomi in her arms. Naomi struggled to stand and then hopped on one leg all the way to the house. The other children followed.

"Samuel," the squad commander roared, "repeat what I have said so far."

"I'm sorry, sir. I was not listening."

"Not listening? What do you mean, 'not listening'? What do you tell your students when they do not pay attention in class?" Benjamin was forced to listen to the tirade for a good seven minutes. He could not take his eyes off the commander and look toward his house across the river. He thought that Naomi had probably broken a leg, and he was sure that she was crying for him. He felt helpless in his inability to comfort her.

Benjamin requested permission to see the officer commanding the camp and was granted an interview at five o'clock. Time seemed to stand still. His frustration began to choke him. Promptly at five o'clock Benjamin stood in front of the commanding officer's desk.

"I believe you wanted to see me on an urgent matter."

"Yes, sir," Benjamin replied. "I live just across the river, and I saw my daughter fall down and break a leg. I want permission to go home tonight."

"Break a leg! Isn't that what actors tell each other before a performance?"

"What do you mean, sir?"

"You should have thought of something better, although you gave a good performance."

"I am telling the truth, sir."

"A broken leg is insufficient reason to ask for leave."

"I'll be back before morning roll call. It is just across the river," Benjamin pleaded.

"No, Samuel. A rule for one is a rule for all. The child's life is not in danger. There is only a week left. The plaster will still be on the leg when you get home, so you will have the opportunity to fuss over her. Army regulations do not consider broken limbs as life threatening. You may leave now."

Benjamin saluted and marched out. After evening tea, he went to the infirmary once again. He hoped to see his children, but it began to rain, and the other side of the river was invisible once more. He returned to his tent and tried to sleep. At around eleven o'clock Benjamin decided to go for a walk in spite of the rain. Flashlight in hand, he prowled around between the tents. He saw a bicycle propped against a tree and made a sudden decision. He would go home. There was a bridge about fifty yards downstream. He had crossed it a thousand times before. He was desperate to see his family. Their proximity maddened him.

Benjamin waited behind some bushes near the gate for a chance to escape. The sentry was as cold and wet as Benjamin was. He had to empty his bladder frequently. As soon as the man faced a tree and unzipped his trousers, Benjamin wheeled his bicycle out of the narrow gap between the bar across the gate and the gatepost. By the time the sentry returned to his post beside the gate, Benjamin was a faint figure on a bicycle that seemed to be in a hurry to get home. He rode as fast as he could. The wind was behind him, so it helped him on his way.

The bridge was deserted and easy to cross. Benjamin's flashlight was almost useless. Its light would struggle for a few feet and die out, but it was enough to show his position to anybody coming from the opposite direction. He could not see the river, although it roared all around him. He just concentrated on reaching home.

Benjamin knocked on his bedroom window. Hannah was surprised to see him. "What's happened, Benny?" she asked. "Why have you come home so late in the night?"

"I can't bear watching you and the children and not being able to touch you or talk to you. I saw Naomi fall and break her leg. I just had to get home and see her."

"You are a silly fellow to imagine the worst. It is just a sprained ankle. I took her to the doctor, and he suggested that an elastic bandage be used during the day but not at night. Come, I'll show you. She is asleep, and the rolled bandage is on the table beside her storybook."

Benjamin and Hannah went into the children's rooms and looked at the sleeping forms. Benjamin turned and touched his wife's shoulder. She smiled and hugged him before she took his hand and led the way to their bedroom.

"You really should not be here," she said as she took out a set of pajamas for him from a drawer. "Aren't you breaking the rules?"

"Yes, I am. I promise you that I'll be back before daylight. Nobody will know." He set the alarm clock for four-thirty before he took his wife into his arms. It rained all night, but the lovers were unaware of it. The harsh ringing of the alarm next morning dragged their relaxed and satisfied bodies into reality. Benjamin struggled into his still-damp uniform. Hannah rose and wrapped a shawl around her shoulders. She ran her hand through her dis-arranged hair. "A week more, sweetheart, and you will be home. I'm waiting," she said.

"So am I," Benjamin said.

The couple made their way to the garden gate. The rain had stopped, and the wind had died down. They could hear the tumult of the river. Hannah clutched her husband's hand. "Benny, the water is over the bridge. You cannot go. It is too dangerous."

"I have to go. I came without permission. I'll leave the bicycle here and hold on to the bridge with both hands. I'll get across."

"Don't go, Benny. If you love me, don't go."

"I do love you, but that will not stop me from doing what I have to do. I was wrong to come, and I'll not be wrong in not returning. What sort of an example will I be to my students? If you love me, help me to do the right thing. Don't stand in my way."

"It's foolish. The right thing is to protect your life."

"Maybe, but I have to return. You have no reason to worry. I am a strong swimmer."

Hannah watched her husband hold on to the bars on one side of the bridge and make his way across the wild river. The water reached halfway up his thighs. Benjamin struggled against the current and made steady progress. Hannah held her breath until he was more than three-fourths of the way across the swollen river. She drew a few relieved breaths before she saw an uprooted tree come swirling down the river, carried by the current and headed straight for her husband. Hannah's scream pierced the morning air, but her husband did not hear her. The river thundered all around him, and the tree knocked him down. He struggled, but it quickly carried him downstream.

Naomi and Eliza ran into the garden. They stared at their mother. She stood at the gate, clutching its bars and weeping. Her shawl had fallen off one shoulder and trailed behind her in the wet mud. The climbing rosebush that arched across the gate had scratched her shoulder, and a few drops of blood stained the nightdress alongside a little tear in the material. The dog had never seen Hannah weep before, and he began to bark at her. Naomi dragged the dog away, while Eliza took their mother by the hand and tried to lead her into the house.

"Your father!" Hannah cried. She stretched one arm toward the river.

The girls looked at the swollen river and saw nothing but mud-colored water rushing and roaring on its way downstream.

"He is not far, Mama. We just have to wait another week to see him again," Eliza said.

Naomi left the dog and took her mother's outstretched arm. The two girls led her into the house, confident that they would be able to calm her down.

A Girl from My Hometown

GERSHON LOOKED AT THE list of names on his desk. He pursed his lips in irritation. An Indian family had been allotted to him once again. His job with the Ministry of Immigrant Absorption in Haifa entailed work with immigrant families. He helped them adjust to life in the new land by helping them find jobs, informing them about their rights as immigrants to tax deductions and health care, and getting them an apartment from the Ministry of Housing. He also helped them with money until they found jobs. Because he was Indian by origin, he usually ended up caring for Indian immigrants. The anxious newcomers always felt better when they were matched with somebody who understood their language and culture. Gershon, however, was not too pleased about this because he found that the Indian immigrants regarded him as "one of our own" and made demands on him that they would never have dreamed of making on another petty government official who came from a different background. He tried to be as fair as possible and treat all immigrants equally, but his former countrymen behaved as though he had a special obligation to them. When he pointed out that he could not favor them over others, they usually accused him of forgetting his origins and being willing to sacrifice "his people" in order to further his career. Gershon could not possibly be pleased that another Indian family was waiting outside his office.

"Come in," Gershon said in response to the timid knock on the door. He busied himself with some papers on his desk. "Sit down," he said, pointing to the chairs but keeping his head down. He looked up only when he felt that the family was seated and looking at him in expectation. As soon as he raised his head, he heard a woman gasp.

"Ching!" she exclaimed. Gershon was startled. He was called by this name only by people he had known in childhood. His older siblings had decided that his chubby cheeks gave his eyes a Mongolian look, so they had taken to calling him by a Chinese name. Gershon's baby fat had melted away as he grew older, but, in Jwalanagar, anyway, the name stuck to him.

Gershon looked at the lady but did not recognize her. He had left Jwalanagar soon after Israel became a state—thirty years ago. People had grown up and changed. If he could not recognize her, he was not really to blame. At least that was what he told himself as he tried to compare the face in front of him with the ones in his memory.

"Don't you remember me?"

Oh, boy! Another person who will make demands on me and all the spare time I've got, Gershon thought. He stole a look at the names on the list in front of him. It said only, "Family Dandekar." This was of no help when Gershon needed the lady's first name.

"I'm Esther. Esther Moses. Don't you remember?"

Gershon was surprised, but if he gasped, he did so silently. Esther had changed. He tried to compare the aging, careworn face before him with the one in his memory, but he discovered that because he had not thought of her for so long the picture in his mind had faded beyond recognition. All he remembered was curly hair that refused to grow beyond shoulder length, a fiery temper, dark eyes, and a slightly upturned nose. He should have remembered more about Esther, but all he could recall were the arguments he'd had with other people in Jwalanagar because of her. She was the girl his parents had chosen to be his bride. Gershon had agreed to the match. Esther was what in Jwalanagar was called his cousin twice removed. This meant that their parents were cousins. Their grandmothers, Elisheva and Ketura, were sisters. His grandfather Joseph and her grandfather Bentzion had always been good friends. As a result, Gershon and Esther had practically grown up together. In spite of this, Gershon had never given her much thought. His parents had suggested that he marry her, and he found no reason to reject their choice. After they became engaged he found himself thinking of her often and convinced himself that the tender thoughts were love. He was also sure that she returned his love because she grew shy in his presence, blushed, and found speech difficult. The wedding date had been set for August, before the Selichot, the prayers of repentance said during the month prior to the Jewish New Year, began.

Trouble for the couple started at a housewarming party given by Mr. and Mrs. Nissim Isaac. At the time there were fourteen Jewish families in town, and the whole community was invited. After prayers and dinner Mr. Solomon turned to Gershon and began to tease him.

"Next housewarming will be yours, eh? I know that you will give us as good a meal as this one, because the Bene Israel women always whip up a fantastic dinner when they get together. I can't wait to taste your grandma Elisheva's *saandans* once again."

Gershon was expected to be embarrassed and bashful about his upcoming wedding. Everybody turned to him with smiles on their faces. But he surprised them all when he said, "I shall have no housewarming. I intend to leave for Israel a few days after the wedding."

There was a stunned silence for a few moments, and then it seemed as though everybody started to talk at the same time.

"Your parents did not tell me that when they asked for my daughter's hand on your behalf," Esther's father said.

"They did not know of my decision," Gershon replied.

"I will have you understand, young man, that I do not intend to give my daughter to a man who will take her far away from me."

"Any man she marries will take her away from you," Gershon said. "Once a girl marries she belongs to her husband's family, and not to her parents. That is the way of the world."

"You are right. Still, a father wants to know when his daughter is well, when she is sick, and whether she is happy or unhappy," Nissim Moses had insisted.

"There are things called letters. Besides that, you must have had some faith in me when you gave your word to my parents and grandparents."

Mr. Moses fell silent, and Mr. Isaac, who was seated beside him, tactfully changed the subject.

Esther had been seated too far away to hear what passed between the men. She remained ignorant of his decision until she returned home. Gershon did not know what she said or how she reacted, but he began to be visited by messengers who acted like lawyers pleading her case. Not only did she not want to go, she also tried to get them to convince him to change his mind about going.

The evening after the housewarming Esther's father came over to Gershon's house to have a serious talk with him. He spoke about a son's duty to his parents. Children were not supposed to abandon their parents in their old age. What would happen to the old people if all the young men and women left them and went to Israel? He quoted passages from the Bible and other holy texts to make his point.

Gershon used the same text against him. "The Torah asks us to honor our parents. It is in honor of what they have taught us that I want to leave. They have taught us to love Israel and pray for her and her prosperity. We even pray for rain or dew in seasons that are suitable for the land of Israel and not the land we are living in."

"You are like the devil quoting the Scriptures. Who do you think you are? The prophet Moses? Are you going to lead an exodus? Already one of my sons and two daughters want to leave like you. What will I do without my children?"

"You could come, too," Gershon said.

"Are you crazy? Do you expect me to give up my job and my home just to go there and starve? Israel is a small place surrounded by millions of Arabs who do not want the Jews there. Do you think that I will risk the safety of my family for a stretch of desert?"

"The people who followed Moses out of Egypt said the same thing."

"Are you comparing me with them? God appointed Moses to be their leader. Who appointed you?"

"Nobody. I do not ask anybody to come with me. It is a choice each man and woman will have to make for themselves."

"Have you stopped quoting God and left the decision making to the humans now?" Mr. Moses tried to sound sarcastic.

"Not exactly," Gershon replied. "These are our lives, and God helps those who help themselves."

Mr. Moses would not give in. He just kept arguing. Eventually Gershon lost patience and quoted the Bible once again to his Bible-thumper of a father-in-law-to-be. He added Jewish tradition to his argument. "At every wedding and circumcision we say, 'If I forget thee, O Jerusalem, let my right hand forget its cunning.' No wife and no son are more important than Jerusalem," he said, infuriating the older man. As a result, Mr. Moses refused to give his daughter to a "smart-arse, loudmouthed man who is determined to break stones in a faraway land." He must have been right about the loudmouth part, because Gershon responded immediately.

"Keep your daughter. And don't be surprised if you can't find a Jewish boy to marry her off to. All the young men will leave, and you will have to pickle your daughters or let them marry outside the community."

"Shut up, you bloody fool," Mr. Moses said as he rose to go.

"Prophecy has been given to fools since the Temple in Jerusalem fell," Gershon replied. He raised his voice toward the end of the sentence so that Mr. Moses would hear it through the door that banged shut behind his retreating back.

It was possible that Esther's grandfather Bentzion had spoken to Gershon's grandfather Joseph. Joseph pretended to be firmly against Gershon's decision. "I will never give my permission for you to leave," he said with finality.

Joseph was a man of few words. He was unaccustomed to being talked back to, much less defied. He always meant what he said, and he expected to get his way in absolutely everything. Unfortunately for him, Gershon was no different.

"I do not need your permission. I am a grown man. You do not have to sign any papers to show your consent. I have decided to go, and I shall," he said as firmly as he dared to the man nobody in the family had ever before had the audacity to oppose.

For the briefest of moments Joseph was taken aback. A glimmer of a smile appeared on his lips, and his eyes twinkled, but this was quickly covered up with a show of anger. "How dare you question my authority? Have you forgotten all that we have done for you?"

"I have forgotten nothing. You prepared me for life; now let me live it my way. I am not questioning your authority; I am merely pointing out its limits to you. Your authority ends with my father. If I need anybody's permission, it is his and my mother's, not yours."

Grandpa Joseph then left the room. He did not say anything to Gershon after that. It was as though for him the young man had ceased to exist. It may have been his way of trying to break the determination of his grandson. Gershon knew his grandfather and his ways well enough to recognize this as a form of pressure and did not bend before it. He also knew that his grandfather would have no respect for him if he did not stand up for what he believed in. Grandpa Joseph admired a fighter and encouraged a strong will in his grandchildren. Then one day Gershon over-heard his grandfather and Bentzion speaking.

"You can tell Esther that I have tried everything. Gershon will not allow himself to be manipulated, especially by the woman who expects to share his life. It would be better if she spoke to him."

"She is as stubborn as he is. She feels insulted that he did not consult with her. Still, Gershon is right. It is the end of life here as we knew it," Bentzion said. "The children are bound to leave one by one. We cannot force them. You are the religious one, Joseph. If it is the will of God, we should accept it gracefully."

"I've never accepted anything without a fight," Joseph said.

"That's your problem," Bentzion said, stressing the word "that's." Gershon did not wait to hear any more.

Gershon's cousin Immanuel was on leave from the army. He tried to dissuade him, too. Thinking that attack would be the best form of defense with this man, Gershon asked him why *he* did not leave and go to Israel, too. Israel needed trained soldiers rather badly.

"Do you think I am a lunatic like you? War is hell. I have seen it. The British have left India now. During their Raj no Indian was

allowed to be an officer and command white troops. Now the way
ahead is open. I will rise to the highest ranks possible in the army.
I do not intend to go to Israel and have some white chap think
that he is better than me because of my color. Believe me, these
people in Israel will even question your Jewishness because of
your color. People are affected by their surroundings. We have
picked up Indian customs and traditions, and they have picked
up European ones. You will be the outsider there. Don't go."

"I must. Other Jews are going there. I want to be a part of a
new land and a new people. I want to help build the Jewish nation
up once again."

"Do you think the others are going there because they love the
land? They are only going because of what happened in Europe.
The Indians have been good to us. Something like that will never
happen here in the East. The people here are different. Their religion teaches tolerance of other religions."

"Can you sincerely believe that after the bloodbath you saw
during Partition? People all over the world are the same. We are
just lucky that our community is not large enough to be a threat
to anybody. Besides, the Hindus and Muslims have each other to
hate, and everybody has the poor untouchable castes to oppress."

"I give up," Immanuel said. He also told every Jewish adult
whom Esther had tried to enlist to her side not to waste their
time. "He has a crazy logic. You will not be able to convince him"
was Immanuel's explanation.

Gershon's parents made no objection to his leaving. His father
said, "If you want to do something, one reason is enough. If you
do not want to, a million reasons in its favor will not satisfy you.
We have heard you argue and reason with those who tried to dissuade you out of fear that their own families will follow your
example. We have seen your conviction and determination, so all
we can do is give you our blessings and pray for your well-being."

Two months later Gershon left Jwalanagar accompanied by five other young men and one family with three small children. There were no young women with them. Parents would not part with their daughters until they were honorably married. Each of the travelers had only the permitted forty pounds of luggage because nobody could afford to pay for overweight baggage. They also had seven American dollars each in their pockets. This was all the money that the Indian government allowed those who were leaving the land to take with them. The families the travelers were leaving behind were very worried.

"Why, Gershon?" his mother had asked. "I am your mother. You can tell me the truth behind your decision."

"I do not know, Mother. All I know is that there is a strange force that is taking me there that I cannot refuse and still be true to myself."

"I believe you, Son," she said, and kissed him on the forehead, signifying her acceptance of the fact.

His father had not objected, but his displeasure and sorrow on losing his son were obvious to everybody. Gershon apologized once again before the train pulled out of the station. He acknowledged the pain he was causing his family. His apology received different responses.

"Don't worry," his sister Shifra said. "You are only the first. We will all follow. At least we will have somebody to come to. You are the fellow who will be alone in the beginning while you find a place for us."

"I don't understand you," his brother Ezra said. "You had a good job and a good girl willing to marry you. You have kicked it all aside for a dream. What can Israel offer you that India can't?"

His father just shook his hand and gave him a bear hug. His mother smiled through her tears and said, "God bless you, Son."

Esther Moses had come to the railway station because her

brother Hannoch was leaving, too. She had not looked at Gershon since she sent his engagement ring back through her mother. All his attempts to speak to her were rebuffed.

"You think that you can steal her heart and life," her mother had said, "but you are wrong. Somebody else will marry her. Esther is right. *Ghar ki murgi daal barabar.* Eating a chicken you have reared is equivalent to eating lentil curry. You do not value it because you did not pay for it. Had you been engaged to a girl from Bombay or some other place you would have asked her opinion in everything. You just took my daughter for granted because she is a girl from your hometown. You thought you could steal her heart, and she would lose her mind to you, too. You were wrong."

"She thought that she could steal my soul from me, but she was wrong," Gershon replied.

"You will have nowhere to lie down." Mrs. Moses cursed him loud enough for everyone to hear.

"Don't worry; where I shall sit, people like you, who stay behind, will find that they have no right to even stand." Gershon's words left his mouth before they had time to register in his brain. He had unwittingly compared himself to Moses, the prophet whom Esther's father had accused him of trying to emulate. He had also used the words that the ancient legends claimed Moses used to the Angel of Death. His greatest regret was that his words sounded like a curse. Gershon had never stooped to cursing anybody. He regretted his words immediately and still did.

Gershon glanced at Mr. Dandekar and then looked Esther full in the face. "Of course I remember you," he said. His memories had taken only a few seconds to pass through his mind. He wondered what had made Esther change her opinions about Israel.

Esther smiled with understanding. Gershon realized that she thought he was being discreet because he did not know whether her husband knew about her previous engagement. She fell silent and let her husband do the talking. Gershon watched her prompt him and add to what he said in an unobtrusive way. There was no doubt in his mind as to who made the decisions in the family. He went through the formalities mechanically while his mind was far away, back in the fateful days of May and June 1948. He remembered the pain he had felt at what he thought of as Esther's non-support of his decision. He had expected that as a woman she would follow her man. He did not expect opposition and was unprepared for it. He had not understood her point of view and had not taken the trouble to find it out. Her messengers had only infuriated him, and tradition had not allowed him to spend time alone with her before marriage.

Well! That's all in the past. It has taken two wars, the death of comrades and a son-in-law combined with twenty-five years of marriage to mellow me enough to realize that other people have a right to their opinions, too, Gershon thought. *Poor Esther would have had a hard time with me the way I was. We were basically unsuited. Perhaps she was part of my education.* The tender thoughts that rose in his breast could not be mistaken for love anymore. This was gratitude mixed with nostalgia for his youth and old hometown.

"I would like to take you and your children home for dinner tonight," Gershon said to the couple at the end of the meeting.

"Your wife may complain of your not giving her enough notice," Esther said.

"No, she won't. It is not every day that I meet a girl from my hometown and bring her home for dinner. I do not have to impress you. You are, after all, *ghar ki murgi.* You are like a chicken that grew up in my backyard. Lentil curry or a meat dish, it is all the same. We know each other well. That can have its advantages."

Gershon was not being sarcastic. He really meant what he said. Although he had once again spoken before thinking, he knew that he would never regret these words.

Esther looked startled for a moment or two at his use of the words she was unaware her mother had repeated to him. His smile reassured her that it was all in the past and that he bore no grudges. She smiled back at him. "There is another saying that chickens come home to roost. My words have come back to me. It could also be that like a chicken that strays during the daytime I have finally come to some understanding of where I belong. The *ghar ki murgi* has returned to her *ghar.*"

Now it was Gershon's turn to be surprised. All his arguments for leaving had in fact been absorbed by Esther and convinced her, even if it had taken her thirty years to realize it. They had, it seemed, learned quite a bit from each other after all.

Old Man Moses

ALTHOUGH YIGAL MOSES HAD strong memories of his childhood and had heard many stories about his grandfather, he was unprepared for the reception he received when he visited him. Yigal had expected to see a grouchy old man with a large twirled mustache who would resent any intrusion upon his privacy and would regard his Israeli grandson as a foreigner, a nuisance, and a drain on the old man's purse.

Yigal therefore had no intention of staying with his grandfather. He and his girlfriend, Galit, booked into the Kohinoor Hotel. They visited the old man only because they thought it their duty and because Yigal's parents had given him a parcel to deliver.

Yigal knocked on the door. "Don't worry, Galit," he said. "We shall stay for about half an hour and then go shopping for souvenirs."

"I don't mind waiting," Galit replied. "Your grandfather will be disappointed if we do not stay longer and tell him about his family and friends who are now in Israel. I have heard so much about him that I want to meet him, too."

"Not if you remember him as I do and have heard the same stories about him as I have from others who had to live with him."

"Perhaps now you will hear things from his point of view," Galit said with a smile.

"I'm not interested in old stories. Let's just give him the present my father sent and leave as soon as it becomes decently possible."

"I've a feeling that it will not be as soon as you hope. We can easily shop tomorrow."

They turned when they heard footsteps approach the door. "Yes? What can I do for you?" a middle-aged man dressed in trousers and a singlet asked.

"I am looking for Mr. Nissim Moses," Yigal said. "This is the address I was given."

"Old Man Moses lives here, but you will have to try the side door. He rented out part of his house to us when his children went away. His wife died a few years ago, so he now occupies just two rooms over there." He pointed to a door that had a beaten path leading up to it through an overgrown garden. Yigal looked around, disappointed. His memories of the house were better than his memories of his grandfather. His eyes searched for the swing that his father had tied to a branch of the jackfruit tree. It had disappeared. One wall of the tank that used to house goldfish seemed to have collapsed a long time ago, because the bricks that had fallen out were covered with grass and weeds.

"Why do you call him Old Man Moses? It seems a rather disrespectful way for an Indian to speak." Yigal was surprised at his own question. The Jwalanagar Jews who had moved to Israel referred to his grandfather in the same way.

"Oh! He likes it. There used to also be a younger Mr. Moses in Jwalanagar. Old Man Moses is the way he speaks about himself. He introduces himself by that name. Come in and sit down. I'll see if he is awake. He sleeps a lot these days. Who shall I say wants him?"

"Thank you, but we'll go to him. I am his grandson Yigal. This is Galit."

The man clapped his hands together. "Of course. I recognize

you now. Your grandfather shows us your pictures quite often. You are much younger in them. You really should send him more pictures. They mean a lot to him." He did not wait for Yigal's response but hurried to Old Man Moses' door and called out loudly, "Hello, Mr. Moses! Hello! Come open the door. See what a lovely surprise is waiting on your doorstep."

The grandfather took his time to come to the door. "What are you shouting about? Do you think that I have gone deaf? Has that silly woman in government exploded the atom bomb and started the Third World War?"

"No, Mr. Moses, this is bigger news for you. Your grandson has come all the way from Israel to see you. He has brought his wife with him. I'll go and buy some sweets for this great occasion."

"*Barfi* and *daalmot*. Sure, we need something sweet for this unexpected honor, but I like something spicy. It makes the tea taste sweeter. Wait. I'll give you the money before you go and spend more than I intend you to. Money doesn't grow on trees."

The man smiled. "Don't be offended," he said to the young couple. "It is just his way of talking. He is happier than I have ever seen him, and I have been living here as his tenant for almost fifteen years."

Yigal and Galit waited on the doorstep while Mr. Moses went in to fetch the money. The old man did not invite them in. "Where are your suitcases?" he demanded from inside the room.

"At the hotel," Yigal answered.

"The hotel?" He sounded thunderstruck. "Why the hotel? Did you think that your grandfather was dead? What do you mean by staying in a hotel when you have a perfectly good home to come to?"

"We did not want to inconvenience you," Yigal explained. His voice sounded weak after his grandfather's roar of disapproval.

"Pandey!" Mr. Moses called loudly to his tenant, who had by

now put on a shirt and was taking his Lambretta scooter off its stand. "Keep the sweets at your place until we return. I'm going with these idiots to the hotel to bring their things home. Have you ever heard such nonsense? Who stays in a hotel when they have family in town? It is an insult to the family. What will the community say about me? They think that I'm a stingy old bastard as it is."

Pandey nodded in silence. He understood the affront to the old man's hospitality. Galit smiled and pressed Yigal's hand. She had never seen him so overwhelmed by anybody before. Mr. Moses strode ahead of them, grumbling and muttering all the way to the taxi stand. "Kohinoor Hotel, and wait for us," he ordered the taxi driver. "We shall not be there for more than a few minutes."

At the hotel Mr. Moses raised his voice and demanded that the receptionist give over his grandchildren and their possessions at once. He then enthroned himself on a sofa in the lobby, held his walking stick between his parted knees, and glared at everybody who passed him. Yigal looked helplessly at the receptionist, who whispered to Yigal that he remembered having had his ears pulled by Mr. Moses when as a young boy he had chased a kite into his garden. The grandfather had claimed that he was trespassing on private property. The receptionist was not going to risk having his ears pulled once again, this time in front of a lobby full of people. Mr. Moses was quite capable of violence to the younger generation in order to enforce his point of view. The receptionist called to a bellboy, who ran upstairs like a frightened rabbit under the hawk eye of Mr. Moses. Galit took the elevator. She wondered whether the bellboy knew Mr. Moses, too. After all, Jwalanagar was a small town. She packed their suitcases while Yigal took care of the bill downstairs, under the stern eye of his grandfather.

"Any more Israelis with you?" the old man demanded.

"Only Itzik Kahn. He does not have a family in town," Yigal said.

"Well, he has family now." He turned to the receptionist and commanded, "Call him down."

"Right away, sir." The receptionist started to dial the number of Itzik's room.

Old Man Moses had no patience to wait or explain the situation to Itzik over the telephone. "What's his room number?" he demanded. "I'll not stand for this kind of nonsense."

Itzik was surprised to see an old man burst into his room and wave a walking stick almost under his nose. "Do you think that you are too good for us and our houses? How dare you stay in a hotel when there are relatives in town? Have you more money than brains?"

Itzik caught a glimpse of Yigal over the old man's shoulder. Yigal spread out his arms on either side and shrugged. Itzik understood the situation.

"I have no relatives in Jwalanagar, *saba*," he said.

"Your parents are Bene Israel. Am I right?"

"My mother is."

"That settles it. You are coming home with me. Our community is so small that I have never met a Bene Israel who I am not related to by blood or by marriage. You will turn out to be a relative of some sort if we go into our family histories. In any case, a friend of my grandson is my grandson. Pack your bags and come down immediately. I shall wait for you in the taxi. Some policeman might make the driver go and park at a taxi stand some distance away, and then we will have to lug your suitcases to it." He marched out, but not before he stopped at the door and said, "Hurry up. The taxi meter is running."

On the way home the taxi driver claimed to have waited for not more than fifteen minutes. Old Man Moses was pleased.

He smiled, leaned back in the seat, and hummed a little tune that seemed familiar but that nobody recognized. The boys were uncomfortable, but Galit thought him the most extraordinary person she had ever met. She leaned toward him and whispered, "I see where Yigal gets his forceful character from." Old Man Moses looked at her sideways and then patted her hand in a most friendly fashion. From that moment on he reserved his smiles for her and his growls for the boys.

Yigal and Galit were given the bedroom, while Itzik and Old Man Moses slept on *khattias*, string cots, in the larger room that served as living room, dining room, and kitchen. Pandey sent an extra *khattia* he had at his house, and Old Man Moses had a low one that he usually kept under his high four-poster. The children were taken to visit every Jewish family in town. Protests were of no use. Galit let Yigal down rather badly. She enjoyed the old man's company and did every possible thing she could to please him. He demanded home cooking, and she obliged. She went to the shops in the area and spent half the morning preparing her specialties for him. After eating a generous portion of every dish the old man was ungracious enough to say, "You call that food? There are no spices in it to speak of. What is that stuff with tomato sauce all over it? It looks like mashed-up brains. If you put a bit of chilli powder and ginger in it, it will not be half as bad. Remember, my dear, the way to a man's heart is through his stomach, and if you intend to keep him you will have to keep filling that stomach with tasty food."

Yigal was horrified, but Galit thought it a sweet outspoken comment. "That is Italian pasta," she said. "My father would consider it quite good, but then he is Italian. Mother is Greek. She would like more garlic, olives, and preferably goat cheese. You want different spices. You must explain what kind of food you would like me to cook for you, *saba*."

"It is not me but your man you have to please."

"Yigal does not fuss. He eats any kind of food I cook. As long as we are here I'll try and cook what you like. You must miss having a woman of the family cook for you."

"Humph," Yigal's grandfather said. "You do not know much about our ways, so I'll teach you a few of the simple recipes. Your mother-in-law will have no reason to complain. Tomorrow is Friday, and you will have to cook for two days. Remember, I do not have a refrigerator and it is summer. Cook something that will not spoil easily. As for you, Mr. Itzik, we shall try and end your bachelorhood soon. There are many nice girls in our community who are unmarried. You shall have your pick of them."

Yigal opened his mouth to say something, but both Galit and Itzik hushed him up. This was going to be a very instructive stay. They did not mind Mr. Moses' ways at all. That night Galit told Yigal that he had heard far too many stories and that they had prejudiced him against his grandfather. He should keep an open mind and not take umbrage at everything the old man said or did. He had the young people's interest at heart. "Don't tell him that we are not married. He will object very strongly, and it will make him unhappy," she said. Yigal thought that perhaps she was right. He turned over and tried to sleep. He could hear Itzik and his grandfather talking far into the night. Memories from his childhood came back very vividly to haunt him. The smells from the garden and the night sounds made him remember things he had forgotten long ago. He relived family quarrels and imagined that he heard shouts followed by weeping. He knew that it was a fantasy, but it made him uneasy. He turned to Galit. She was fast asleep.

On Friday evening the entire community collected at the Samson house for prayers. Theirs was the largest house owned by a Bene Israel family. Two rooms and a covered veranda were set aside as the prayer hall. Almost all the Jews of Jwalanagar attended. Everybody wanted to meet the children and grandchildren who rightfully belonged to the community but whom they either had never met or had last seen a long time ago. Yigal felt as though he was being put on exhibition until he realized that the local girls were in a worse situation. They were being pushed forward by their well-wishing community elders and their virtues extolled to the "bachelors." Yigal felt as though he was at an auction and held Galit's hand tightly. If people thought that he was married, it would save him from the embarrassment that showed clearly on Itzik's face. Mr. Moses was delighted when Itzik showed an interest in Naomi Samuel, and he hurriedly introduced them. Itzik got invited to the Samuel house for dinner, and Mr. Moses went home with Yigal and Galit.

Trouble started at kiddush. Mr. Moses asked Yigal to read the prayer and kept finding fault with his pronunciation of certain words, when in reality it was he who was pronouncing them wrong. He was reading from a book in the Devanagari script. Not all the letters sounded the same. Yigal controlled his temper and read the way he thought was correct. Then Mr. Moses poured sherbet made from currants into a wineglass and filled it until it overflowed. Yigal lifted the glass and read the benediction over it. He handed the glass to Galit, but his grandfather objected.

"In our house the wife drinks from the saucer. Hasn't your father kept any of our traditions?"

Yigal's mouth fell open. Galit spoke quickly, before he had a chance to recover and say something he would regret. "Why, *saba*? Why does the woman have to drink from the saucer?"

"How do I know that you do not have your menses? If you do, you defile the cup. No man who is clean can drink from it. It makes him unclean, too."

"Ohh! *Uus ko cootth lag jaiaygee kiya?* He will become an untouchable?" Yigal asked sarcastically.

Mr. Moses had forgotten that when Yigal had left Jwalanagar he was ten years old. He had retained some Hindi and now used the language to ask a derogatory question about a practice that annoyed him. Mr. Moses was furious. He considered himself an authority on Bene Israel traditions, and now the traditions he valued were being questioned by his own grandson.

"A woman has her proper place in a man's life. Keep a tight rein on her or she will run wild. She must be constantly reminded that she is not equal to a man. Her biology makes her different, even in God's eyes."

"Different is not the same as unequal," Yigal said. "Poor God! He is given all the views men want Him to have. He made two creatures in His image, and now one part of His divine image is supposed to be better than the other. In whose eyes, *saba*? Yours? What makes you such an authority on what God thinks? Perhaps all your trouble started because of the way you treat the women in your life."

"How dare you question my behavior? What do you know about me, anyhow?"

"I saw the way you treated my mother and my aunts. Who stopped Aunt Esther's wedding just because the boy wanted to go to Israel?"

Mr. Moses looked flabbergasted. His mouth fell open for a second before he shut it so tightly that it became a straight, compressed line under his nose. Yigal did not look at the changes in the old man's facial expression. He continued shouting at his grandfather. Galit thought that they sounded exactly the same when they were angry.

"Your family left because you gave them no freedom. You treated all of them as though they were complete idiots and you were the only one with brains, the only one with a proper understanding of things. Don't console yourself by saying that it was the will of God. It was you everybody wanted to be free of."

"Yigal." Galit tried to calm him down.

"That's right. The woman keeps the peace of the house," Mr. Moses continued as though he had not been interrupted. He was fully in control once more. "I have lived longer than you. My hair did not get bleached in the sun. Unlike you, I know what I am talking about. I know what happened here. You were only a child. You know nothing. You would not recognize the truth if it stared you in the face."

"You know nothing, either. For one thing, Galit is not my wife."

Old Man Moses really looked like an old man when he heard these words. He did not believe his ears. "In my house," he said in a shocked voice. "You slept in the same bed without being married, in my house?" He stressed the word "my." "Have you no shame? Where is your respect for the older people of the family? Is this what you have learned in the Holy Land?"

"We did nothing except sleep. There was not much privacy, anyway," Yigal said as nonchalantly as he could.

"That does not matter. You are not married. You don't sleep together. Some things are right, and some things are wrong. This is wrong. What sort of a grandfather would I be if I allowed this immorality under my roof?"

"We shall return to the hotel," Yigal said.

"Go. And good riddance to bad rubbish." Mr. Moses sounded disgusted.

"I shall not go, saba," Galit said. "If Yigal wishes to leave, he can do so. I have accepted you as my grandfather, and I shall stay with you as long as we are in Jwalanagar. Yigal has to learn to start respecting other people and their opinions."

"You are strong for a woman. It will lead to much pain and trouble. But you know something? In spite of your immoral conduct, I like you. Marry him and become a respectable woman.

Now I shall go and borrow another *khattia* from Pandey for my grandson. He shall sleep beside me where I can keep an eye on him."

Yigal was furious, but Galit would not give in. He wanted to leave immediately, but she wanted to wait at least until Shabbat was over. Mr. Moses would be spared the embarrassment of telling the community why his grandson had left. They went into the garden to discuss the situation and were still arguing when an excited Itzik returned from the Samuel house full of plans to visit the caves with Naomi on Monday. She would probably not go out with a boy unless another person accompanied them. He practically begged Galit and Yigal to go with them and oblige him. Yigal saw no way out, so he agreed to stay in Jwalanagar until Monday evening. They would leave for Khujarao on the train that left at midnight.

On Saturday, the Jewish community gathered at the Samsons' prayer hall once again. Even Mr. Moses was pleased when Itzik went up front to give everyone assembled *birchat cohanim*, the priestly blessing. This was a tremendous event for a community that had no *cohanim*. Before the blessing began, Mr. Moses had walked up to Yigal and covered his head with his *tallit*. He told Galit that he had been blessed by a *cohen* only once before in his life, when a *cohen* from Cochin had visited the community. His happy mood made the walk home more pleasant than it would have been without the *cohen*'s blessing.

Yigal took his leave midway to visit the Jirad family; one of their sons had fought with him in the same unit during the war. The young man had been wounded, and Yigal wanted to show them pictures taken after his release from the hospital. He was sure this would help to alleviate their worry. Galit went home with Mr. Moses.

At kiddush, Mr. Moses offered Galit the glass and not the

saucer to drink out of. "If you were my wife and I was saying kid-dush, I would not let you drink out of my cup," he explained. "You would be the joy that makes my cup overflow. I hope Yigal appreciates you."

"Overflow but not share, eh? Only what you can spare after the men had their fill? Never mind that now. Yigal has no problems with how the wine is drunk and by whom. It is just symbolic of an attitude he does not like, share, or appreciate. You do not have to take it so hard. He believes in God and religion. Now, for my information, please explain one thing to me. In the Bene Israel wedding ceremony, the bridegroom holds the glass he has just drunk out of to the bride's lips. Why is that different?" Galit asked this with real curiosity. She did not mean to be critical. Mr. Moses looked at her and reassured himself of her intentions before he answered.

"That's different. That signifies that they are not two persons but one now."

"What if she is menstruating at that time? Her nervousness could bring about a change in her usual dates. If she still drinks out of the same glass, why does that change after marriage?"

Mr. Moses thought about it for a minute or so. "Yes," he said. "Why does it change?" Then he asked, "Now why can my family not take that line of reasoning with me? They just try and force their opinions down my throat. I cannot be blamed if I refuse to let that happen."

"You and Yigal are alike in far too many ways to live quietly with each other. You insist on head-on collisions without ascertaining the truth or trying to understand the other person's position or reasons for anything."

Mr. Moses smiled when she said this. "Go lie down for a while. It is too hot a day to do anything else," he said before he lay down on his *khattia* and began to fan himself with a palm-leaf fan.

Galit went to the bedroom and lay down to rest. She found that she was quite upset by everything that had happened. She closed her eyes, but images of the old man's shocked face kept appearing in her mind. After some time she decided to go and have a talk with Mr. Moses. Perhaps she could explain the situation between Yigal and herself from her perspective. She could not find him anywhere. A muffled sound from the garden drew her attention to his hunched-over figure sitting on the bench under the jackfruit tree.

Galit hurried to the old man. He did not hear her footsteps. He was far away in a world of his own. She looked at his face and discovered that he was weeping. "*Saba?* What is it, *saba?*" she asked as she touched his shoulder.

"Only my memories, child," he said. He moved over and made a place for her on the bench beside him. "Once, when I was a small child, I was very nasty to my mother. Every time I have trouble in my family it is that incident that comes to my mind. I am sure that God is punishing me for what I did."

"What did you do that was so bad?"

"The worst thing ever. I was a young child of about five. A vendor who was selling *buddi ka baal* came down our street. It means old woman's hair because that is what it looks like. I think you call it candy floss. Well! He stood outside our gate and called out his wares. The children of our locality came with their pice, and he made some floss for them. I wanted my mother to give me one paisa, too. She said that she did not have any money to spare. I cried. I sat on the floor and banged my feet as I wailed. I screamed. Nothing moved her. She tried to explain to me that there were other, more necessary things that she needed to buy. My father was not a rich man. Money could not be wasted. I kept crying that she was mean and stingy. She did not love me. It was only one paisa. It was a very small amount I was asking for. She refused for some time, but my persistence eventually wore her down. I had cried for so long that I even forgot what I was crying about.

"Eventually she got fed up with my wailing and untied a knot at the end of her sari *pallo*. She gave me one paisa. It was not the kind of coin you see these days. It was as large as an English penny and it had a coppery color. There was a hole in the middle. I had cried so long and so hard that the *buddi ka baal* did not matter anymore. I threw the coin at my mother. 'Keep it. I don't want it now,' I said. The coin struck her on her forehead.

" 'I don't need it now!' I screamed at her once again. She did not say a word. She put her hand to her forehead. It came away covered with blood. She picked up the coin, retied it in a knot in her sari *pallo*, and returned to her work in the kitchen. I remember very clearly the way she sprinkled dry flour over the board and resumed rolling chapatis as though nothing had happened. I began to weep once again. This time it was not the crying of a spoiled child. Every Yom Kippur this is the first sin I ask forgiveness for. I struck my mother. It is the worst thing I've ever done."

"Perhaps it is time you forgave yourself," Galit said. "I'm sure that your mother forgave you. Parents usually forgive children almost immediately, especially if they promise never to do it again."

"Then why has my family left me?" Mr. Moses did not raise his head. He was still trying to find an explanation for his present woes in his actions of the past.

"Your family left to build a new home in a new land. That is the way life is. Things move on. Nothing remains the same. Why don't you come to Israel and stay there, too?"

"Nobody wants an old grumbler who insists on having his own way in everything. No, child. I'm too old and set in my ways. I'll stay here. It's all over for me."

"Nothing is over unless you want it to be. I'd love to have you stay with us."

"You are a good girl. I hope Yigal has enough sense to value you and take care of you. I'll make you a promise that I've never made to any of my children. I'll come for your wedding. You have the word of Old Man Moses."

Galit kissed the old man on the cheek. "Thank you, *saba*. I'll look forward to it. We are getting married in June, as soon as I get my second degree from the university. We have not told the others as yet."

"I'm glad that you will soon become a real part of my family." Old Man Moses sighed as he rose and went back into his house.

The Courtship of Naomi Samuel

A FEW MONTHS AFTER THE Yom Kippur War a group of Israeli boys and girls visited Jwalanagar. The town did not ordinarily get many tourists, but one of the boys, Yigal Moses, had emigrated with his parents from Jwalanagar as a ten-year-old, and his parents expected him to visit his grandfather, who still lived there. Yigal, his girlfriend, and another Israeli boy named Itzik stayed on longer than did the others in the group, who simply visited the local sights and continued on to other towns. Itzik's mother had grown up in India, and he wanted to spend time with the local families and absorb some of the traditions he had heard about during his childhood.

Nissim Moses was delighted to see his grandson. He took Yigal around to all the Bene Israel families, introducing him as "my Hannoch's boy, Yigal." The local Jews were very interested in meeting Israelis who had fought in the war. On Friday evening almost everybody came to the prayer hall with the intention of seeing these curiosities.

Itzik, whom the locals called Isaac, took one look at Naomi Samuel and was smitten. She was dressed in a lightly starched mauve cotton sari that had a small print of a geometric design on it. The end of the sari was drawn over her head as a covering, out of respect for the holy place and prayers being said. This accentuated her large brown eyes and curving eyelashes. Her eyes seemed to shine each time she smiled. Itzik took Yigal outside during the service and told him that he was interested in meeting the girl.

"I'll ask my grandfather to make the introductions, but you must remember that things are different here. You can't just ask her out on a date. We will have to organize an outing and include her. You will have to look for, or make, an opportunity to speak to her. After that we'll see what happens."

Itzik waited impatiently. Everybody in the prayer hall was watching the strangers. Since most of the older people had died and there had been nobody to teach the younger generation Hebrew, the congregants wanted Yigal and Itzik to do most of the reading. After the service they plied the boys with questions. But Yigal must have found a chance to speak to his grandfather because the old man pushed through the crowd that had gathered around Yigal and Itzik.

"We must not let a young bachelor escape," he said. "The ladies will never forgive us." He dragged a rather red-faced Itzik by the elbow to the area where the women and children were waiting.

Itzik thought that he must have shaken hands with everybody in the room before he reached Naomi and her family. He kept racking his brains about what to say to her, but he was extremely lucky because her brother Gabriel immediately invited him to have dinner with the family. Mrs. Samuel seemed embarrassed, and Itzik thought that she did not like being caught unprepared for a guest. He looked at Mr. Moses, who immediately said, "Go ahead, my boy. I have my grandson and his wife with me."

The group began their long walk home. Gabriel did all the talking, and Itzik gave him as much attention as he could. Naomi walked a little behind them with her mother, Hannah, and her sister Eliza. Itzik tried to include Naomi in the conversation, but it was Hannah who replied each time. Naomi only smiled. Itzik gave up. He decided to wait until they got to the house.

The Samuel family lived in a dingy flat in the run-down part of town on Shastri Road. In Israel, Itzik had seen the houses immigrants had been given, houses they had never been able to move out of even as their family grew in size, but he had never seen a family live in such crowded conditions. There was one medium-sized room that served both as a dining room and a bedroom. It led to a tiny kitchen on one side and a small bedroom on the other. A covered balcony had been enclosed with old packing cases to make another room. A bamboo cot covered by a hand-loomed cotton counterpane stood silent witness to the fact that somebody slept there. Itzik's dismay must have shown on his face, because Hannah said, "If you think this is bad, just go and take a look at how people in Bombay live. There are whole families to just one room. This includes sons, daughters-in-law, unmarried daughters, and grandchildren."

Itzik had no time to cover his embarrassment. A middle-aged lady dressed in a white sari came out of the bedroom leading a young girl of about seventeen or eighteen by the hand. The girl obviously had some sort of mental disability. Her bright eyes lit up when she saw her family, but her loose mouth kept drooling. "Eva has been a good girl," the lady said. "She helped me to pit the dates and cut the bananas for prayers tonight. Look, here is a picture she drew for Eliza."

"Oh! How nice!" Eliza exclaimed as she took the piece of paper into her hands. All Itzik saw was a mass of scribbles, mostly circular, but nothing else.

Eva seemed happy with the praise Eliza doled out rather lavishly.

"Thank you very much, Selma," Hannah said as she walked the lady to the door. "It was really nice to be able to take Eliza out for a while."

"It was my pleasure. Eliza needs to get out of the house a bit more."

"I almost forgot! Mr. Kahn, please meet Mrs. Youssuf, our good friend and guardian angel. This is Isaac Kahn from Israel."

"Khan? You have Khans, too, like the Muslims of Afghan descent?" Selma Youssuf asked.

"No, my name is Kahn. It is one of the European variations of the name Cohen. My father's parents came to Israel from Latvia. I owe my dark skin to my mother, who is a Bene Israel from Bombay."

"I see," Selma said, and left the flat.

"I suppose we will be able to get the *cohen*'s blessings from you tomorrow morning in synagogue," Hannah said. "Do you know that we Bene Israel have no *cohanim*? Everybody will be very glad that you have come. We will remember this for a long time."

Everything was new to Itzik. Perhaps he spoke a little too much to cover his earlier embarrassment. "My mother described to me the sherbet made from dried black grapes, which is used instead of wine for kiddush." He saw the surprise on Gabriel's face, so he hurriedly added, "That's okay. It is perfectly kosher as long as there is very little water used to soak the currants or raisins, and the bulk of the sherbet is grape matter."

"We know that," Eliza said. Her voice sounded a little cold, but Itzik did not notice. He saw that Naomi was looking at him.

"Are you very learned in the Scriptures and in religious matters?" she asked.

"Not very, but I did study with a rabbi for a short while after army service and before I found a job," he replied.

"Weren't you in the army during the war?" Gabriel asked.

"Everybody was in the war," Itzik said. "We were all called up. It is not like India, where there are enough people to have a volunteer army."

As the oldest male present, Itzik had to read the service. All through prayers and dinner he was conscious of Naomi and her quiet way of doing things for the family. Eliza was fully occupied with Eva, who needed all the attention she could get. She sat twisting a cotton scarf, while Eliza knotted a handkerchief into the shape of a rat to amuse her. Gabriel did very little to help out. Before he left, Itzik invited the family to accompany him on a visit to the local Buddhist caves on Monday. He claimed that he had not yet seen them, and was very eager to. He did not get an enthusiastic response. Eliza could neither leave Eva nor take her out on a long trip. Hannah had to go to work. Gabriel had promised to meet a friend after work. Monday was Naomi's day off, but she would not go alone. Itzik guessed that she thought it would ruin her reputation. "Yigal and Galit are coming, too," he lied.

"In that case she can go," Hannah said. Itzik felt his face flush. He realized that he should have asked for the mother's permission first.

Itzik reached the Moses house after eleven o'clock. He opened the door on a very angry Mr. Moses, who was involved in an argument with his grandson about some Bene Israel customs. Itzik realized that this was not the time to bring up another problem, especially because it involved a local girl of the same community. He went to bed quietly. Early the next morning he cornered Yigal and Galit in the garden and told them that they had to accompany him to the caves once more. "Let's go on Monday. Then we can visit Khujarao later," he said.

"Why not do it on Sunday? It is a holiday and more people will be around. Then we can also leave a day earlier," Galit said.

"Exactly. It is a holiday, so her mother will come, too. I don't want the older lady's company when I am courting her daughter." Itzik did not understand why his friends had not realized this. They just smiled and agreed to spend another day in Mr. Moses' house.

The Saturday morning service passed like a dream. The tiny

congregation was delighted to have a *cohen*'s blessing. Some people were openly weeping. Fathers and sons came up to Itzik to speak to him after the service. The older men invited him to have lunch with their families. Itzik watched Hannah and Naomi open the compound gate and start their long walk home. He could not follow them without attracting attention, so he accepted the invitation of a Mr. Rohekar, who had been the first person to invite him.

Itzik spent a pleasant morning and most of the afternoon with the Rohekar family. As soon as he got away, he went to Naomi's house. The long walk in the hot sun made Itzik sweat a great deal. His shirt was stuck to his back by the time he climbed the stairs to her flat. Instinctively he looked for a doorbell before he realized that it was Saturday, and as the religious Jew that he said he was, he could not use electricity on Shabbat. He breathed a sigh of relief that he had not made this mistake, then realized that there was no doorbell, anyway. He knocked twice and waited. He was wiping his face with his handkerchief when Eliza opened the door.

"Yes?" she asked.

"I came to tell Naomi that we will pick her up at seven o'clock on Monday morning," he stammered.

"Okay." She began to close the door, but Hannah's voice called out, "Who is it?"

"Mr. Isaac Cohen," the girl replied.

"Please come in," Hannah said.

"You watch it, mister," Eliza whispered fiercely as he walked past her. "Don't you play with my sister's feelings. We are poor but not for sale."

Itzik was surprised at the vehemence of the words. Hannah and the rest of the family were beside him before he had a chance to react.

"What were you saying?" Hannah asked.

"Just that the name is Itzik Kahn, not Isaac Cohen. There is no need for 'mister,' either. We Israelis are not formal people."

The room was too small for a sofa, and the dining table served to receive all visitors. Itzik pulled out a chair and sat down. He noticed that every article in the house was functional. Nothing was pretentious or ornamental. He wished that there had been a functional electric fan as well. He was offered a fan made from woven date leaves, and Eliza brought him a glass of ice-cold water from an earthenware *surahi*. Eva followed Eliza and suddenly grabbed the glass Itzik was drinking from. This caused most of the water to spill down his shirtfront. Hannah quickly pulled her away, and Eliza got him another glass of water.

"It's okay. I was hot, anyway." Itzik laughed.

"You mean you were feeling hot," Eliza corrected.

"Yes. My English is not too good," he said. It occurred to Itzik that the girl did not like him. He took it for a good sign. *She is afraid of losing her sister to me,* he thought.

Exactly at seven o'clock Monday morning, just as he had promised, Itzik stood at the Samuels' front door once again. Galit was with him, while Yigal waited in the car they had rented for their stay in India. Naomi had abandoned her sari for a *salwar kameez* and *dupatta*. She also wore sensible, strong *kohlapuri chappals* on her feet. She was dressed for walking. Her hair had been let down from the bun she wore when dressed in a sari. Itzik noticed the long plait and the soft curls at the nape of her neck for the first time. It had been her smile and the way her eyes lit up when she spoke that had attracted him at first. Galit went over to the table, and Hannah gave her a basket, while Naomi went around saying goodbye to her family. "Chapatis, pea and potato *bhaji,* and a thermos full of tea," Hannah said. "You will not have to spend more than the entrance fee."

"You did not have to take so much trouble," Itzik said.

"No trouble at all. We just made a little extra when we prepared the lunch we usually take to work and the food we leave for Eva and Eliza. Have a nice time, and don't pay for a guide. Naomi can explain everything."

Naomi and Galit left the flat together. Itzik noticed that Naomi was as tall as Galit. *That means that she reaches my earlobe,* he thought as he wished the family goodbye. Eliza glared at him. Hannah came to the door and stood watching them as they went down the stairs. Itzik looked up at the building after he placed the basket and thermos in the *diggi,* the baggage compartment of the car. Hannah and Eliza stood at the window watching them. He waved to them, and they waved back.

"You sit in front with me until we pass out of sight," he said to Yigal in Hebrew. "The mother might call her daughter back if she thinks that I'm trying something with her." Yigal moved to the front without a word. Galit smiled and opened the back door for Naomi.

When they had driven about a mile out of town Yigal asked Galit if she would not mind moving to the front. He wanted to drive and wanted his girlfriend beside him. Itzik gave up the wheel and moved to the back. He wanted to reach out and take Naomi's hand but thought it prudent to wait a bit. "What shall we talk about?" he asked with a smile. "Tell me about yourself."

"There is nothing much to say. You have seen the family. I am a nurse."

Itzik gave a low whistle. "A nurse," he said. "You are not only beautiful, you are also clever." A small voice inside him said, *Don't overdo it, you idiot,* but he did not pay too much attention to it.

"I could have been a doctor like Yigal's cousin Judy Moses Avaskar. I had better marks than her all through school. Eliza could have become anything she wanted, but things did not work out for us."

"Why?" Galit asked. She turned around in the front seat and looked at Naomi.

Naomi took a deep breath before she answered. It was as though she was preparing to perform a task that was unpleasant. "My father died when we were quite small. My mother got a job at the college where he used to teach, but the principal will not give her a promotion, although she manages the office almost alone. It is obvious what he wants in return. Jobs are not easy to find in our town. Men cannot find employment, so women naturally do not find anything at all. Hardly a year after my father's death, Eva was knocked down by a car in front of her school. She was standing on the pavement. The driver lost control of the car for a moment and destroyed her for life. He regained control quickly enough and drove off. He was never caught. Eliza stayed home to take care of Eva. I don't know how she does it. Eva would tire a person who has the strength of a Titan and the patience of a saint. I wish I could do more for Eliza. All I can do is earn a living and make the financial situation at home a bit less tight. Mother and I managed to take leave and take care of Eva while Eliza appeared for her matriculation examinations as a private student. She got a first class in spite of the little time she had to study. It is a pity she cannot go to college or make a life for herself."

"Perhaps it is God's plan that something else that is good will come out of this situation," Itzik said with the intention of giving her hope.

"How does a disabled child who has never harmed anybody glorify God? How does Eliza's sacrifice make Him greater than He already is?" Naomi asked. She looked him full in the face for the first time, and her eyes demanded an answer even as they filled with tears.

"I don't know, but I believe," he answered honestly.

She looked away without saying a word, but her lips tightened into a grim line before they relaxed again. Galit tried to change the topic without being too obvious. "So you work in a hospital," she said.

"No. I work in a family-planning center. I specialized as a midwife, but instead of delivering babies I now try and stop their conception. In Israel you pay people who have babies. Here we pay those who do not."

"Come to Israel, then. You can work as a midwife once again," Yigal said.

"If I could take care of my family I would go there like a shot. We do not want to become charity cases, not even those your state takes care of. I have responsibilities. My mother will retire next year. Once she is home I plan to go to Chawhanganj, a small town in Rajasthan, and resume the work I like. A doctor I worked with has offered me a job there. I will have a small flat of my own on the hospital premises. The salary will be higher than my present one, and the family needs the money."

"What about Gabriel? Doesn't he help?" Galit asked.

"He is the one with all the rights and none of the duties," Naomi said bitterly.

Itzik reached out and took Naomi's hand. "Not all men are like that," he said.

"I didn't say they are." Naomi let her hand stay a moment before she took it back. Itzik took it as a sign of encouragement. For want of a better topic he began to talk about Israel and his life there. Naomi asked a few questions, so he continued speaking. He commented about the countryside they drove through, and she told stories and legends about different sites. They spent an enjoyable day together. They had lunch at a small restaurant near the caves. The food they had brought was given to a group of beggar children.

"Don't tell your mother," Itzik said, and Naomi laughed. The sound of her laughter delighted him. It reminded him of the bells Bedouin shepherds put around the necks of their sheep.

"My mother is the sweetest person I know, and I never hide anything from her," she said. "You do not have to worry. I won't tell her as long as you are here, so you do not have to be afraid that she will scold you."

After lunch Yigal and Galit wandered off. Naomi found a seat on a bench under a gulmohar tree that was in full bloom. The ground was covered with orange and red petals from the flowers. She brushed a few petals off the bench and sat down. Itzik sat beside her. For a few moments there was silence between them, as neither knew what to speak about. "What did you like best in your trip so far?" Naomi asked.

"Do you have to ask?" Itzik replied as he took her face in his hands and looked into her eyes.

Naomi blushed. She looked away and removed his hands. "What was the worst thing you found here?" she asked in a softer voice.

"The horrible caste system that still prevails."

"That is no doubt the worst thing you can find in India," she agreed.

"How do people explain the injustice to themselves? How can a person, made by God like the rest of us, pollute our food just by touching it?"

"That's simple. Unlike other religions, Hinduism does not consider all men to be born equal. The lower castes rose from the feet of the creating god and the higher castes from other parts. The Chitpavan Brahmins are said to have risen from his mouth."

"Then why is it the desire of all men to reach the 'feet' of God?" Itzik asked.

"That is a paradox," Naomi replied. "All religions are full of paradoxes, because not everything can be explained by the priests. After all, religion was made by them for their own gain and livelihood."

Itzik was shocked. He had met the girl in a prayer hall. He had attended Friday service at her house. Did she believe or didn't she? He remembered something his rabbi had once said, and he decided to put it to use. "We believe that God created the whole world from a single set of parents so that no one can say to somebody else, 'My parents are better than yours.' We believe that all men are equal."

"I must remember that," Naomi said.

They spoke of other inconsequential things for a while before Itzik decided to grab opportunity by the forelock. He would probably never be alone with the girl again.

"I want to marry you, Naomi. What do you feel for me?" He put his arm around her shoulder and moved closer.

She took his arm off gently and moved a bit away from him. "I hardly know you," she said.

"In your tradition, you would not know any man well before you decide to consent to or refuse his offer of marriage. You have spent more time with me than you would with any other prospective bridegroom."

"That is true. I've told you everything about myself and my family, but you do not know that I am not as young as I look. I am twenty-seven years old."

"So what? I am thirty-two."

"I will have to speak to my mother first."

Itzik was happy. She had not refused him. He looked at her and said nothing.

Naomi began to speak. "I cannot leave my family. They need me."

"All of you can come to Israel. The family will be given a house, and an institution for the mentally disabled will take care of Eva. Eliza will be free to live her own life. She will find work and, in time, a husband, too. Your mother will get a national pension. You will not have to worry anymore."

"You must give me time to think about it," Naomi said. "Marriage has to be more than just a set of arrangements. I don't know what I feel about you."

"I'll go away with my friends for a while. You think about it. In the meantime, we will see the places we planned to see, and I'll ask for an extension of my visa. I'll be back on Friday three weeks from today, and I'll come for dinner and your answer."

Itzik returned on the day he had promised. It turned out to be a bad day for the few Jews who were left in Jwalanagar. Mrs. Abigail Samson, the revered "old lady" of the community, had died that morning. Absolutely everybody was busy. Yigal's grandfather was annoyed that Yigal had not returned. He did not mean to be rude when he said to Itzik, "What use will you be? As a *cohen*, you cannot enter the cemetery, and we need ten men for the Kaddish to be said."

"I'm sorry about my birth," Itzik said.

"Mr. Moses is just worried. Don't be offended," said Jonathan Samson, the only son of the dead lady. "We are seven men, and you are the eighth. Gabriel has gone to Nagpur, where there are two Jewish families. Perhaps we will have ten men. The problem is that we must bury my mother before Shabbat."

The funeral took place at three o'clock. The body was washed and waiting by the time the two men from Nagpur arrived. Another Jew was found in the Kohinoor Hotel, which had been recently built. This man was an American businessman on holiday. "That's appropriate," Hannah said to Itzik. "Auntie Abigail was the first Bene Israel woman who stepped out of the house, opened a business, and made a success of it. She started with one shop and owned four by the time she died. All the women admired her."

Itzik listened to the praise of the dead woman with only half an ear. His eyes searched for Naomi, and he strained his ears to try and catch her voice. She remained busy. Then, in defiance of local custom, the Bene Israel women decided to accompany the woman they loved to the graveside. Mr. Moses refused to allow it, but Jonathan said that it was his mother's wish to have women present. "She said that if the men objected, they could stay behind and the women would bury her" was his explanation.

"That's ridiculous," Mr. Moses said, but he raised no further objections. Itzik waited for the people to return from the cemetery. He left his backpack at Mr. Moses' house. He had promised to have two auto rickshaws waiting for Naomi and her family. Nobody wanted to be late, because the Shabbat candles had to be lit by sunset on Friday. As soon as the lorry that had carried the funeral party drew up in front of the Samson house, Itzik rushed forward to help the ladies descend. Twenty minutes later he entered the Samuel flat.

The smell of mutton curry cooking in green spices greeted them as the door opened, and Selma Youssef came forward to meet them. She had heated water for everybody's bath on two Primus stoves and a charcoal fire. The table was set for dinner, and candles had been fixed in the candle stand. Eva was seated on a stool beside the window with a string of beads in her hand. She looked up at them and began to cry. "Very long," she said between sobs. Eliza moved forward to comfort her.

"I've got everything ready. Hurry up and have your baths. There is only an hour to sunset," Selma said. "I've placed a tub with water outside the bathroom. I know that you will not wash clothes on Shabbat, but you can just rinse them and hang them out. The wash can be done later."

Hannah leaned forward and kissed her on the cheek. "Thank you, Selma," she said. Selma touched Hannah's cheek and went into the kitchen.

Itzik looked at the table. "The kiddush wine," he said, "and the Hammotzi bread. That woman prepared the things for Friday prayers."

"Yes, isn't she very thoughtful? She believes in praising God no matter what happens," Hannah said.

"You can't use that." Itzik pointed to the covered plate and the little teapot on the table.

Hannah lifted the cloth and looked at the *papardi*. She shook the teapot a little and lifted its lid. "Why not? She has watched us do it a hundred times. Everything is the way it should be."

"It is unclean. She is a goy."

"A what?" a voice from the kitchen door asked.

"Not Jewish," Itzik answered before he turned around and saw that it was Selma who had spoken.

"*Main achouth hoon kiya?* Am I an untouchable?" she asked in a soft, rather shocked voice. Itzik watched her eyes fill with tears as she placed the plates with the bananas and dates on the table. She made her way to the door.

Before Selma could reach the door Naomi's voice rang out. "Please leave our house, Itzik, and never show your face here again."

Itzik turned to face her.

"You spoke of one set of parents for the whole world, so that nobody can say he is better than his brother," she said. "We all worship the same God. Auntie Selma has made it possible for us to praise Him with prayer today, too. I will quote something else you said. You said that insulting a person is the equivalent of killing him. You have insulted the only real friend we have, and we will not stand upon our brother's blood. Please leave."

"But the halacha says—"

"Is that the law from Sinai? You are more involved with ritual than with God and common humanity. I could never live with a man like you." She pointed to the door with a hand that held a large white bath towel.

Itzik was stunned. He had to lean against the front door for a minute or so after he made his exit. He heard Naomi say, "That is the end of the courtship of Naomi Samuel. I'm sorry, Mother. I did try, but it is better this way. I was tempted to use him as an escape. The thing that stopped me was that he wanted to place Eva in an institution, with strangers to care for her. In other ways he is nice, and I know that I could easily have fallen in love with him and then been forced to choose. I do not want to abandon my responsibilities. Not ever. But more than anything else, I don't want a man who thinks he is better than other people."

Itzik was shocked, and he did not wait to hear any more. He now realized that there had been a lack of understanding between them from the beginning. Naomi was obviously unaware of the quality of life disabled adults were able to maintain in institutions that were run by caring professionals. But it was too late. Itzik was hurt to hear that instead of feeling about him as he felt about her, Naomi had simply felt compelled to see if she could grow to like him as a way of escaping her current situation. And he was sorry that Selma took offense, but the halacha must be followed. Itzik hurried down the stairs. He had to get to the Moses house and pick up his backpack before he went over to the hotel to register, and he had only forty-five minutes before Shabbat set in.

Her Three Soldiers

MICHAEL TURNED TO URIEL and said, "I've accompanied you this far, but I shall go no farther. I'll sit on the bench under that tree while you make your macabre visit."

"As you wish," Uriel replied. "I want you to know that I appreciate your taking time off for my strange fancy, as you call it."

Michael smiled. "You probably think me stupid, but I have an odd fear of crazy people."

"They are people like you and I. They are just unfortunate enough to be ill in the mind. It is something we all fear, mainly because we do not understand it."

"Enough of your lecture. Go into the office. I'll wait for you out here," Michael said.

Michael made his way to the bench and sat down. He had come to India from Israel on holiday with his brother Uriel, who was a medical student, and several companions. In Jwalanagar they found that they had plenty of spare time because some of their companions were obliged to visit with relatives, whereas they had no family left there at all. Their mother had been taken to Israel when she was still a young child, and their father came from a different part of India. Since they had no obligatory visits to make, Uriel decided to go and see the local asylum and compare the methods of treatment there with those in Israel. Michael accompanied him rather unwillingly. The doctors at the asylum had been very friendly and cooperative, but Michael did not want to go on doctors' rounds. Uriel could spend time in the office reading medical files. Michael would sit in the open air. In his mind, mental asylums were associated with straitjackets, padded cells, electroshock treatments, and injections that put a person to sleep so that he could be overpowered and then tied to a bed. Michael had no intention of going to see anything of that sort. Even if things were different than what he had imagined, he would not know how to behave around a person who was mentally ill.

Michael sat in the garden and looked around. A gardener was weeding a bed of violets. The flower beds produced a riot of color. He remembered his mother saying that February was the month of flowers in Jwalanagar. Michael rose from the bench and wandered around the garden. The gardener looked at him and smiled. He said something in Hindi that Michael did not understand. Michael raised his hand in salutation, and the man returned to his work. Then he saw an artificial pond built of cement and bricks. White and purple water lilies floated on the surface, and a few black bumblebees hovered around them. He began to walk toward them when he felt a hand on his shoulder.

"The man asked you not to touch the flowers," a woman's voice said.

"I have not touched anything yet," Michael answered.

"Please don't. Shayam gets very upset when anybody plucks flowers from the garden," she said.

The lady fell in step beside him and continued to talk. "Do you want to see the place?" she inquired. "I can show you around without any difficulty. I know everything here quite well."

"No, thank you. It is a kind offer, but I'd rather sit on the bench there. The garden is much more pleasant."

"I'll tell Shayam that you like the garden. He will be pleased. The poor man works very hard and gets very little appreciation." She said something to the gardener in Hindi. The man spat out a stream of red *paan* and betel-nut juice and then grinned, revealing his few black teeth. Michael had seen this result of the tobacco-and-betel-nut-chewing habit before. The red juice made him think of patients who suffered from tuberculosis and coughed up blood in the advanced stages. Although it disconcerted him, he smiled back.

"This is a nice spot you have chosen," the lady said. "It is quiet and a person can think here. The rest of the place is not too bad, but there is no privacy for our patients. Here they can be seen without being heard. I suppose I will see you a lot here."

"No. I have only come on a visit. My brother is talking to the doctors. I do not want to go in."

"I see. You are one of the quiet ones. You will not have much trouble here. The violent crazies are kept in another ward. The people here are all manageable. They present no problems to our staff."

"You are mistaken. I am not mad." Michael laughed. He had never been in a similar situation before. It was funny, but it made him angry, too. "My brother is studying to be a doctor. He is just inspecting the place for his own curiosity."

"Relatives fool our patients in many different ways simply to bring them to the hospital. Come along. We were expecting you to arrive around eleven o'clock. Your people couldn't wait to be rid of you and brought you in early. Isn't that so?" The lady shook her head in sorrow.

Michael and the lady walked to the bench but found it already occupied. A young man was seated there. He held a book in one hand and a long fishing rod in the other. A plastic cup full of earthworms sat on the ground at his feet. The fishing line disappeared into a bucket of water. Michael wondered why the man had not chosen the pond as a fishing site. Before he could say anything, the lady greeted the man.

"Hello, Raman," she said. "What are you doing?"

Raman looked over the top of his book and said, "Can't you see? I am fishing." He returned to his reading.

"Are the fish biting today?" Michael asked.

"Are you mad? Who has ever caught a fish in a bucket?" the man replied. His book must have been very interesting, because he gave it all his attention. He did not look in their direction or speak another word to them.

"Come, I'll show you where you will eat and where the laundry is," the lady said. "The more you can do for yourself the easier it will be for you to pass the time."

Michael lost patience. "I tell you I am not going to stay here. I have come to visit from Israel with my brother. We will return within a few weeks."

"Israel!" the lady said. Her eyes widened, and a smile of pleasure appeared on her lips. "What is your name, my boy?"

"Michael. My brother is Uriel."

"Ah! The names of the archangels! Do you have the other two archangel names in the family, too?"

"Only one more. Our youngest brother is named Gabriel. We also have two sisters, and Mother decided that five children were enough. She did not care to try for a 'Raphael.' What is your name?" he asked. The woman seemed to be acquainted with the Bible, and this aroused his curiosity.

"Ruth Samuel. You can call me Auntie Ruthie. Everybody, especially the Bene Israel children, call me that." After a pause she added, "Tell me something. Did you fight in the last war?"

"Yes, I did. Uriel and Gabriel fought, too."

"Where did you fight?"

"Why do you want to know?" After the war, morbid curiosity similar to the kind the lady displayed never failed to annoy him.

"Three brothers in the army." The lady sighed. "It is just like my boys. I lost my three sons in Israel. Did you ever meet Nathan, Shalom, or Tzion Samuel?"

Michael's attitude changed immediately. Here was a grieving mother. He had seen far too many of them recently, and his heart ached each time he met one. Ruth Samuel had remained in India and had not even seen her boys before they went off to serve their country and defend her inhabitants. She had been here in Jwalanagar, alone with her worries and fears. He lowered his eyes for a minute before he looked up and asked very gently, "In which units did they serve?"

"Nathan was a paratrooper. His parachute did not open, and he fell to his death. Shalom was guarding his base when an intruder slipped in behind him and slit his throat. Tzion, the baby of the family, was a submariner." There was a definite pride in her voice and face, especially when she mentioned the submariner.

Michael was confused. "We did not use parachutes or submarines in this war," he exclaimed.

"Now you are mistaking me for one of the demented ones. Nathan died while in training, and Tzion drowned trying to save a sailor who was so badly wounded in the neck that he did not survive, either."

The lady, whom Michael now thought of as Auntie Ruthie, asked several questions and displayed a deep knowledge of the war. She had followed the battles very closely. She also knew a lot about the geography and history of Israel. Michael did not realize how quickly two hours passed. He was surprised when Uriel appeared and announced that it was time to return to town.

"Meet Auntie Ruthie," Michael said.

"Pleased to meet you," Uriel said as he shook hands with the lady.

"Can we offer you a lift back?" Michael offered.

"No, thank you. I must wait for my husband. He will come for me in the evening when I go off duty. It was a pleasure meeting you both. Say a prayer for me when you pray at the Wailing Wall."

"What should I ask for?" Michael inquired.

"Mercy. God does whatever He wants. Just ask Him to have mercy on His creatures."

"I will," Michael promised.

Michael was silent on the way back to Jwalanagar. Uriel drove quietly for a while before he asked his brother what was bothering him.

"It's Auntie Ruthie. Poor lady! She has lost three sons."

"I know."

"How do you know? I haven't mentioned a word about her to you."

"I read her file."

Michael drew back. He stared at his brother. "You don't mean—" He found himself unable to say the words.

"She is one of the inmates," Uriel said.

"No."

"Yes. Why is it so surprising?"

"She seemed so normal. What is her particular problem?"

"She has lost touch with reality. She had a nasty shock when her three children died, all within a few minutes of each other. She thinks that her husband blames her. The worst part for her is that she blames herself."

"What happened?"

"It is a really weird horror story. She comes from a religious Jewish family. You know that the Jewish community in Jwalanagar slaughters a goat or two every Tuesday and Friday. This is done in the garden of the Samson house, and one of the older uncles koshers the mutton for those who want it done properly but do not want to go to all the trouble themselves. One day Ruthie's little boys watched the whole procedure. Nobody thought much of it. Children had always watched, and nothing worse than their not being able to eat any kind of meat for a time had ever occurred. This time things were different.

"Ruthie was alone at home. She was bathing her baby in a bathtub when she saw her eldest son fall past the window. This was followed by a thud and a woman's scream from downstairs. Ruthie ran to the window. She saw her son lying in the street. His head was at an impossible angle. She ran downstairs, but it was too late. The boy was dead. She looked up at the roof to see where he had fallen from. Blood was dripping down the walls. One of the neighbors went onto the roof to see what had happened. He found the second son lying on his back. There was a deep gash in his throat. His father's sharp *shichita* knife lay beside him. This boy was dead, too.

"It could have been put down to children's thoughtless and stupid games, but there was worse to follow. Ruthie had left the baby unattended in the bathtub, and he drowned. People in the community held her responsible for at least that death. There were those who said she was an inefficient mother. She should have known where her children were and what they were doing.

"Ruthie did not go mad overnight. It took some time. Anything anybody said was interpreted by her as a reference to the incident, and any mention of it was seen as an accusation. Her husband supported her for a few years, but then he wanted them to go ahead with their lives. Ruthie remained fixed in the past. One day he also blamed her for the deaths. At that point, something inside her snapped. She has never been the same since."

"Is there no cure for her?" Michael asked.

"I don't know. All I can say is that I have learned one thing today. I shall never specialize in mental diseases. I wouldn't want to cure her even if I could. She asked you to pray for mercy. Her condition now is a mercy."

"How can being mad be a mercy?"

"She has forgotten what really happened," Uriel replied. "She always wanted to go to Israel, but her husband would not emigrate because he was afraid his children would meet violent ends there. It is ironic. His wife consoles herself and gives her children's death some meaning by imagining it happened in a war, in defense of the Jewish homeland she always wanted to live in. Realization of the truth will only bring back the pain. Someone once said that memory is like a purse. When it is too full, things just fall out."

"Not completely," Michael said. "She imagined that the boy who fell was a paratrooper. The boy who had his throat cut had it done by an enemy intruder, and the boy who drowned was a submariner. She has not forgotten the manner of their deaths." After a few minutes of silence he asked, "What about her husband? She said that he was to pick her up in the evening after she finished work."

"That is the lie he told her when he left her there. He did not want a scene."

"She is still waiting for him to take her home. Doesn't he visit her?"

"Not anymore. He pays her hospital bills regularly, but he is in Australia with his new family. In India you are allowed to have a second wife while the first is still living only if she is childless or mentally ill. Her husband found a second wife. That is another reason I would not bring her back to reality even if I could."

Michael looked out of the car window. The passing scenery had lost all its charm. He wished that he was a child once again so that he could lie in bed, cover his head with a pillow, and weep silently.

The Funeral

THE TRAIN FROM BOMBAY reached the outskirts of Jwala-nagar at around four o'clock in the afternoon. Joseph Naor stood at the open door of one of the carriages, looking at the passing scenery with interest. The little town of his childhood had changed beyond recognition. Slums had grown up everywhere. Houses that had once stood on large plots of land had given way to blocks of flats. Joseph had never imagined so many people living in his sleepy little town.

"Anything you recognize, *motek*?" Maiya, his Israeli-born wife, called from her seat.

"Only the river, and it has dried up. I suppose that the dam upstream is responsible. I can hardly imagine that Benjamin Samuel drowned in the floodwaters of this miserable little stream. We used to bicycle up on Sundays to fish here. I wonder whether there are any fish left. The water used to be brown and muddy only during the monsoons. Now it looks oily and brackish."

"The price of progress," Maiya said.

"Whose progress? That is the question. The poor people who lived on the land beside the river have certainly not become the middle-class people who occupy those flats."

"Come on, dear, don't start our holiday in a sour mood. Enjoy your homecoming," she coaxed.

Joseph closed the door and went to sit beside his wife. He

did not want to look at the town anymore. There would be time enough for that during the five days he planned to spend there. The rest of the vacation would be used to see parts of India he had never seen when he lived there. His parents had had no money to spare for sightseeing. Now, as a tourist, Joseph planned to see the Taj Mahal and the famous Ajanta and Ellora Caves for the first time. He hoped to include Jaipur, Khujarao, and South India in his tour.

The train pulled into the station an hour and a half after its scheduled time of arrival. Trains still ran late. That had not changed. Joseph instinctively refused the red-shirted coolie who tried to pick up his luggage. The man's hopeful expression changed to one of disappointment and pleading. He touched his belly, and Joseph relented. He did not want to employ a human beast of burden, but the man needed to earn an honest living. Joseph went through the motions of noting the number on the coolie's brass armband. He took his wife by the arm and guided her past the legless, armless, blind, or leprous beggars, many of whom were children. He practically had to drag her past the food stalls and bookstalls, the water carriers, and the restrooms. A mixture of different smells attacked his nostrils. These smells had excited him when he was a child; now they nauseated him. He did not follow the smell of cooking food to its source. He followed the coolie off the platform to the taxi stand instead.

"Has it changed much?" his wife asked.

"I'll say it has," he replied. "There are three railway platforms where there used to be only one. There is a taxi and auto-rickshaw stand instead of the place where bicycle rickshaws and tongas waited for passengers." He paid the coolie much more than the man expected. Joseph looked around but saw no familiar faces, and he realized that he had left Jwalanagar more than thirty years ago. But that did not explain the feeling of disappointment that at first crept into him and then completely overwhelmed him. Everything seemed strange. He had come to visit an unfamiliar town.

"Dead," he muttered. "Everything I loved is dead, and we have come to bury my memories."

"Don't be like that," Maiya said. She put an arm through his affectionately.

"Not here," Joseph said pulling away. "Couples do not show affection in public."

"Those boys are holding hands. Is homosexual affection not frowned upon?"

"Don't be silly. If they were homosexuals they wouldn't dare to be seen together in public. Friends show their friendship out in the open; lovers don't."

Maiya found this funny, and she laughed. The sound of her laughter turned Joseph's disappointment into anger.

"Keep quiet. You are attracting attention. A woman your age in jeans is bad enough. Must you attack people's ears as well as their eyes?"

Maiya was offended. She stopped laughing and entered the taxi. She did not comment on anything she saw. Joseph saw different expressions flit across her face as she looked out of the window, but she asked no questions. She had locked him out, and he resented it.

"What are you thinking?" he asked.

"What can I think? Everything is new to me. I'm only gathering impressions that I'll sort out later."

Joseph did not like her way of throwing his question back at him. Her partial reply was not an answer to his question, either. He sulked all the way to the hotel, and Maiya ignored him.

"Are you Joseph Nawgaonkar?" the receptionist at the hotel asked.

"Yes. I changed my surname to Naor. It is more Israeli," Joseph replied.

"Ah! The price of progress." The receptionist sighed. Before Joseph could react to the same comment he had heard earlier from his wife, the receptionist held out his hand and introduced himself. "You may not remember me, but I was one year junior to you in school. The name is Satish Verma."

Joseph looked at the man closely and smiled. "Yes, of course. Your family lived close to the railway level crossing on Elgin Street."

"That's right."

The two men asked about each other's families. Joseph introduced his wife and then asked about old friends and members of the Jewish community. Satish did not know everybody, but he did have a lot of information. "There is nobody from your community left in Jwalanagar except for Miss Eliza Samuel. There is also a Jewish lady here who comes from a different town. She married an insurance agent friend of mine, a Hindu named Rajgopal. Eliza Samuel is very ill in the Victoria Hospital. You should go and see her. She will be glad to see a Jewish face at her deathbed."

Joseph turned toward Maiya but looked into an empty space. She had accompanied their luggage to their room. The receptionist pointed toward the stairs. "Room 313," he said.

Joseph mounted the stairs muttering, "Three, thirteen, nine, eighteen." According to Indian folklore, these numbers were omens of bad luck and destruction.

Joseph and Maiya visited Eliza in the hospital. The lady had trouble recognizing him but was pleased to meet his wife, an "authentic Israeli." She raised a trembling finger in Joseph's direction and spoke to Maiya. "I once knocked him down into a patch of cactus for troubling my elder sister, Naomi," she said.

"That was a different Joseph, much older than I. He was the grandson of Bentzion and Ketura Avaskar. I am from the Nawgaonkar family."

"Are you a Samuel, too? Uncle Jacob's son?"

"No, but I am a Jew from Jwalanagar. Is that not as good as a blood relative?"

"Yes, thank God it is. It makes it possible for me to ask you to promise to see to the proper disposal of my body. It is important to me."

"Don't talk rubbish," Joseph said. "You still have a long time to live."

"Just promise me," Eliza insisted.

"I promise." He then said, "You will come and visit us in Israel. It is time you saw some place other than Jwalanagar."

"I wanted to, but now it is too late. At first my mother could not afford even a short holiday with cousins who lived in different towns. The railway tickets and presents for the family we would stay with were too much for her pocket. Then Eva had her accident. She actually died, but the doctors managed to revive her. Her brain was damaged from the lack of oxygen, and our family was never the same after that. Medicine has made progress, but sometimes it makes suffering worse. I gave up my education and cared for Eva so that Mother could go back to work. Our father died when we were very young. Mother had to provide for us."

"Couldn't she have kept a servant?" Joseph asked.

"She tried, but Eva recognized only her family. She made it very difficult for a stranger to take care of her. When Mama found bruises from a beating on her body, she allowed me to stay home. Naomi was the clever one, and Gabriel was the boy. I was the obvious choice."

"Weren't you angry about it?" Maiya asked.

"No. I was the one who volunteered in the first place, and I kept insisting on it later. There was no alternative. It was better than accepting my grandfather's charity. My father's family moved to Israel one by one. We were essentially alone, and we had to manage as best we could. Eva died five years ago. By then it was too late for me to do anything like move to another place. I am the last Jew left in Jwalanagar, and soon even I will be gone." She saw some expression of protest on Joseph's face. "Don't say anything, Joseph. It is true. I can speak clearly now only because of the medicines, but it is not always so. I'm glad you came when I am lucid. Soon it will be over, and I cannot say that I am sorry."

Joseph and Maiya stayed until visiting hours ended. Eliza asked questions and let Joseph or Maiya talk. Speaking became difficult for Eliza, but she did not want them to leave until they had to. When the nurse came into the room, she turned to Joseph, raised her hand, and said, "Remember your promise."

The telephone in the hotel room rang at six o'clock in the morning. "We are sorry to inform you that your relative, Miss Eliza Samuel, passed away ten minutes ago," a woman's voice announced. "Please come and take the body."

"Can't you keep it until I can make arrangements?" Joseph asked.

"We do not have the facilities. You will have to come."

"Wait a minute. Don't hang up. What is her address? I am not a relative, and I live abroad."

The lady gave the address, which Joseph repeated before he wrote it down. He turned to go to the bathroom to wash.

"What's happened? Where are you going?" Maiya asked.

"Eliza is dead, and I have to go and fetch the body. I hope one of the neighbors has a spare key to the house. We will have to clean the place before I get the body home. According to custom the house cannot be swept for the seven days of mourning. Scraps will have to be picked up by hand. Who knows how long she was in the hospital and how much dirt has collected? Fine screwup of our holiday! I don't know where the rest of the family is. I don't want to be the person to have to say Kaddish and stay the full week in this town."

"She is a Jew," Maiya reproached him.

"She is not my responsibility."

"As a fellow Jew, she is. Besides that, you promised her."

"Did I have a choice?"

Maiya dressed quickly and accompanied him to the house Eliza had lived in. Joseph paid the auto-rickshaw driver in front of number 18, Shastri Road. He looked up at the unpainted, crumbling facade of the block of flats. There were morning noises and smells all around him. Crows pecked at piles of rubbish beside the road. Every kitchen seemed to send out the smell of frying eggs, chapatis, and cooking vegetables. The children would leave for school soon, and the mothers had to have their tiffin lunches ready. Joseph remembered all this from his childhood. A man carried freshly baked bread in a basket on his head. *"Double roti,"* he called out, announcing his wares. Maiya caught sight of a milkman with his milk can and quarter-liter measuring cup coming down the stairs of Eliza's block of flats. She pointed him out to Joseph as someone to ask about Eliza's flat number.

"Doodwallah, milkman," Joseph called out.

The man stopped. *"Ji,* sahib?" he asked.

"Which is Eliza Samuel's flat?"

"Third floor, first on the right. It is flat number nine. But she is not at home, sahib. I heard that she is in Victoria Hospital."

"I know, I have been there. Do you know which neighbor may have a key to that house?"

"Are you a relative, sahib?" the man asked.

"A sort of a relative," Joseph answered.

"She owes me eighty-one rupees for the milk she took before she went into the hospital. As a relative you should pay me, sahib. I am a poor man. I support a family through this milk business."

Joseph took out his wallet and paid the man, after which the milkman said, "Come, sahib. I'll take you to the house of the Bhatnagar family. Bhatnagar memsahib and Eliza memsahib were friends."

Joseph and Maiya followed him. "Did you have to pay him? How do you know how much she owed him?" Maiya asked.

"It was too ridiculously low a price to be untrue. Besides that, I need to know where the keys are."

"Perhaps there is a set with her things at the hospital."

"Imagine bringing the body home to a flat that has not been cleaned for who knows how long. There may be food on the table and sprouted onions and potatoes in the *dooli*. We have to clean the place before people begin to arrive."

Mrs. Bhatnagar provided the keys when she heard the news. She promised to come and help once she had given her husband his breakfast and sent her children to school. "I cleaned the place and aired it on Sunday in the hope that Eliza would come home soon," she said. "She was a very clean and tidy person. It is a small place, only two rooms and a balcony that they enclosed and used as an extra room. There will not be much to do."

When Joseph brought Eliza's body to her flat, the place was clean. Maiya was explaining to a Christian lady that the candles she had brought could not be lit beside the body. They could be lit only after the funeral. And the flowers she had brought would have to be placed in a neighbor's house. Jews did not display flowers in a mourner's house. They were a sign of joy. She could, however, take the flowers to the cemetery, because many Jews placed flowers upon graves.

"Anybody know where Naomi or Gabriel lives?" Joseph asked the people who had gathered in the flat. "I can't find any diary or notebook with their address or phone number."

"You won't find them," Mrs. Bhatnagar said. "Naomi married a non-Jewish man who worked with her in a hospital in a small town called Chawhanganj in Rajasthan. Her family disowned her. Eliza started to speak about her only after Eva died. I have informed her by telegram because I have her address. She used to send me money from time to time to help with Eva's expenses— things like diapers, talcum powder, and the sweets she liked to eat but Mrs. Samuel could not afford. The family knew nothing about it. I do not have Gabriel's address. He had a big fight with his mother and left for Australia when she made a will leaving the flat to Eliza. He thought that as a son it was his right to inherit, even though he did nothing for any of his sisters. Naomi does not have his address, either."

"Any Jews anywhere?" Joseph asked. "I need help with the funeral service. We need at least ten Jews."

"After the Jewish boys left for Israel or jobs in big cities, a few Jewish girls married outside their community. Mrs. Rajgopal still follows her religion. I do not know where she lives. Eliza once mentioned her to me, that's how I know."

"I'll ask the hotel receptionist to inform her. He mentioned that she is married to a friend of his," Joseph said.

"That makes three of you. If Naomi comes it will be four," somebody said.

"That won't do. We need men," Joseph answered.

"My husband does business with a Jewish man from Indore. Maybe we can contact him by e-mail. It may be quicker than the telephone he has at home, because he travels a lot and we may not find him there. I have his e-mail address but not his mobile number." This was from another lady, before she departed for the post office from where she could call her husband with her request. The post office was barely a hundred yards away, on a street that ran parallel to Shastri Road.

Eliza's body was placed on a cotton dhurrie on the floor. It was covered with a sheet. Blocks of ice were placed around it so that the body would not begin to smell in the heat. Table fans were brought in from the neighboring flats to circulate the cold air and slow down the body's decomposition. Somebody emptied a bottle of eau de cologne on the body. The smell soon became overpowering and sickening. Nobody seemed to mind. That was a smell they all connected with death.

Mrs. Rajgopal arrived carrying a large parcel. After introducing herself as Edna, she said, "I'm sorry I'm late, but I had to wait until the stores opened, and then I had to come all this distance by rickshaw." She went over to the dining table and opened her parcel upon it. Ten yards of unbleached white cotton cloth, a pair of scissors, white thread, and a few needles were taken out. Mrs. Rajgopal was going to prepare the funeral clothes for Eliza.

"I have a sewing machine," Mrs. Bhatnagar offered.

"Thank you, but we can't use it. Funeral clothes are sewn by hand. It will not take much time. We do not have to use a fine backstitch or a hemstitch. A close running stitch is all that is required. I'll cut out a pair of pajamas and a kurta, and then you can all help."

Maiya sat down to sew. After the clothes were ready, Edna asked Maiya to help her bathe the body. Maiya hesitated. She had never done anything like this before, and it seemed unpleasant to her. As the only other Jewish woman present, she had no choice

but to follow Edna into the bathroom. She carried in the two
sheets Edna had cut out to serve as a shroud.

A coffin maker appeared mysteriously. He said that somebody
in the hospital had given him the address, for a small commis-
sion. This man knew all about Jewish coffins. "You want one
where the lid slides in and out. You will not want a coffin with a
lid that is nailed down," he said. He then added, "Half payment in
advance, sir, second half on delivery."

Joseph paid quietly and counted the money left in his wallet.
Another hole in my pocket, he thought as he handed the money
over. *Who knows? Perhaps I really will be repaid on the other side.
Her family for sure will not do so over here.*

There was nothing to do but wait for the Jewish businessman
from Indore to respond to a message left by another businessman, who would then send someone with a message to his wife,
who would then bring the message to the flat. It might take
hours. Joseph decided to go to the cemetery and dig the grave in
the meantime.

The cemetery was in a sad state. Huts made of every kind of
material imaginable clung to its walls. The gate had disappeared.
Joseph recognized it as the roof of a hut because of the Star of
David engraved on it. He recognized old tombstones in the walls
of some shanties. But in spite of all that, he was unprepared for
what he saw inside. Bushes had sprung up all over the place.
Graves that did not have a tombstone could not be identified
between the piles of rubbish that had gathered over the years. A
mother pig with a group of piglets was eating human feces that
lay scattered around the area near the wall that offered some privacy from the street. In the absence of lavatories, the cemetery
served as one for the shanty dwellers.

Joseph looked around in despair. He had hoped that there
would be a map of the place in Eliza's flat but found none. Then

he had an idea to visit the rooms that once served as the Jewish prayer hall, which had become part of a pickle and chutney factory. A Parsi gentleman had bought the property from the Samson family. Joseph had a wild hope that a cemetery map might have been overlooked in some corner of the prayer rooms. The new owners denied all knowledge of any documents pertaining to the Bene Israel community, but they gave him permission to search the premises for anything that he thought would help him. Joseph found the rooms full of raw mangoes, lemons, and green chillies. The shelves that once held prayer books were stacked with packets of salt, turmeric, and other spices. Nothing remained that could be connected to the old place of worship, unless a person looked hard enough and saw two hooks on the ceiling. Two big glass bowls holding oil lamps used to be suspended from these hooks. Joseph was disappointed and dejected. He thanked the workers at the pickle and chutney factory and left.

Joseph looked around at the cemetery in despair. He had heard stories of people being buried in graves that were already occupied, and he did not want to be responsible for disturbing the rest of somebody who already slept there. He had a superstitious fear of that. The area close to the gate would be the place least likely to have graves and would be the safest place to bury the body. Joseph began to dig. Soon he had an audience: three ragged children stood around him. They watched whatever he did with interest.

"This is a cemetery. You have no business being here. Where do you live?" Joseph tried to shoo them away.

"We live there." One child pointed to the old pavilion that was once used to place the Jewish dead while part of the funeral service was read. It had sides now, made of pieces of cardboard, plastic sheeting, and a battered asbestos board. It had become somebody's home.

"That's not your home. That is part of the cemetery. I will have you turned out," Joseph threatened.

"Where will we go, sahib? Here at least the rain does not fall on us. Somebody else will move in as soon as we leave."

Joseph realized the truth of the statement. He had forgotten the grinding poverty of his old country. The children told him that their old home had now become a lake and their whole village had been uprooted. Joseph understood that these children were part of the hundreds of people displaced because of the new dam. There was little—often no—compensation given for fields and homes lost. Self-sufficient people had become beggars. The ragged, hungry condition of the children told its own story.

"Can we help you to dig, sahib?" the eldest of the children asked. "Only five hundred rupees."

"You have learned how to cheat people in the city," Joseph said.

"It is not too much these days, sahib. Think of it as a good deed done in the name of the dead person. It will get him or her into heaven and add to the list of your good deeds. You will need it when your time comes."

Joseph looked at the children. He saw three heads crawling with lice, three pairs of big, staring eyes, one runny nose, and three bright, hopeful smiles. He did not have the heart to refuse. He dug into his pocket. "Here, take these twenty rupees and buy something to eat first. I'll rest a little under this tree until you return, and then we will dig the grave together. Three hundred rupees will be enough."

When Joseph returned to Eliza's flat he was greeted with the news that a Mr. Enoch Japheth would be down by the night train from Indore. It meant that the funeral could not take place until the next day. Mr. Japheth had mentioned the taxi stand outside the station as the rendezvous point.

A young girl of about ten came to Maiya and asked, "May I sit with the body tonight? It is not our custom to leave it unattended until the funeral."

"Aren't you a bit young for that?" Maiya asked. "Do you even know what death is?"

"Only babies are too young to know that. Death comes to all of us, even to children. Everybody knows that."

"You can stay," Maiya said.

The girl smiled. She began to walk toward the coffin, but stopped in midstride and turned to Maiya once again. "Auntie Eliza taught me to sew and embroider. Could I have the box she kept her sewing things in, in memory of her? It is not expensive, just an old biscuit box with her threads, needles, and stuff."

She knows what death is, all right, Maiya thought as she said, "It is not mine to decide. You will have to ask her sister when she arrives."

"I did not realize that there were any Jews left in Jwalanagar," Mr. Japheth said as he shook Joseph's hand later that night. "How many men have you collected?"

"You are the second."

"So there will be no mourner's Kaddish. Poor lady! She really should have moved to a place with a Jewish community." He paused and then smiled. "Who am I to talk? There is only one other Jewish family in Indore, and the man there is never home. I tried to bring him with me, but he is out with a group of tourists acting as their driver and guide."

"The neighbors informed us that she wished to be cremated," Joseph said.

"Out of the question. It is the duty of the community to deal with the body. The dead person has no say in the matter. I did not travel so far and cancel all my plans for today to have a Jewish funeral in a non-Jewish way. I did not spend time searching for the funeral service not to do my duty as a Jew. I had a hell of a time getting Jerusalem sand. The fellows who come from Israel forget our needs, and hardly anyone brings any."

Maiya took an instant dislike to Mr. Japheth. He took her for a Jew of European descent who knew nothing about the Bene Israel. One of the remarks he made was "I hope you do not wear black to the funeral. Christianity is new to India. It arrived only with the British. We follow the older custom of wearing white. Look around you; most of the people are wearing white out of respect for the dead woman."

Maiya checked the retort that rose to her lips. She did not want to say anything that Joseph could interpret as disrespect for his people. She looked at Joseph, but he was talking to Mr. Bhatnagar and had not heard. "God only knows what the original Jewish custom was," she said.

"It was sackcloth and ashes. Black was worn only by the chief *cohen* when he had a wet dream. He had to wear it from morning to sunset, when he purified himself and returned to his usual white clothes."

"Is that so?" Maiya said before she turned away to speak to somebody else, which effectively stopped the conversation from going any further.

At around ten o'clock the next morning, Joseph and Enoch each took one end of the coffin and, after much maneuvering, carried it downstairs. The staircase was too narrow to allow four men to carry a coffin through it. Other men relieved them from time to time. The coffin was placed in a truck that Mr. Bhatnagar had hired. Only the men climbed in after the coffin and accompanied Eliza Samuel to her resting place. Maiya, who had bathed and dressed a corpse for the first time in her life and had followed Edna's instructions in preparing the shroud, felt sad to think that her handiwork would soon be underground. She had watched in horror as Edna poured sand from Jerusalem onto the eyes of the corpse.

"You people are lucky. You are buried in the earth of Israel. We have to make do with just a little bit of its holy sand," Edna said by way of explanation. Maiya tried to control the expressions on her face. This was not the time for questions.

Maiya had assumed that she would be present at the funeral, but Mr. Japheth informed her that Indian Jews, who had lived in India more than two thousand years, had naturally adopted many customs of their Hindu and Muslim neighbors. Women did not attend funerals. Maiya resented this but did not argue. She and Edna handed the flowers to the men in the truck and returned to the flat to await the funeral party's return.

The funeral service was a sad, cut-to-pieces affair. Because there were only two Jewish men in attendance, no mourner's Kaddish was said. The coffin was placed three times upon the ground on its way from the truck to the grave. After the service was over, Joseph and Enoch slid the coffin open, placed the lid beside the open coffin, and then threw a shovelful of earth into the grave. Everybody present did the same. The men took turns in helping to fill the grave. Candles were lit and the new grave was covered with flowers. A group of squatters stood outside, where the gate once was, and watched. *"Ram, Ram, Satya hai,"* some of them chanted. "God, God is true." After a neighbor spoke about what a wonderful lady Eliza was, everybody climbed into the truck and returned to the flat.

"Did anybody from the family arrive?" Enoch asked Maiya when they returned.

"A sister lives in a small town, not far from Udaipur," Maiya replied. "She sent a telegram saying that she could not come. I am to leave the key with the neighbor who had it before. The sister will come when both she and her husband can get leave."

Joseph came up to Enoch. "I have a question," he said. "If I light a memorial candle and place a glass of water beside it, will I have to sit here for seven days? I don't want to do that. There is nobody here to read the prayers, so what is the use of my staying?"

"Do what you want to do," Enoch replied. "I have to take the night train back to Indore."

"I planned to stay in Jwalanagar for five days. Three are already over," Joseph said. "We'll stay in this flat tonight so that we can clean it up early tomorrow. Some people may still want to visit. We shall leave the day after tomorrow. There is nothing left in Jwalanagar for me. Everything is changed. For me, it is all dead. We also want to see other parts of India and are not so rich that we can make another trip here."

"We have done what we could do," Enoch said.

Late that night Joseph had a dream. He saw Eliza standing behind the bushes in the children's area in the cemetery. Only her head showed above the foliage. "Joseph," she said, "you promised decent disposal of my body. I dressed modestly all my life and now my body lies naked on the top of my grave. Take a big bedsheet from the cupboard and cover my remains. Joseph, I'm depending on you."

Joseph woke with a start. In the dim candlelight he looked at the sleeping form of his wife. He imagined that he saw it quiver and shake. Suddenly, Maiya uttered a soft scream and sat up. "Joe, I had a most horrible dream," she said, clinging to him. "Eliza asked me to take a big bedsheet from—"

Joseph stroked her hair and completed her sentence with her. "—from the cupboard and cover her naked body."

"She came to you, too."

"Yes. It can't be only imagination. There must be some truth in it. I'm going to the hotel immediately to rent a car. Go get the sheet."

It was a moonless night, and the cemetery was pitch-dark. Joseph and Maiya drove up to the place where the gate had once stood. The headlights of the car shone upon the area of the new grave. "Oh, God," Joseph said when he saw the open grave. The flowers and candles placed there a few hours earlier had disappeared. Eliza's naked body lay facedown upon a heap of mud beside the open grave. The coffin was missing, too. Maiya clutched her husband's hand hard for a moment. Then she went quickly to the body and covered it with the sheet.

"Shall we rebury her?" she asked.

"She will only be dug out again, this time for the sheet," Joseph answered. "Let's take her back to her flat. I'll see the mayor about this tomorrow."

The next day found Joseph in the mayor's office. He had insisted on seeing the man. The clerks said that it was impossible, the mayor was a very busy man, but Joseph announced that he would wait. Eight hundred rupees paid as a bribe and three and a half hours of waiting did not do much to improve Joseph's temper. He narrated the whole story to the mayor in rather forceful language.

"What do you want me to do about it?" the mayor asked. "You are asking me to assign police, who are needed elsewhere, to guard a plot nobody is using. I am sorry, but I cannot do it."

"Have you no respect for the dead?" Joseph asked.

"And have you none for the living? You saw those homeless, hungry people. Where are they to go? The tap you Jews installed outside your graveyard is the only source of clean drinking water for that *bustee*, that settlement. If they took the clothes from the body, they have more need of them than the dead person has. They are not evil people, just desperate ones. The flowers the dead person cannot smell have definitely been sold to provide a piece of bread for the living. Do the decent thing. Cremate the body. Leave the land for other people."

Joseph took a deep breath and began to explain his position in a calm, controlled voice. "It is our belief that the souls of the dead will rise on the Day of Judgment together with their bodies. Their graves must be respected."

"You will not own this land until the Day of Judgment," the mayor said. "The law mentions seven or fourteen years, I forget which, from the date of the last interment, as the period during which the graveyard cannot be used for other purposes. We plan to build blocks of flats there."

"But the land belongs to the community," Joseph argued.

"What community? We have laws about absent landlords. Even when you were here, all the land had to be used. I am not talking about graveyards now. It had to be cultivated before, but now that the area is urban it has to be lived upon. Your people are all in Israel and other places. As for this piece of land, it has served its original purpose. There will be no more Jewish funerals in Jwalanagar. If you want to bury Miss Eliza Samuel, bury her. My advice to you is to cremate her. Now if you please, I have another appointment."

"What about the rising of the dead and the Day of Judgment?" Joseph asked in bewilderment. "My ancestors are buried in that place."

The mayor rose from his chair. He walked over to Joseph and placed a hand on his shoulder. "Tell me, Mr. Naor, do you believe that the millions of innocent Jews whom Hitler had killed and then burned in his crematoriums will not come to life with their bodies? If you do, you have very little faith in the powers of your God."

Joseph looked at the mayor for a minute. Then he rose, shook the proffered hand, and walked out.

ABOUT THE AUTHOR

Sophie Judah was born in India in 1949. Her parents were born in Jabalpur, but her father was an officer in the Indian Army, and she grew up in many different cities without claiming any of them as her hometown. She graduated from Marathwada University and worked as a teacher and as a flight attendant for Indian Airlines. In 1972 she married and moved with her husband to Israel, where they now live with their five children. In 1997 she received a master's degree in English literature and creative writing from Bar-Ilan University.